EAST IS EAST

John Putnam Thatcher of the Sloan Guaranty Trust flies to Japan to head off a possible takeover. Meanwhile, a US electrics giant is planning an assault on the lucrative, and almost impregnable, Japanese market. The company's president arrives in Toyko at the same time as Thatcher to announce a distribution deal with the Yanezawa Trading Corporation. But the decorous negotiations are interrupted . . . by murder. Tangled in an ever-widening web of unscrupulous business practices, corruption in high places and violence, Thatcher must travel to England before a conundrum can be solved . . . and the killer found. *East Is East* is vintage Lathen: a complex, satisfying murder mystery set against the fascinating background of international finance.

EAST IS EAST

Emma Lathen

CHIVERS PRESS
BATH

First published in Great Britain 1991
by
Victor Gollancz Ltd
This Large Print edition published by
Chivers Press
by arrangement with
Victor Gollancz Ltd
1993

ISBN 0 7451 7506 6

British Library Cataloguing in Publication Data available

East
Is
East

Chapter 1

Wall Street has always been a workplace with a high incidence of occupational hazards, and these days the perils range from OPEC to computer viruses to the Chicago Board of Trade. Eternal vigilance is the price of survival, let alone success.

John Putnam Thatcher, executive vice-president of the Sloan Guaranty Trust, knew this better than most. Even so, there were moments when he felt that his sharp-eyed staff was verging on paranoia. This sunny morning in July was proving to be a case in point.

"We have just heard that you are planning to go to Japan," said Everett Gabler sternly. A senior man in every sense of the word, he set uncomfortably high standards for himself and for everybody unfortunate enough to be within reach.

Charlie Trinkam, Thatcher's second in command, was cast in a different mold, but today he, too, sounded censorious. "God, John, with currencies on this roller coaster, is now the time for you to take off?"

"My trip to Alaska has been scheduled for

some time," Thatcher defended himself. "I am merely prefacing it with two and a half days in Tokyo."

But Gabler did not budge, and Thatcher's secretary, a zealous guardian of Thatcher's time, was nodding grave approval.

There was no doubt in Thatcher's mind what was really troubling all of them. This morning's mail had included the current issue of the *Journal of the American Bankers Association,* together with the news that the Sloan Guaranty Trust, once the third-largest bank in the world, had been nosed out of the money by some behemoths in Tokyo. His subordinates, for all practical purposes, were accusing him of fraternizing with the enemy.

Thatcher, who usually found it wise to deal with palace revolts as they arose, pushed aside a memorandum.

"Let's take a break for fifteen minutes or so, Miss Corsa," he suggested.

Gabler barely waited for the door to close before continuing his indictment. "No doubt this is George's doing," he complained. "Having just completed his own Pacific tour, he now wishes to dispatch you."

A specialist himself, Gabler tended to undervalue generalists. George Lancer, the Sloan's chairman of the board, was also its statesman-in-residence. He was the one who testified before Congress and attended the international conferences, while John Thatcher took care of the hands-on banking.

"In spite of the fact," Gabler continued inexorably, "that Japan is almost the one area where the Sloan is in no danger of encountering default or problem loans."

"The danger," Charlie interrupted, "is that they come here and buy the store out from under us."

The Japanese miracle being what it was, yen-holders could well be prowling Exchange Place in search of tempting banks and skyscrapers to devour.

"George is not taking your defeatist attitude," said Thatcher, injecting a reproachful note of his own. "Instead he's convinced we should step up our efforts to sell the services of SloanCorp in Japan."

There was a respectful silence. The Tokyo branch of the Sloan's investment-banking arm was a relatively recent undertaking, but already it had produced gratifying results. On Thatcher's trip to Anchorage, he would be overseeing the union of Japanese and American money in a joint venture arranged by the Sloan.

"In principle that is certainly desirable," Gabler hedged.

Trinkam was quicker off the mark. "It's

9

the timing I don't get. Why is George so hot to have you eating sushi right now?"

Thatcher's reply was commendably brief. "Recruit."

The Recruit scandal enveloping Japan had gone from strength to strength. It had begun when an ambitious entrepreneur had transformed his start-up company into a commercial giant overnight. Along the way there had been handouts in many forms to many elected officials. By rights the story should have caused a momentary sensation, then died away. But the combination of a newspaper intoxicated with investigative reporting and a crusading public prosecutor had created a nonstop uproar. The disclosures had reached higher and higher into the seats of the mighty, until cabinet members awaited arrest and prime ministers trembled.

"But that's been going on for over two years," Charlie protested. "Sure, the research department sends us memos about what will happen to the Nikkei Average if the government falls. But beyond having the Treasury auction killed dead, where does the Sloan come in?"

Thatcher examined his subordinates over his fingertips as he did his best for the absent George. "Japan has been run for forty years by a coalition of the big business interests and

10

the conservative politicians in the form of the Liberal Democratic Party. It's not really a political party, however, so much as a vast aggregate with many internal factions. Until now a scandal has merely meant that one faction had to step down. But this Recruit pressure has been so unrelenting that, for the first time, it's conceivable that a fall could involve the entire apparatus of the LDP."

Everett always grew restive when someone else gave the lecture. "Surely the possibility of such a crisis has abated, John," he reasoned. "The LDP seems to have weathered the storm and achieved some kind of equilibrium."

"At at price," Thatcher rejoined. "The establishment figures are walking warily, reluctant to do the kind of favors for each other that were commonplace a short time ago. George feels there's a window of opportunity for the Sloan, not only to consolidate its position in Japan, but to make substantial gains."

No proposition could have been more appealing. Years of taking it on the chin from Nomura Securities and Sumitomo Trust made most red-blooded American bankers itch to hit back. Even Everett Gabler was not immune.

"Mmm," he said with a splendid facade of dispassion. "No one can deny the benefits to the Sloan if that were possible."

"Score one for George," murmured Charlie.

Everett ignored this provocation. "That is precisely why we have opened an office in Tokyo. And there, the Sloan is very ably represented by a man who speaks the language and has had years of experience in a notoriously difficult business environment."

Tributes to colleagues did not fall lightly from Gabler's lips, even to the ones many miles distant. Both Charlie and Thatcher recognized this accolade for what it was worth.

"And therefore Gene Fleming is surely the ideal person to direct the Sloan's efforts," Gabler concluded ringingly.

"On the whole, I agree with you," Thatcher said, feeling as if he were seconding a nomination. "In fact, that's what I told George."

Charlie already knew George had won. "And I'll bet he had a snappy comeback for that one."

"He thinks that with the Japanese emphasis on status, someone senior to Fleming should set the initial tone," Thatcher reported dutifully. "He wants to send a signal of our degree of commitment. For all I know, he may be right."

"Don't be too sure of that," Trinkam warned. "When I was over there last year, the emphasis was on the bottom line. It's still money that talks."

He might be diverted, but no power on earth could deflect Everett Gabler.

"I am sure both you and George have gained many insights as visitors to Japan, but Fleming has been living with Recruit since its inception," he said, turning like a compass needle to his own magnetic north. "He is the one who really understands the situation there, and he's the person whose opinion is worth hearing."

Thatcher could not have been more sympathetic.

"But, Everett," he said mildly, "this is all Fleming's idea."

When Thatcher began canceling several appointments, he was reminded that world travelers are routinely asked to perform minor chores. Often it is a duty-free bottle of perfume for Aunt Sally, but sometimes it takes more elevated forms.

"All right, we'll scrub lunch on Monday and make it the nineteenth instead. Is the Lawyers Club okay?" Leonard Solletti began, before pausing thoughtfully. Then: "Say, are you going to be in Tokyo on Wednesday too?"

"I am due at an embassy reception that evening," Thatcher replied, hoping this would scotch whatever suggestion was coming.

But it was not to be.

"Oh, this would take place during office hours," Solletti said instantly. "Carl called me from Japan yesterday, asking if anybody from the committee was going to be over there."

Carl was head of Lackawanna Electric Industries, and the committee in question was composed of Lackawanna's creditors. Thatcher was chairman of the committee; Solletti was its secretary and general dogsbody.

"Why in the world does he want one of us in Tokyo?" grumbled Thatcher, reluctantly jotting himself a note.

"It's for the creditors' authorization to sell that R&D outfit in England. You must remember, you all approved at our last meeting."

"Of course I remember, but it's a minor transaction. I was planning to mail the affidavit."

The sale might be minor, but it involved interests that were fully worthy of the Sloan's attention. Since the turn of the century, Lackawanna had been synonymous with electricity all over the world. Whenever a shaft turned, an element heated, an electromagnetic field appeared, or a humble sixty-watt bulb lit up, Lackawanna was, more often than not, integral to the process. With manufacturing capability in Europe and South America as well as twenty states, its reach embraced so-

14

phisticated equipment for rockets, sleek appliances for the home, heavyweight generators for industry, and the street lighting of Idaho Falls. The rise of Lackawanna had been the stuff of history; its fall had been chronicled by *Barrons* and FNN. The flabby giant, burdened by out-of-date facilities, inefficient management, ancient labor regulations, and the firm conviction that Lackawanna was immortal, had staggered into bankruptcy and precipitated a national convulsion.

When Carl Kruger had been handpicked to lead the salvage operation, hopes had not run high. Against all odds, however, he had succeeded. Subsidiaries disappeared, antiquated plants closed, labor practices changed, and executives, as well as hourly employees, took home pink slips. Within three years, Lackawanna was out of intensive care. By the end of the fourth year, Lackawanna was again a force to be reckoned with, and Carl Kruger had become a national hero.

There were, however, still plenty of matters to occupy Lackawanna's creditors.

"At our last meeting," Thatcher recalled in a puzzled tone, "we agreed they should offer early retirement to one thousand workers in Terre Haute and Akron, while we insisted they delay installation of that new information system. Offhand, either of those items is worth

15

more of Kruger's time than this sale of Midland Research."

"Nonetheless you gave him the go-ahead."

"We were delighted to," Thatcher admitted without hesitation. "Any R&D operation eats up a fair amount of money every year. But Kruger always claimed that if we let him nurse MR along, he could recover his costs, and he was right. I am merely surprised that he's handling it in person."

Solletti lowered his voice conspiratorially. "If you ask me, Carl is up to something."

"He almost always is," Thatcher rejoined, bracing himself for the familiar litany.

Leonard Solletti's gift for meticulous attention to detail made him the ideal man for his job. Under his magic touch, compliance with endless legal formalities occurred on time, mountains of paperwork moved smoothly through the system, and the lowliest creditor knew what was going on. But these same talents made dealing with Carl Kruger a penance. Solletti had so often been affronted by Kruger's airy dismissal of red tape and his blithe disregard for time-honored methods that Solletti was now chronically dismayed by everything Kruger did.

"Sometimes Carl seems to forget that he's the bankrupt and we're the creditors," he began. "He just steams ahead, making decisions and expecting automatic concurrence when we don't really know what's going on. Approving this sale may have been a big mistake."

Thatcher appreciated prudence as much as the next man, but there is not absolute safety in an imperfect world.

"On paper it looked as if Kruger is simply getting his investment back with a modest profit," he pointed out.

"Ah ha! But I heard last week that Midland Research has produced a dynamite advance in industrial robotics. And that," Solletti concluded, "means that it's worth more than Carl is selling it for."

"Then he's getting something besides money," said Thatcher, remaining calm. "Say what you like about him, Carl doesn't run around making free gifts to purchasers of his property."

"Of course he's getting something — and without bothering to inform the creditors. Once again he's taken the bit between his teeth and is planning some slapdash move that should be studied by us with a good deal of time and care."

Thatcher knew time had been a luxury that Lackawanna could not afford.

"It's precisely because Kruger isn't hidebound that he's made so much progress these past few years. I admit he tends to ignore the rulebook, but he gets results. Who are we to complain?"

Solletti was disappointed.

"At the very least he should have consulted us," he insisted.

"With his track record, Carl knows that the creditors are willing to give him all the latitude he wants."

Solletti was not a lawyer for nothing.

"This might even be actionable."

"It wouldn't surprise me at all," Thatcher confessed. "But you will bear in mind, Leonard, that we are far more interested in getting our money back than in litigation. Or even in trying to run Lackawanna."

Solletti still saw trouble ahead.

"Carl not only went to Japan himself; he took his production vice-president and his chief financial officer. He's planning something big."

"It certainly sounds like it," Thatcher agreed.

"I can't make out what he's up to."

By this time Thatcher thought that he did. Nobody had ever claimed that George Lancer was endowed with superhuman vision. When a window of opportunity opens, quite a few people are apt to notice.

"Well, I am scarcely in a position to find

fault. Unless I miss my guess, Carl Kruger is on the same errand as I am. No doubt I will discover the details in Tokyo."

"Then I'll let Carl know you're coming?"

"Yes. After all, what harm can it do?" Thatcher reasoned. "Whatever Carl has in mind will require the sanction of the Japanese government. If he gets it, he can go ahead with his plans. If he doesn't, he can sell MR for more money."

This well-meant attempt at reassurance missed the mark.

"And when it's all over, he'll let us know what he's done," said Solletti, stiff with disapproval.

"You can always make space for these details in the agenda for our next meeting," Thatcher suggested with a straight face.

But playfulness did not exist in Solletti's scheme of things.

"That would be completely irregular," he protested. "It would be tantamount to recognizing that the disclosure came a month after the approval."

"Of course, of course. What can I have been thinking of?"

It was all beyond Solletti, but he could identify parallel lines.

"You're both zeroing in on Japan at exactly the same time, and I don't see why."

Thatcher was unwilling to do more for him than for the staff of the Sloan.

"Recruit," he said briskly. "See you on the nineteenth."

Chapter 2

"Well, will you take a look at this? Thatcher himself is coming over!" Carl Kruger exclaimed, continuing to commune with himself as he thrust a cable at Bennet Alderman. "Talk about lucky breaks. We've got the chairman of the Creditors Committee right up front, and Thatcher will impress the government bigwigs more than somebody they've never heard of."

Kruger was too wrapped up in his own schemes to wonder about this happy coincidence. As for Alderman, he had no idea what Kruger was talking about. He was a public relations man and a good one, so he merely consulted his watch and said:

"It's about time to get started, Carl."

Not many corporate heads travel with their own personal publicity specialist, but it was no accident that Lackawanna's struggle and victory had become powerful symbols. At the very outset Carl Kruger had realized that he could save Lackawanna only by asking many institutions to do things they preferred not to do. Accordingly he had hired Alderman to manufacture a climate in which saying no to

Lackawanna was the equivalent of stabbing American industry in the back. Working day and night, Alderman had succeeded to such a degree that by now, sample results showed the American public thought Kruger would make a better President than any politician.

In line with Lackawanna's new tradition, Carl Kruger had descended on Japan like a meteor. From the moment of touchdown he had been followed as if he were a major celebrity, right up there with Princess Di. Today, even though Lackawanna was merely hosting a simple press conference, it had been necessary to rent a large function room equipped with translation facilities and upscale refreshments. After seven days of tantalizing hints from Kruger, the usual mob of reporters had been swelled by all the stringers from the worldwide press and crews from every television station in Tokyo.

As Kruger made his way to the lectern, he stopped to shake a few hands and smile down from his six feet four. Trailing behind, totally overshadowed, was Alderman, thin, bespectacled, and prematurely bald.

"Can you all hear me in the back?"

Kruger was relaxed, his voice carrying the assurance that comes from almost five years of public appearances.

Listening critically, Alderman was joined by

another American.

"You got a great turnout," the attaché said enviously. His own releases about Japanese quotas on Florida grapefruit went from the press pool to oblivion.

"With Carl, it's easy," Alderman replied. "He's a winner, and people always grab the chance to see him."

Every PR man knows he should keep the attention on his client. So Alderman did not mention his own efforts or his impressive track record. But false modesty aside, Alderman was singularly fortunate in his man. First there was Kruger's background, which distinguished him from the normal corporate nabob. He had graduated from West Point, spent ten years in the army, then left to establish the Kruger Corporation. In addition, he was an imposing physical presence, with youthful blue eyes belying a grizzled crop of hair. Most important of all, he had taken to television like a duck to water. Without this raw material, Alderman could never have painted Lackawanna as a beleaguered outpost and Kruger as John Wayne riding to the rescue.

Kruger always liked to work his audience up by degrees, and he was doing so now.

"First of all, I want to thank you for coming to listen to me explain what Lackawanna is doing here and why . . ."

There were journalists in the room assigned to cover yet another personality, but there were others who knew, quite as well as John Thatcher, that the divestiture of a small firm was not responsible for Lackawanna's high-visibility trip to Japan.

". . . pleased to announce the development of a new generation of robots. In acquiring Midland Research, the buyer gets technology vital to his interests and any further advances from a high-tech outfit based in the Common Market. And all this at a price that's a real bargain."

He paused to let his audience catch up in its furious scribbling.

"Some of you are probably wondering if Lackawanna's getting anything out of this," he continued blandly. "We certainly are. As part of the overall package, the Yonezawa Trading Company will undertake the distribution of certain Lackawanna products in Japan."

Everyone had been waiting for a now-familiar corporate proclamation. Lackawanna would build a new facility in West Virginia with Japanese participation. Either that or Lackawanna would manufacture a new washing machine with Japanese components. Nobody expected Kruger to launch a solitary head-on assault against Fortress Japan.

There was a collective intake of breath. Then all hell broke loose in a multitude of languages.

"But that means you want to compete with the Japanese in their home market."

"What products are we talking about?"

"What about opposition to this agreement?"

Kruger had deliberately arranged this chorus of howls so that he could choose which questions to answer and in what order.

"The product line subject to this agreement includes our heavyweight basic electrical equipment — generators, motors, industrial circuit breakers."

"Does that include the output from your state-of-the-art plant in Oregon?"

Kruger ignored the reference to the plant. Instead he named the product.

"Those are our Orion generators you're talking about. Yes, they're part of the package."

"Then aren't Japanese manufacturers going to scream?"

Kruger shook his head gently. "We're not exactly asking for a free ride. Lackawanna technology will enable the Japanese steel industry to be competitive again. If Japan loses something on one end of the deal, it gains a hell of a lot on the other end."

"Are you attacking Japanese trade policy?"

"Certainly not! I've never had any sympathy for those American businesses that whine about Japanese competition and ask for government intervention. The companies that are going to survive are those that are willing to compete with the Japanese. We've got to be ready to admit when somebody is doing something better than we are and to learn from them. Lackawanna made a lot of mistakes along these lines, but now Lackawanna is better than ever."

Reporters with questions are, however, rarely satisfied by generalizations.

"Do you think the Japanese would have welcomed you with open arms if they guessed you wanted this kind of deal?"

"They knew damn well I was coming for some kind of deal," Kruger returned, smiling. "One of the Japanese traits I admire is their realism. They've got a big market. They know people like me want a crack at it."

He was gliding over a nice distinction. It was the press that had been conveying every Kruger encomium to Japanese enterprise. It was the press that had rolled out the red carpet. Realism about Kruger's motives lay elsewhere.

Nonetheless the press was familiar with its own headlines.

"Mr. Kruger," demanded an earnest Japanese, "have you timed your proposal because you think the Recruit scandal will make things easier for you?"

Kruger shook his head at this wild speculation. "Scientific discoveries — like MR's robots — make their own schedule," he explained. "We came as soon as we could formulate a deal so attractive for both parties that it wouldn't make sense to turn it down."

"But the heavy-electrical industry here is already vulnerable to foreign competition. How are they going to react?"

"Well, I certainly hope they're not going to start trying to get more special treatment. As I've said all along, it's best for everyone to let honest competition take its toll."

The pack seized on one word instantly.

"Honest? Are you hinting at favors from government members?"

"Isn't that the same as exploiting Recruit?"

With questions being hurled at him from all sides, Kruger slowed the tempo of his response. As a result, he sounded like the only reasonable man in the room.

"You're talking about glitches in the political arena, and I'm talking about long-term economics."

"But your long term has come at a pretty convenient time."

"The convenient time," Kruger said, unruffled, "is when you can put a deal together. And all Lackawanna ever asks is a level playing field."

Bennet Alderman, listening intently, was learning a great deal. Politics and personalities always meant more to him than turbines and circuit breakers. But suddenly Alderman realized that he was working for a man willing to take big risks.

It was something worth remembering.

Other members of the Lackawanna family had made that discovery a long time ago. Two of them, Don Hodiak and Pamela Webb, were in one of the Tokyo Hilton's lounges that evening. The TV over the bar was bringing them the Carl Kruger they knew so well.

When the Recruit scandal emerged, Hodiak groaned aloud. "God almighty, I'm sick of that name."

"If you feel that way, think of how the Japanese must feel," Pamela retorted. "And you have to admit, Carl's doing a beautiful job. He's mentioned the benefits to the steel industry at least three times. And he's skated over the tricky parts."

"I only wish he'd done as good a job selling me," Hodiak said. "Even if this is a great idea in itself, how am I supposed to hammer out a sensible distribution system with this kind of scramble? Basically we're relying on the competence and good faith of a Japanese company we don't know anything about."

"*We* may not know anything about them, but I'll bet Carl has been quietly dickering with Yonezawa for months. Besides, how would you like to try selling over here without them?"

He was not in the mood for questions to which they both knew the answer.

"That would be suicide," he acknowledged grumpily. "But you don't rush into unloading subsidiaries because you get an unexpected market break."

"It's a lot more than that, and you know it, Don. This may be the one moment in time that the local opposition can't tank right over Lackawanna."

Seeing he was unconvinced, she ended more lightly. "Don't let eating all this rice get to you. We really do have a solid deal going."

"That remains to be seen," he replied. "But I'll hand you this, Pamela. You make a better case for Carl than Carl does."

They were a study in contrasts. Hodiak, a heavyset sixty-year-old, bore the marks of chronic anxiety. A longtime Lackawanna production expert, he was a company man to the core. No one valued Kruger's lifesaving results more than he did, but he was too much

29

a traditionalist to appreciate the razzle-dazzle.

He was not too hidebound, however, to accept Pamela Webb, even though she represented one of Kruger's more radical innovations. A stunningly photogenic blonde who had yet to see thirty, she had risen to become Lackawanna's chief financial officer and Carl Kruger's closest confidante. Speculation about their intimacy was widespread, and articles about Lackawanna always featured a photograph of the two of them boarding an executive jet or emerging from a hotel. Pamela herself responded to the publicity by working hard and maintaining her composure, but she appreciated Don Hodiak's uncomplicated willingness to judge her by results.

"Say, where's Ali?" Hodiak asked suddenly. "I feel sorry for that kid, wandering around at loose ends."

Ali Khan was the wizard responsible for Midland Research's technical breakthrough. He had been summoned from England to support Kruger's mission, but his skills were confined to electronic engineering. Business sessions proceeded without him, and so far, his time had been his own.

"He's seeing Tokyo," Pamela replied indifferently. "After all, he's an Asian. It's probably very meaningful to him."

"In a pig's eye!" Hodiak guffawed. "Ali was

born and bred in Birmingham, England. He's about as Asian as I am."

She acknowledged the point with a shrug. "Then he's playing tourist. Thousands of people pay good money to visit Japan."

"They don't do it alone. Hell, the poor kid doesn't even drink."

"What makes you think Ali's doing it alone? He's a very good-looking boy, or," she asked with a challenging lift of the eyebrow, "don't you notice that sort of thing?"

Hodiak grinned good-naturedly. "It may surprise you, Pamela, but twenty years ago, when I had a lot more hair and a lot less weight, I knew all about that sort of thing. If Ali's found himself a girl, I say good luck to him. But it doesn't look like it to me."

He nodded toward the entrance of the bar, where a tall, lithe young man had halted to inspect the gloom. When Khan finally located his colleagues, a brilliant smile lit his dark-skinned face, and he moved toward them with the grace that accompanied all his movements.

"I was shopping in the Ginza, and the TV sets were on," he announced. "Do you know who I saw?"

"Give us three guesses." Pamela laughed.

It was Hodiak who explained the Kruger press conference.

"Well, it doesn't make much sense to me,"

Ali confessed unconcernedly. "Of course I understand why they want my robotics, but I don't see how it's going to help Lackawanna sell American machinery in Japan."

"You," said Don Hodiak, "and a whole lot of other people."

Among those who understood exactly what Carl Kruger was up to were Japan's elected representatives. Two of them watched Kruger's performance with an eye to their own interests.

"The man is clever," the first conceded. "He said over and over that his proposals were attractive to both parties because the steel industry will get its technology and Lackawanna will sell in Japan. He never admitted there was a third party, our own electrical industry."

"He has probably convinced half the nation that he is suggesting a rational and mutually profitable arrangement. And what will the result be?"

The question was rhetorical, but it was answered.

"If we lift a finger to protect the electrical people, our own press will suspect corruption."

Two wily heads cocked in thoughtful silence. Then:

"On the whole, I think the entire problem should be left to MITI."

"I agree."

But the speaker could not maintain the lofty note.

"I only hope," he added bitterly, "that they do not regard themselves as so far above the battle they fail to recognize exactly how sensitive this situation is."

There was no danger.

The Ministry of International Trade and Investment — or MITI, as it is known around the globe — is as distinctively Japanese as Mount Fuji. Nowhere else in the free world is there a single agency so widely empowered to create and implement economic policy. MITI regulates business practices, enforces industrial coordination, and guarantees that domestic and international commercial activity conform to its national goals. Nothing is too large or too small for its consideration. Rice farms and the Toyota Motor Corporation alike fall under its purview. Widely credited with having masterminded the Japanese miracle, MITI is regarded with respect bordering on awe.

Formally, MITI's staff was composed of civil servants. In fact, they were an elite beyond the dreams of Washington or Whitehall.

Amid the scandals convulsing Japan, they strode, untouched and impregnable, like the aristocrats they were. One of them, Tomaheko Matsuda, was presiding over the Midland Research application. He knew that he had been presented with both a great danger and a great opportunity. The result of his actions could be either a career setback or a golden future.

Therefore he studied Carl Kruger's press conference with a critical acumen that exceeded any other viewer's. If Kruger succeeded in beaming the spotlight of public attention on a MITI hearing, then Tomaheko Matsuda intended to showcase his own talents. Everyone, from the Prime Minister down, would witness a display of painstaking attention to detail, consummate mastery of all factors, and scrupulous impartiality.

Matsuda never doubted that he was up to the task. Others in his office, however, were not.

"This report of yours, Ushiba, is unacceptable," he said coldly the next morning. "It is nothing more than a précis of the material supplied by the interested parties. I should not have to remind a man with your years at MITI that we judge on the basis of our own research. Our specialists have performed their separate analyses. It remains only for you to utilize them and integrate their results into your final treatment."

The subordinate bowed too deeply, then broke into fulsome apology.

"I will have an exhaustive study ready for your next session," he promised in conclusion.

"I shall expect it on my desk."

Both men spoke in the even cadence of established ritual. Each turned an impassive face to the other. But in that instant, twin decisions were born.

Matsuda had realized for some time that the obsequious Mr. Ushiba was lazy and incompetent. He had always been an irritant; now he was a peril. Ushiba would have to be shipped to some distant outpost of MITI.

Tomaheko Matsuda was in almost every way the more intelligent and perceptive man. But in one minute area, Ushiba was the more experienced. His ineptitude had been noticed before. During the past ten years Ushiba had been posted to every single department of MITI. By now he had developed a sixth sense for recognizing when his superiors arrived at the moment of truth. And he was tired of annual transfers. Behind his expression of dutiful receptivity, Mr. Ushiba vowed to bestir himself into uncharacteristic activity.

This time he was staying put, no matter what he had to do.

Chapter 3

High over the Pacific, John Thatcher had ample time to digest Carl Kruger's game plan. Instead of a run-of-the-mill transaction, he was hoping to score a touchdown in the Japanese market, with Yonezawa Trading Company running interference. On the whole, Thatcher wished him nothing but luck. If the gamble paid off, Lackawanna would make bigger and better profits. And if it did not, the failure would be cost-free for the company's creditors. Lackawanna's domestic activity was their real collateral.

Fair-mindedly willing to share the gold on the streets of Tokyo, Thatcher regarded his own schedule as basically unaltered. The first order of business was to nudge the Alaska deal forward. Then he and Gene Fleming would swim through the embassy reception, touting the services of SloanCorp. In between these serious endeavors, he would make time to attend the MITI hearing on Wednesday and formally present his affidavit.

But, at Narita Airport, newsstand after newsstand displayed the same face. There was

Carl Kruger gravely testifying before a congressional committee; Carl Kruger in shirtsleeves, conferring across a desk with Pamela Webb; Carl Kruger in a hard hat at Cape Canaveral; and, on three separate covers, Carl Kruger standing at the top of an airplane's steps, his arms outstretched in wide greeting.

The driver in the car waiting for Thatcher was the first to confirm the prevailing fervor.

"I myself saw Mr. Kruger's arrival," he began chattily before sweeping to his impressive conclusion. "And I even saw Pamela Webb."

In the back seat, Thatcher grimaced. By the time Miss Webb was a household name, his own agenda was threatened. Instead of being recognized as the visible symbol of the Sloan Guaranty Trust, he was all too likely to be viewed as a bit player in the great Kruger campaign.

This premonition received support when he followed his luggage into the lobby of the Hilton, where the staff was galvanized by his name.

"Yes, yes, Mr. Thatcher," they chorused. "We have been anticipating your arrival and are holding a letter for you."

There was no question of rummaging through the everyday pigeonholes. Instead the desk clerk reached into some more hallowed recess to produce a thick, creamy envelope addressed in calligraphy so beautiful that it was a rebuke to the entire Roman alphabet.

"And," he continued eagerly, "the messenger from Yonezawa Trading Company awaits your reply."

Glancing in the direction indicated, Thatcher encountered the deepest bow of his life.

The communication was just as stately. Would Mr. Thatcher do Fumitoshi Arai the inestimable honor of lunching with him today? Since Thatcher's sojourn in Japan was to be lamentably brief, might Mr. Arai be pardoned the discourtesy of such short notice? His driver would, of course, hold himself ready to await Mr. Thatcher's convenience. With profoundest respect, etc., etc.

Thatcher could recognize high-pressure tactics, even when they came gift-wrapped, but usually he knew what was being sold. Today he was baffled. A giant of Japanese industry, with whom he was personally unacquainted, had not only ascertained his flight time and hotel accommodation but also stationed a messenger with obvious instructions to preempt other overtures. Curiosity dictated his reply, but prudence suggested an interval to permit other developments.

Lifting a finger, Thatcher fetched the driver to his side.

"Tell Mr. Arai it will give me great pleasure to lunch with him, and you may pick me up in one hour."

Thatcher normally allowed himself a substantial breather after a major flight. With this indulgence seriously curtailed, he decided to soak himself in a steaming tub. He had just enough time to review what he knew about his luncheon host. Yonezawa was not one of Japan's ancient trading companies, with a Baron This or a Baron That in its lineage. It was a postwar phenomenon, the single-handed creation of Fumitoshi Arai. Having started as a maverick, he was now, after forty years' unbroken success, a pillar of the industrial establishment.

But what did he want with the Sloan Guaranty Trust? Lunch, presumably, would tell.

Yonezawa was headquartered in an industrial park north of the city. At the arched entrance from the highway, small letters beneath the exotic script read YONEZAWA TRADING COMPANY. Thereafter the limousine cruised past *Yonezawa Concrete*, *Yonezawa Steel*, *Yonezawa Marine*, and *Yonezawa Financial Services* before arriving at another *Yonezawa Trading Company*. The individual buildings were not inordinately large, but the massed effect was impressive.

The autocrat responsible for all this was a fragile, parchment-thin patriarch who moved haltingly. After initial courtesies, Fumitoshi Arai apologized.

"I very much regret that I do not speak English," he said through an interpreter.

The private dining room to which he led Thatcher was furnished with museum-quality Louis Quatorze, and the paintings on the wall had come by way of Sotheby's.

A waitress materialized, bearing a bottle of champagne and glasses.

"You may be amused to learn that this comes from a vineyard that I own," said Arai in a silvery whisper. "It is not a first-rate champagne, but I enjoy indulging in it."

"Very natural," said Thatcher, reflecting that if it had been single-malt Scotch, Arai would probably own the distillery.

They reached consommé topped with caviar before Arai raised any relevant topic.

"I am told that the Sloan Guaranty Trust has dealt with Carl Kruger and Lackawanna in many capacities," he said.

"Quite correct," said Thatcher, thinking that he saw light. "In addition to the loans we made during the emergency, we have a long history of acting for Lackawanna."

Thatcher delivered his testimonial unresentfully. Arai had a legitimate interest in

Lackawanna. If Kruger's scheme to distribute through Yonezawa bore fruit, the two companies would be marching in lockstep. Before he took the plunge, Arai wanted reassurance that Lackawanna could pull its weight.

Thatcher was willing to provide a banker's general endorsement. Whether this was enough for the enigmatic Mr. Arai remained to be seen.

"There are many indisputable advantages in the acquisition of MR," said Arai. "However, the case for our distributing Lackawanna's products may be somewhat more problematical."

Bracing himself, Thatcher continued eating his excellent sirloin. To his surprise, Arai did not press for privileged information. On the contrary, he divulged some of his own.

"There is, as you may know, considerable opposition to the introduction of the Lackawanna product line," he said. "It is necessary to obtain official sanction. In addition, there is political pressure involved as well. Fortunately I think I may confide that Yonezawa has useful friends in the government."

He paused for a sip of iced water, making comment from Thatcher necessary.

"I am sure that bodes well for the likelihood of your coming to terms with Kruger," said Thatcher cautiously. Arai's candor struck him as out of character.

"However, other people also have friends in high places." Arai resumed, looking into space. "They are organizing a major campaign to convince certain members of the ministry that it is critically important to protect the domestic electrical equipment industry from American competition."

"Is that so?" said Thatcher helpfully.

"And the leadership of these forces has been assumed by Shima Trading Company, which has been successful in the past in ensuring this protection."

Thatcher realized that he should have seen this one coming. Shima was the Japanese partner that the Sloan was bringing together with Ridgeway, Ridgeway & Hall of Anchorage. By fair means or foul, his aged host had gotten wind of this arrangement.

"It would be highly unfortunate, indeed disastrous, if Shima prevents Lackawanna from selling in Japan," Arai observed. "And we would go far toward deflecting protectionist sentiment in your great country by liberalizing the Japanese market."

Rather than rehash arguments about quotas and trade deficits, Thatcher struck out for new ground.

"The Sloan has not had the honor of dealing with Yonezawa," he remarked. "But our preliminary discussions with Shima have impressed us very favorably."

Arai inclined his head.

"However," Thatcher continued, "our involvement with Shima is confined exclusively to a projected wood-pulp undertaking in Alaska. I know, of course, that they are a major manufacturer of electrical equipment and, hence, a potential competitor to Lackawanna. But in that area, we at the Sloan do not envisage doing any business with them."

If the interpreter was worth his salt, the verbiage would convey a simple message: What did Arai expect Thatcher and the Sloan to do?

Once again the old man took refuge in indirection.

"It is always difficult," he philosophized, "when, in balancing many interests, a conflict appears to arise. Then true wisdom is required."

Thatcher was left to make of this what he could.

"Obviously he is a man who appreciates the exercise of power," Thatcher was saying late that afternoon.

Carl Kruger, when finally tracked down, denied instigating the overture from Arai.

"Hell, I didn't even know the Sloan was

43

involved with Shima. And I don't see what difference it makes."

"To anybody not familiar with American banks, it might seem like a conflict of interest. And these days I suppose they're sensitive about that kind of thing."

Kruger veered off on a tangent. "I don't know about that, but it seems as if you've spent more time with Arai than we have. I met him for about fifteen minutes and then got shuffled downstairs. You'd think that MR and Lackawanna weren't worth his attention."

"I doubt if he would be preparing to ram through a major revolution in Japanese practice if that were the case."

The famous Kruger grin surfaced. "That's what I'm banking on. I want this deal so much I can taste it. But believe me, we walk soft when it comes to Fumitoshi Arai. It's practically like dealing with the emperor."

Thatcher agreed that Japanese formality, carried to the nth degree, could be unsettling.

"Oh, it's not that." Kruger waved broadly. "I've got nothing to complain about with the Japanese. They've done very well by me. We know what we're proposing goes against the grain with a lot of them, but everybody in the government has bent over backward to be cooperative."

Examining his companion critically, Thatcher recalled the atmospherics of the great Lackawanna bailout. Unrelentingly optimistic, Kruger had stage-managed a major restructuring without admitting for one moment the scope of what he was doing. The same process seemed to be going on now. Kruger's public line was that the Japanese were wonderful, simply dying to be of assistance to this stranger in their midst. Like Arai, Carl Kruger was not going to say one single word about the Recruit scandal. The sunshine approach had worked once, and it was being tried again.

"I'm sure they're cooperating," Thatcher said. "Otherwise you couldn't have progressed so rapidly."

"If you think the Japanese feel they're being rushed, you should hear my people. Don Hodiak — you've met him, haven't you? he's the head of production — is so busy seeing all the obstacles, he can't see the benefits."

Kruger's tone was indulgent, but Thatcher was interested to learn of a nonenthusiast in the Lackawanna camp.

"Pamela says she's barely had time to scrape the financials into shape, and Benny Alderman, our PR man, said a couple of days wasn't enough to prepare a media blitz." Kruger laughed outright. "If this isn't a blitz, I'd like to see one."

Thatcher agreed that the unknown Alderman had done a smashing job.

"What about the people at MR?" he asked. "This means the most to them, after all."

"That's Ali Khan. He's the boy genius at MR who developed these robotics. He's still in shock at being tumbled into a plane at Heathrow and dumped down in Tokyo. But he's never pretended to understand business decisions, and he's tickled pink that the whole world wants his brain-child."

"That's certainly understandable," Thatcher murmured, wondering if an unnerved staff was what Kruger needed.

But communication with Carl Kruger was pursuing a familiar course. Even as Thatcher thought of a problem, Kruger was moving to dispel it.

"None of this really makes any difference," he argued. "Ali was getting ready to speak at some technical conference in England next week, so he could handle our presentation here in his sleep. And Pamela is our liaison with Midland Research. She had to rush a little to update the last quarter's figures, but nobody gives a damn about MR as a company. It's their robotics that Yonezawa wants."

"I'm surprised they're buying the company. Wouldn't acquiring the technology satisfy their needs?"

"It would satisfy theirs but not mine," Kruger said bluntly. "Arai would have been pleased to shell out a mint just for a license and call it quits. But I want the Japanese market for Lackawanna. MR's technology is the bait to get it."

How typical of Kruger! Enormous frankness about his deal with Yonezawa while he allowed one member of the Lackawanna team to slip away from consideration.

Matching innocence with innocence, Thatcher sounded as if he were automatically running down a list.

"So that leaves Hodiak."

"Don doesn't really enter the picture until we have MITI approval. Then, of course, he'll be central to the final arrangements with Yonezawa, which gives him plenty of time to adjust."

In other words, everything was for the best in this best of all possible worlds.

"You see, Don's the kind of guy who doesn't like novelty," Kruger continued. "Propose something new to him, and his first instinct is to dream up every possible contingency that can go wrong. But by the time you've talked about it so long it doesn't sound new anymore, he climbs aboard."

A lesser man might have misjudged Kruger. But Thatcher was inclined to think that he was like an actor who insists on staying in

47

character, even off the set. How the performance was viewed by someone like Fumitoshi Arai, it was impossible to say. Either the Japanese were baffled by the success of this smiling simpleton or, more likely, they ascribed to him depths of cunning that would boggle the Western mind.

"Hodiak will have to, won't he?"

Kruger's grin was a challenge. "Show me the division manager who seriously objects to skyrocketing sales with a healthy profit margin."

Here, at least, they were on solid ground.

"You have a point," Thatcher conceded.

"I'm not worried about my people. But I sure as hell would like to know why Arai is suddenly nervous. Three days ago he was so calm, he was practically dead."

Thatcher reviewed his séance at Yonezawa. "Not exactly nervous," he corrected. "Thoughtful and very alert. I made a point of emphasizing that the Sloan's connection with Shima began long before I knew of Lackawanna's application to MITI. But while that may have assured him of our good faith, he is certainly expecting some action by your opposition."

Kruger nodded. "I'd better get my people fanning out in case there are any rumors floating around."

Surprised, Thatcher pointed out that the Japanese grapevine was not likely to be accessible to transient visitors.

"Hell, no. That wasn't exactly what I was thinking of."

Kruger proved his point ten minutes later, when they were joined by two of his staff.

"How did things go at Yonezawa?" he asked, immediately after the introductions.

Don Hodiak accepted a drink and sank into a chair. "Oh, they seem cooperative enough," he said grudgingly. "On paper, we've got a reasonable program for spare parts and warranty compliance. What it would be like in practice is something else again."

After depositing a mountain of financial data on a table, Pamela Webb joined them. "The accountants over there are right on target. We got through more than I expected."

"Well, they've already seen most of the figures for MR," Kruger remarked.

"Come off it, Carl." She laughed. "Nobody cares about those figures. If Shima has a brain in its head, it will present Lackawanna as an undesirable element in Japan. That's sure what Yonezawa is anticipating."

Suddenly Hodiak's expression lightened. "You should have seen their faces when they realized that lunch was going to have to include Pamela."

"They adjusted fast enough," she said with amusement. "I've had more trouble with Austrians."

Silently watching the threesome at work, Thatcher was impressed by the camaraderie of the Lackawanna team. Differences in opinion, age, and sex seemed immaterial. Kruger was lounging lazily, while Hodiak slumped on his spine, with his legs outstretched. Pamela added to the general informality by kicking off her shoes, plumping down on the settee, and neatly folding her long legs beside her.

With his staff ready and waiting, Kruger moved to the matter at hand.

"Something else has come up," he began, explaining Thatcher's audience with Arai. "Don, why don't you use this program you worked out with Yonezawa as an excuse to go over to MITI tomorrow morning? And, Pamela, they say that Zaretski, the commercial attaché, keeps his ear to the ground. You'd better touch base with him. If there's anything really out there, one of you should pick up tremors."

As it happened, John Thatcher got there before either of them.

The unexpected eruption of Mr. Arai had forced Thatcher to delay contacting the Sloan's Tokyo office. But as he returned to his hotel room later that evening, he decided it was time to call in his secret weapon on the Pacific Rim.

Eugene Fleming was a unique member of the Sloan's far-flung empire. He not only bridged a vast cultural chasm, he had learned to do it as an adult in a commercial context. Twenty-five years before, he had been snatched by his draft board and assigned for two years to Japan. An enthusiastic motorcyclist, he had spent his time off at local rallies, at one of which he met the daughter of a small motorcycle manufacturer. Ultimately Fleming returned to Buffalo, taking his bride with him. By the time he earned his MBA, the Japanese motorcycle was making its first foreign inroads. Fleming's mother-in-law missed her daughter, and her husband conceded that an American in the business might be useful. From these small beginnings Gene Fleming never looked back. He was worth every penny of the exorbitant sum he demanded from the Sloan.

He was also quick on the uptake. Before Thatcher had shed his tie, the phone rang and Fleming was apologizing for the lateness of the hour.

"I've been trying to get you since five o'clock," he explained.

"Something unexpected came up, Gene, or

I would have gotten in touch with you earlier," Thatcher said briefly. He was curious to learn the reason for the late-night urgency.

"The pot beginning to boil?" Fleming suggested cheerfully. "I figured something must be up when Noriko Iwamoto called, inviting us both to play golf tomorrow. He's the head honcho at Shima, and I could practically hear the tom-toms beating."

Was this the contact that Arai was so eager to forestall?

Thatcher had no intention of being rushed into a hasty review of the situation over the phone. "I probably should meet with Shima, but not before I've had a chance to talk with you."

"Absolutely." Fleming was way ahead of him. "I rejected the offer of their limo. If I drive, we'll have well over an hour to ourselves. At the very least."

Thatcher found himself grateful for the urban sprawl that was forcing Japan's golf courses into the hinterland.

"Good. I have a fair amount to tell you."

Chapter 4

In spite of early stirrings the next morning by every member of the Lackawanna camp, the Japanese were at work before them. Tomaheko Matsuda began his day at a conference with his cabinet minister, in which he had no difficulty deciphering the high-minded sentiments uttered. When a hearing threatened to become a confrontation between two great trading companies, the utmost sensitivity was required. But the ministry must also remember that Carl Kruger, a good friend of the Japanese government, had earned the right to the utmost consideration.

As a result, Matsuda was outraged, when he returned to his office, to learn that a vice-president of Lackawanna was being entertained by Mr. Ushiba.

"How did this happen?" he demanded.

The receptionist had already washed her hands of the entire affair. Foreigners were not supposed to wander casually into MITI, and she had never received instructions for such eccentricity.

". . . and then Mr. Ushiba passed and insisted that it was improper to keep Mr. Hodiak here." Her sniff at this point spoke volumes. "He introduced himself and invited Mr. Hodiak to his office."

The minister's *utmost consideration,* Matsuda knew all too well, did not mean a lowly clerk. There was only one way to retrieve the situation.

"Tell Ushiba that I will receive Mr. Hodiak immediately," he thundered, "and summon an interpreter."

When Ushiba appeared with Hodiak in tow, Matsuda was presented with further cause for embarrassment. Ushiba was pelting his guest with English phrases so halting and freakish that Matsuda winced. Breaking right through his subordinate's babbling, he jerked the conversation into Japanese.

Unfortunately it was normal procedure for Mr. Ushiba to report.

"I have explained to Mr. Hodiak that my synopsis of the MR application will be ready for distribution on Wednesday," he said proudly. "There remains only a final analysis of the latest Midland Research figures added by Miss Webb and a review of these new schedules Mr. Hodiak is offering."

By now Matsuda bitterly regretted his failure to transfer Ushiba months before. The clerk was prattling as if MR's past finances had any significance, ignoring the one element worthy of discussion.

"New schedules?" Matsuda queried.

"That's right," Hodiak said. "At our last meeting you expressed reservations about the distribution of Lackawanna products. So we've arrived at an agreement with Yonezawa that spells it all out."

"The material will, of course, be entered into the record, but there was no need to add to your no doubt busy schedule by coming here today. We would have been pleased to handle this at our next meeting."

The implied rebuke passed over Hodiak's head. "Just making sure you've got enough time to give it the once-over," he replied.

Matsuda had raised the question of distribution in order to give Shima Trading Company its opportunity to criticize. The last thing he wanted was to have the issue resolved before Wednesday's open meeting.

"That is extremely considerate of Lackawanna, and I only regret that you have suffered personal inconvenience."

"No trouble," Hodiak said gruffly.

In spite of the casual approach, Hodiak's next words confirmed Matsuda's growing suspicion that he was dealing with a crafty player.

"Just let me know what else we can do. If any areas of our proposal give you trouble,

I figure we can knock them off, one by one."

They were now at complete cross-purposes. While Hodiak only wanted some clue to Fumitoshi Arai's sudden edginess, Matsuda saw an obvious attempt to limit his freedom of action. If he said there were no problems, the statement could be used against him. If he admitted doubts, Hodiak would promptly try to short-circuit Shima's input to these hearings.

As he pondered, Matsuda's eye fell on Mr. Ushiba, projecting birdlike interest in the proceedings.

"We appreciate your offer, but as Mr. Ushiba has explained, our final review will not be complete until Wednesday. It is impossible to say what arguments may be raised at that time."

Hodiak had never hoped for direct information. But the more he lingered, the greater the possibility that Matsuda might let something fall.

To Ushiba, however, Matsuda's words constituted an invitation to join the discussion.

"All necessary files have been forwarded to my attention," he said earnestly, "with the sole exception of your own, Mr. Secretary. I have hesitated to interrupt your study of these documents, but it would be most helpful at this juncture if they could be incorporated into my final draft."

The constraints imposed by the presence of an outsider prevented Matsuda from annihilating his subordinate with a look of fire. The idiot was actually taking these remarks at face value. Thank God only a foreigner was witnessing this absurdity.

"Yes, yes."

Hastily Matsuda reached for a folder on the desk, shoveled several loose sheets into its bulging cover, and handed it over.

"And now we will not keep you from your important work any further, Mr. Ushiba," he said.

But Mr. Ushiba proved unexpectedly useful. By taking an elaborate leave of Hodiak, he created the dynamics of departure, on which Matsuda was swift to capitalize.

"It was good of you to allow us to impose on your time, Mr. Hodiak," he said.

When Hodiak had finally been levered out of the office, Tomaheko Matsuda was as wary of Lackawanna as any minister could wish.

The other meeting scheduled that morning would have shocked everybody at MITI, from Matsuda down to the receptionist.

Pamela Webb knew nothing about the individual she was going to meet, beyond his credentials. Stanley Zaretski was reputed to be the star U.S. official for American companies with designs on Japan. The embassy in Tokyo struggled with the balance of power in Asia, nuclear armaments in the Pacific, and the life expectancy of the Japanese cabinet. The commercial attaché, who operated out of Osaka, engineered things like the surprising success of Pepperidge Farm cookies.

In person, Stan Zaretski was certainly welcoming. Genially bellowing for coffee, he simultaneously offered a chair and took one appreciative glance. Then, in a move that would have paralyzed Matsuda with embarrassment, he commented:

"No wonder you get so much coverage in the business weeklies. They've never had such photogenic material."

Pamela was far too experienced to mistake this for an overture. Zaretski was signaling the lines along which he wished to conduct their discussion.

"It doesn't hurt," she semaphored back.

She, too, had been making a visual inspection. God had given Zaretski the build of a football player, with a bull neck, massive shoulders, and a barrel chest. The rumpled shirt and open tie were his own contributions.

By the time the inevitable foam cups arrived, they were on first-name terms, but Zaretski was still feeling his way.

"I like your boss's touch," he remarked. "Eight weeks ago, when he sprang this on us, I thought he might have missed the boat. But this turns out to be perfect timing."

One small piece of information deserves another. Pamela instantly acknowledged that she knew the rules of the game.

"Eight weeks ago! I wish to God Carl wouldn't play things so close to the chest. He opened up to us forty-eight hours before we caught the plane."

"He was absolutely right," Zaretski said decisively. "Kruger's always been a favorite here. If there'd been rumors that he was planning to bulldoze his way onto the local market, at least some of the press could have started backtracking. Instead he just descends from the clouds."

Pamela shook her head. "It's a little more complicated than that, Stan. As well you know," she retorted.

"Sure, but that's the way it looks to the outside world."

He was agreeing to more than her statement. They were both now established as knowledgeable, worldly equals, with the understanding that they were operating on his turf. Guidelines in place, Zaretski got down to business.

"So what's up, Pamela?" he asked, quirking

his heavy eyebrows. "Why the sudden rush to Osaka?"

"Yonezawa has started to get fidgety, and we don't know why. They practically kidnapped the man from the Sloan when they found out he was working with Shima on some project in Alaska."

"They kidnapped Gene Fleming?" Zaretski repeated blankly.

"Who's Gene Fleming? I'm talking about John Thatcher." In New York the man from the Sloan might be called Thatcher, but in Tokyo he was definitely called Fleming. When this snarl had finally been untangled, Zaretski scrubbed his jaw thoughtfully.

"Let me get this straight. Thatcher is representing Lackawanna's creditors at your MITI meeting, then he goes to Alaska to finalize this pulp deal of Shima's."

"That's right."

Pamela watched the slow birth of a smile on Zaretski's battered features. She could almost hear the wheels turning as he factored this information into some equation unknown to her.

"It would be a great ploy," he said at last. "Everybody would be off the hook."

"Would you like to enlarge on that to a simple country girl?" she asked sweetly.

Zaretski grinned. "Look, Arai and Kruger

have worked things so that on the surface, it's to almost everybody's advantage to go along with them."

"Not to Shima's," she pointed out. "Or any other Japanese heavy-electrical producer."

"Naturally. I'm talking about the government boys. Now, in spite of their current problems, they're just as leery as ever about letting foreign competition into the country. They've maintained a balance here between the industries that are genuinely competitive worldwide and the ones that need protection in the home market. Everybody's afraid Kruger would be the thin end of the wedge for a pack of foreign invaders."

This was nothing new for Pamela. "We all realize that it's just a temporary political scandal that's giving Lackawanna any government tolerance."

"From their point of view, it would be wonderful to get the reputation for cooperation without having it cost them a plug nickel."

Now she was hanging on every word. "Go on," she urged.

"What if an American institution blew the whistle?"

"You mean the creditors?"

Zaretski leaned back, his muscular wrists locked behind his neck. "It would be beautiful," he crooned. "Look at the script they'd have. Total helpfulness by the Japanese government, eager participation by Yonezawa, enthusiastic endorsement by the media. And then, boom! The whole thing crumbles because the creditors won't support the deal. That way, Tokyo can tell Washington it's not their fault it got blown out of the water."

The frown that had been etching fine lines on Pamela's brow disappeared.

"Restrain your enthusiasm," she advised. "There's just one little problem — it won't wash."

"You and I are pretty sure about that. But if I were Shima, it sure as hell would be worth the old college try. And if I were Yonezawa, I'd want to know all about this guy from the Sloan, particularly when that bank is already making waves."

That was enough to bring her bolt upright.

"This is some backyard you've got, Stan. It's more like a minefield. Don't tell me the Sloan has screwed up?"

"No way. Japanese investment abroad is growing every day. To the surprise of some of their banks, it's the Americans who are picking up the big bucks. That's bad enough, but the double whammy is provided by our own little Gene Fleming."

"Somehow I thought we'd get back to him," she murmured.

But Zaretski was now serious. "You've got to understand that over here, the ideal world is split into two parts. In the first, everybody is pure Japanese. In the second, everybody is pure non-Japanese. There are no crossovers, no half-breeds. They still get real shook up when a foreigner takes on Japanese coloration. From the start Fleming was connected to the grid, and these days the connections have multiplied. Besides all that, he's bilingual."

"So are lots of people," she protested. "The place is filled with European kids studying Japanese."

"They don't count. The Japanese are used to Westerners trying to go native. Would-be Buddhists are just comic. But Gene makes no bones about being an American. He looks like one, he acts like one. The trouble is that after fifteen minutes, he can seduce them into forgetting it. And this in a country where people are physically startled by fluent Japanese coming out of a white face."

Trying to maintain her footing, Pamela fell back on what she knew.

"Fleming must be doing something right."

"Enough to make people sit up and take notice. I'll bet Mr. Arai thinks Gene is some kind of mutant. That would explain why he wanted a real quick gander at the big boss from New York."

"Well, if that's all it is," she reasoned, "he should get reassured on Wednesday. Thatcher's role is just a formality."

Pamela had what she had come for; Zaretski was still waiting for his *quid pro quo*.

"Why don't you catch a later train and stay for lunch, Pamela?" he suggested.

Her eyes sparkled with amusement. "Someplace quiet and out of the way?" she said in mock innocence.

"Like hell!" he retorted cheerfully. "We'll go where all the local commercial types hang out. I want to see their jaws drop."

Pamela exploded into a gale of laughter.

"One of my favorite occupations."

Chapter 5

John Thatcher's day also began early.

"My sole connection with Carl Kruger's deal will be the delivery of my affidavit," he explained to Gene Fleming as they were trying to break out of Tokyo's cluttered streets. "The only reason I'm representing the creditors is that I was coming here anyway for the Alaska pulp venture. But it was a mistake not to bring you into the picture beforehand."

Fleming did not share the defensiveness of so many overseas managers. His position was too strong.

"That doesn't make any difference. But I can see why Shima wants to play golf with us. They've got a hell of a lot at stake."

"Presumably so does Yonezawa. At least that is how I interpret Mr. Arai's sudden invitation to lunch yesterday."

Fleming whistled appreciatively.

"So the old man is coming down from the mountain. You know Arai's become pretty much of a recluse the last couple of years."

"Perhaps he's husbanding his strength," Thatcher suggested.

"You mean because of the frail appearance? Don't you believe it!" Fleming snorted. "Arai looked that way twenty years ago. Personally I think he does it for effect. The Japanese may not go in for press conferences, but they've got their own brand of image creation. Arai likes to play the invisible man most of the time. Then, whenever he does emerge, he packs a hell of a wallop. Tell me, was he using a cane yesterday?"

Thatcher was intrigued by the question. "No, he was not."

"Wait until the trade reception tomorrow night. He'll be the elder statesman incarnate," Fleming prophesied.

"I'll look forward to it. In the meantime, what should I know about Shima?"

"They're being shafted. This deal has been set up so that Yonezawa and Lackawanna get all the profits while Shima does the paying. For the life of me, I don't know if Kruger has been very clever or just plain lucky."

"In what respect?"

"In choosing his partner. Arai is the only one who would dare pull something this raw. He must have been planning it for months, waiting for just the right moment to strike. And of course he came up with a format that gives him a fighting chance of success."

Thatcher understood the nature of the timing. "You're referring to Recruit, aren't you?"

Fleming had to delay his answer until a fleet of eight-wheelers thundered past them.

"Yes; no one in the government wants to interfere," he said in the ensuing quiet. "A lot of Shima's friends are lying low."

"And Kruger's done a good job with the publicity, judging from the magazine covers I saw at the airport."

Fleming grinned. "He's pretty damned colorful to Japanese eyes. And this personality treatment of a business executive is new to them. I saw one story on what he likes to eat. The net result is that he's on his way to canonization by the media."

"Surely that can't be decisive."

"Not by a long shot," Fleming said energetically. "But Kruger's come flitting in here at a time of turmoil that's bigger than Recruit. Everybody's uptight about how to keep the country booming. There's a national debate going on. Some of them want to open up the economy, some of them want to seal the doors tighter than ever. But they're all scared at the prospect of Japan losing ground. Korea, Taiwan, Malaysia — you name it. They're all threats. Yonezawa's trying to sell Kruger as one way to keep Japan competitive."

As he defined the forces arrayed against Shima, Gene Fleming casually scanned the incomprehensible road signs, swung around a cloverleaf suspended over a spanking new satellite town, and sped off in a different direction.

"And to protect their interests, Shima's got to wade in and start an all-out fight to upset someone else's applecart. That sort of confrontational move doesn't get a lot of sympathy here. The received truth is that they should resolve their differences with Arai behind the scenes. Fat chance! Poor Rick has been put in a position where he's pressuring a lot of bureaucrats and politicians who won't thank him for it."

"Rick? Is that Noriko Iwamoto? Are you familiar with him?"

"Oh, Rick and I go way back to the days when Shima started him in their motorcycle division. But don't be fooled by the nickname. He went to school in the States because his father was stationed there, and he likes to pretend he's one of the boys to innocent Americans."

Clearly today's meeting was going to be a sharp contrast to Arai's luncheon, with its formality and its interpreters. Even the pictorials helped, as they discovered when they finally arrived at the course.

As far as the eye could see there were men who seemed dressed by the same outfitter as

Arnold Palmer. Thatcher was under no illusion as to what they were doing here on a workday. Golf, after all, is a worldwide lubricant. Strangers can spend hours together, and small talk is no problem.

Noriko Iwamoto — tall, rangy, and at least fifteen years younger than Thatcher expected — took full advantage of the ambience. After vigorously pumping hands and introducing one of his vice-presidents, he launched into a discussion of the clubs awaiting Thatcher, which took them through the pro shop and onto the first tee. The vice-president, who spoke minimal English, was amiable, and Gene Fleming did his bit by describing difficult holes.

"It's a good course," Iwamoto said earnestly, as if he really cared. "The only trouble is that it's so far away."

Thatcher, who knew that today's game was being stage-managed, was willing to wait upon events.

"The same thing is happening around New York," he replied politely, getting on with the round.

To an outsider the scene would have seemed idyllic. There was a clear blue sky overhead, and the sunshine was tempered by a mild breeze. The greens were in perfect condition, and according to their handicaps, the four men were evenly matched. But Thatcher, who had noticed the smooth, practiced swing of the vice-president, together with the extraordinary pains he required to miss several easy putts, confidently expected developments from him.

At the third hole the language barrier was allowed to intrude. The vice-president addressed a remark in Japanese to Gene Fleming, and the foursome dissolved into two couples. Even then Iwamoto was in no hurry. Chatting about the Burning Tree Club outside Washington, he continued to take Thatcher's measure. It was a full half hour — by which time Thatcher was coming to the end of his resources about the different grasses required by Japanese grounds keepers — before the vice-president plopped his ball into the water hazard.

Instantly Iwamoto brought down the first-act curtain and suggested that he and Thatcher move into the shade while they waited. Confident that the vice-president knew his duty, Thatcher prepared for a lengthy session. It began with their forthcoming trip to Alaska.

"We've been very pleased with the service provided by the Sloan. Len Ridgeway seems like the ideal partner for us, at least on paper. But I'll be glad to meet him."

Thatcher said that while some questions still

had to be ironed out, he foresaw no real problem in Anchorage.

"The sooner we can increase production, the better, as far as Shima is concerned. The demand for pulp here is skyrocketing," Iwamoto said with an expansive thrust of his hand.

Thatcher obligingly nudged them forward.

"There seem to be ten times as many magazines on the stand as during my last visit," he said.

"And every single one of them featuring Carl Kruger," Iwamoto replied tartly.

"He does tend to grab the limelight."

But Rick Iwamoto was simply using Kruger to get to the point.

"We all realize his technology can be a godsend to the steel industry. There's no argument against acquiring it. The question is, how?"

Now they were getting down to it. Thatcher cocked his head receptively.

"There are alternatives?"

Iwamoto grinned. "For starters, what's wrong with old-fashioned money? Kruger could license Yonezawa and charge a hell of a lot. What's more, that way Kruger would still have the benefit of future advances."

"I expect that possibility has been considered."

Iwamoto leaned forward persuasively, giving Thatcher a clear view of Fleming and the vice-president trudging off behind a screen of trees.

"Kruger may have considered it, but have you? I would think the creditors would be happier with a substantial addition to Lackawanna's income, coupled with the retention of a valuable asset. That way, they're taking no chances. Kruger's plans to enter the Japanese market are a gamble at best. He has no familiarity with domestic practices; he's bound to take a lot of time getting off the ground."

It went without saying that Shima's mighty apparatus would be busy raising a host of obstacles to Kruger's success.

"That would certainly have been a major consideration if Kruger did not have Yonezawa's contacts and distribution system to support his efforts," Thatcher pointed out.

"Arai may not be able to deliver as much as he has promised," Iwamoto warned. "He probably expects the usual resistance from us. But his own proposal is so radical and it affects us so directly that we may be forced into more far-reaching opposition."

"Speaking of far-reaching," Thatcher said mildly, "how do you think your vice-president has managed to get into that sand trap?"

Iwamoto spared only a perfunctory glance at his subordinate's predicament before returning to the attack. "I am trying to suggest that you, being on the scene, may want to revise your assessment of Kruger's plan."

Thatcher took a deep breath to deliver the speech he had come to make. By American custom, the creditors were not concerned with the broad picture. If Kruger's sale of assets did not materially lessen his ability to meet his obligations as due, then the creditors had to yield the right of decisionmaking. And Lackawanna's current performance effectively reduced Thatcher's role to one of automatic compliance.

As the well-rehearsed phrases dropped from Thatcher's lips, he observed a change in his companion. Until now Iwamoto had been a robust, outgoing person. His voice had been inflected, his face had mirrored one expression after another, his hands and arms had been in constant play. As he listened to Thatcher, he became Japanese. His hands were stilled, his face was a mask, his brief queries were monotonic. The overall impression was not one of placidity but of great nervous energy under restraint.

"I cannot, of course, propose that you depart from your customs," he said stiffly.

Thatcher was prepared to counter any such

effort by forcing conversation back to RR&H, but the moment passed. With the best will in the world, the vice-president had been able to manage only a quadruple bogey.

"Did you see that last putt?" Gene Fleming marveled. "It must have been at least ninety feet. And I could have sworn that Jiro hit it all wrong. It was damn near miraculous."

Under the shower of congratulations, Jiro produced a tight smile.

"Miraculous," he echoed painfully.

"Well, did we give you enough time on the eighth hole?" Fleming asked when they were finally back in the car.

"Yes, thank you. Your man seemed to be working hard."

"He did everything but hire a dog to steal the ball. And then to have that putt take that crazy break." Fleming laughed. "I thought he was going to swear when it went in."

Thatcher was reassuring. "Oh, the job was done by then. Theoretically, Iwamoto was trying to promote a creditors' strike or at least a demand for further review. Actually he was warning me that he is far from through. He feels that Yonezawa is playing so dirty that from now on it's street fighting with no holds barred."

"That's no way for Rick to talk," Fleming

said disapprovingly. "Maybe he's beginning to fall for his own act. Because the American clothes and the American slang are just a put-on. Rick thinks by Japanese rules, and it's a big effort for him to plan anything outside them. Now, with Arai, it's second nature. He's been a rogue elephant from the start. People prefer to forget that little fact now that he's a symbol of national success. He may have been head of the Tokyo Rotarians, but he hasn't changed a bit. With him, it's the conservative act that's the put-on."

"In America people would say the same thing about Kruger. I notice you don't consider him when you're weighing the odds. You feel he won't have any impact?"

Fleming was apologetic. "Well, of course, I don't know him. For an outsider, he already has had an impact, so I shouldn't overlook him. I guess I've read too many stories about him and his lady companion."

Gene could hardly have missed them, Thatcher reflected.

"It's hard to know what's going on there. The simple explanation that she's his mistress may be correct. On the other hand, given Kruger's gift for publicity, he may have deliberately made an unusual choice of financial officer as part of the general picture. It has certainly succeeded in capturing the attention of the American media."

"And the Japanese," Fleming retorted. "Everybody here is wildly curious. 'Is she the power behind the throne?' 'Is it true he doesn't go anywhere without her?' You know the sort of thing. What's she really like?"

Thatcher recalled his impressions of Pamela.

"Very good-looking, very efficient, very motivated," he summed up. "I don't know what the facts are, but the two of them have created a situation that is beneficial for both of them. Offhand, I'd say they have most to gain by keeping everybody guessing."

Fleming had not previously considered it from Pamela Webb's point of view. "What's she getting out of it, if not a sugar daddy?"

"She's a household name with the Fortune 500 at the age of twenty-nine. That's worth a great deal by itself, let alone the opportunity to create an impressive résumé. What's more, I'd say she rather enjoys the speculation. She's quite an open young woman. She doesn't hide the fact that she's ambitious."

Gene Fleming nodded comprehension.

"She also doesn't hide a certain underlying sense of mischief," Thatcher added.

This was going too far.

"Mischief!" said Fleming, appalled. "That's the last thing we need."

Then, for the remainder of their long drive back to the city, he turned his attention to the future of SloanCorp.

Chapter 6

Bennet Alderman was sticking with his proven strength as he, too, did his bit for Lackawanna. Having already saturated Japan with Carl Kruger, he had now scheduled Ali for an interview with several technical monthlies. But for these purposes, Ali was still an unknown quantity.

"You have nothing to worry about, Ali. This won't be as tricky as Carl's press conference. It's just a bunch of people coming here to talk."

Ignoring the reassurance, Ali said: "Did you get me the easel with the blackboard?"

"Listen, I'm not sure a blackboard is such a hot idea. You're just giving a general talk."

"I need a blackboard."

Bennet took a deep breath. "Okay, okay. Now, another thing. I don't suppose anybody will ask you about the business details. If they do, just say frankly you don't understand."

"What's so bloody difficult about it?" Ali sighed. "Carl wants to sell me to the Japanese."

"For God's sake, don't say that! Particularly

in that tone of voice. We're all supposed to be enthusiastic."

Ali, still in his sweatsuit, was lounging against the door frame, munching an apple.

"Not me," he said briefly.

"But the sale won't change anything in Birmingham," Alderman protested. "Are you worried by those TV stories about how they do calisthenics and sing the company song together? That's only here. When the Japanese take over a foreign company, they're very tactful. They're supposed to be a lot better at it than we are."

It was impossible to tell whether the speech had any effect. Instead of answering, Ali tossed his apple core into a wastebasket and said:

"I have to shower and dress."

"Just remember, Ali, there's nothing to be nervous about."

"I'm not nervous, Bennet. You are," Ali countered, disappearing into the bathroom.

Alderman winced. The actor was supposed to suffer stage fright while the director remained calm. This role reversal was unsettling.

Half an hour later, Alderman welcomed his guests with professional cordiality and profound misgivings. If anything went wrong, there was no way to retrieve the situation. Carl Kruger at least was adept at trimming his wings in midflight. He could soft-pedal a previous statement, increase his emphasis, or toss out a modest disclaimer — all in response to barely perceptible cues. With Ali, it was foolhardy to expect such control.

But from the first handshake, Ali took charge. Bennet Alderman had overlooked the obvious. After graduating from the University of Birmingham, Ali had done postgraduate work at Cambridge. For three years he had moved in a circle where the exposition of technical matters was an everyday occurrence.

Without a shadow of diffidence, Khan explained the practical aspects of his work. "You can see, from these diagrams of the steel process before and after the introduction of MR's robotics, that there's been a giant saving in labor costs. But that's not all. What may not be so obvious is that we've reduced the need for a very expensive environment."

His audience had been following intently. Now one of them frowned.

"I don't understand that."

Ali scrubbed his nose thoughtfully as he considered possible simplifications. The resulting chalk mark on his forehead completed the professorial picture.

"Stop thinking about robots and think about human beings instead," he directed cheerfully. "Your traditional plant has to protect human respiration, human eyesight, even human skin. And so long as you throw in a robot here and there on a piecemeal basis, you don't change any of that. But by robotizing a major segment of the production line, you can get rid of those requirements in over half your plant. And that means you're saving a hell of a lot of pounds, shillings, and pence."

Even when somebody strayed from the technical arena to ask about the capital investment required for the changeover, Ali did not miss a beat.

"You can see from these figures," he said, "the speed with which you could recover your start-up costs."

For Alderman it was a humbling experience. At the end of twenty minutes he had to shake himself mentally. He was not in Japan in order to admire technical advances — or even to understand them. For a variety of reasons it was desirable that Carl Kruger should score an international victory. That was Bennet Alderman's goal, and he had better remember it.

Meanwhile Ali was nodding approval to a query from the local equivalent of *Scientific American.*

"Sure, there are applications beyond the steel industry."

"Electronics? Machine tools? Isn't that what

Yonezawa is after?"

Ali shrugged. "Offhand, I'd think the older, resource-based industries offer better opportunities. But we're just in the first generation of our work. God knows where we'll end up.

He achieved the ultimate triumph of the salesman. The final burst of optimism came from his audience.

"You were great, Ali, just great," Alderman said the minute he closed the door after the departing visitors. His imagination was fired by the discovery of a new weapon in his armory. "Look, I might be able to get you on some talk show. Or maybe they have a kind of science panel. Do you think you could handle it in twenty-four hours? I'd work overtime with you."

Ali was the expert now. "Bennet, I invented MR's robotics, remember? It's not something where I have to stay up late and cram. I know more about the subject than anyone else in the world."

"I know, I know," Alderman apologized hastily. "It's not the subject matter. It's how you communicate."

"You're talking about transmitting information. People were doing that long before someone invented publicity agents."

Chastened, Alderman tried to justify himself. "Of course you can explain it all; I know that now. But with you being reluctant about the Japanese deal, I was afraid it would show."

"I wasn't telling them about any deal. I was describing my work."

Alderman dismissed petty distinctions. "If I can just get you some TV exposure, then the big-circulation magazines will want their innings with you. Christ, with luck, I can blanket Japan a second time around."

Carl Kruger's thoughts were ranging further afield.

When his call to Washington came through, he greeted the familiar voice eagerly.

"Mike? Glad I caught you."

"Any problems, Carl?" the senator from Ohio asked. "From where I sit, it looks as if you're doing fine."

"No complaints so far," Kruger said buoyantly.

Mike was envious. "I wish I could say the same. Around here things are pretty grim. In fact, if you pull this off, they'll want to hang medals on you."

"It's a long way from being in the bag, but I'm happy with the way we're moving."

"Of course you won't be so popular in this town," Mike continued reflectively. "Everyone's going to be on our necks, wanting to know why it's possible for you to do what

Washington can't."

Sometimes Kruger could be a realist.

"Tell them it's because I get to pick and choose what I tackle," he said crisply. "But, Mike, I'd like to keep the ball rolling by giving the brass here something to chew on."

The two men were ancient allies, their association dating back to shared military service and their fledgling efforts in the business and legal worlds. Now, after twenty-five years of favors given and received, Mike was the one who owed the most.

"Just what did you have in mind, Carl? After all, I've been making speeches against Japan-bashing as long as I can remember."

"Sometimes what you say isn't half as important as when you say it," Kruger drawled. "The thing is, Mike, we've got one of those big, fancy receptions tomorrow night. . . ."

Mike understood. "I'm flying out to L.A. this evening to talk to the Chamber of Commerce. I could give them a barn-burner about how it's getting harder for the U.S. to defend open markets without a show of good faith from our trading partners. Would that do it?"

"Perfect. And it's sure to be picked up by the wire services."

Mike could do better. "I'll have my people release the text real early."

Kruger had learned the importance of political homework. At the embassy gala he might not be able to pronounce the names, but a mental printout would enable him to identify new acquaintances as For, Against, or, most important of all, Undecided.

"Right now the establishment's thinking in terms of the domestic heat," he enlarged. "Whether or not they want to side with Yonezawa against Shima. I'd like to remind the fence sitters about the rest of the world."

"I get your drift, Carl. So why don't I end by saying we've all waited a long time for a signal from Japan. If we don't get one soon, we may lose the fight."

Kruger's voice was velvet with satisfaction. "I do like hitting them on the blind side."

"I haven't forgotten." Mike sounded rueful. "Before the bailout, you had every single private lender, bondholder, stockholder, subcontractor calling Washington. And while we were fielding that flak, you threw the unions at us."

Carl Kruger was not apologizing for his tactics.

"If you hit people from different directions, they're too busy ducking to mount a counterattack. It works in war, and it works in business."

But Mike had known his friend a long time.

"There's more to it than that." He chuckled. "Because while they've got their heads down, Carl, they can't see what you're really up to."

Chapter 7

On Wednesday morning Tomaheko Matsuda was already in the chair when John Thatcher and the other participants arrived at the critical MITI hearings. Ignoring the flurry of bowing and handshaking, Matsuda consulted subordinates until the newcomers sorted themselves out.

At the dramatic last moment, Fumitoshi Arai appeared in the doorway, sketched a salute, then allowed aides to help him to a chair. A gentle wave of his hand indicated that the proceedings could now begin.

Mr. Matsuda remained imperturbable.

"We are ready to open these hearings," he announced through an interpreter. "However, before addressing the first items on today's agenda . . ."

One leftover from earlier sessions was Yonezawa Trading Company's wish to introduce statements from other firms about Japan's urgent need for robotics.

"I, too, have a supplementary filing," said Noriko Iwamoto. From Mr. Matsuda's cautious study of the signatures on these documents, Thatcher inferred that both sides had found additional allies.

"These items shall be entered into the record," said Matsuda, preparing to move ahead. Then he flicked through the contents of his portfolio and frowned. "Summon Mr. Ushiba."

Almost immediately, a small, worried-looking man appeared.

"Ushiba, your report was supposed to be available for distribution this morning," said Matsuda sternly. "Where is it?"

"I deeply regret that the material will not be ready for several hours," Ushiba said. Then, after a pause, he added: "Unfortunately the delay was unavoidable. The drafts submitted by the financial and technical staff did not address the nonprofitability of Midland Research. In the interests of comprehensiveness, I am including study of this point."

Matsuda frowned magisterially. "This matter is not central, but I agree it must be considered. We will therefore study your report *after* Mr. Ali Khan's demonstration of his work. Three o'clock at the latest."

"Without fail," said Ushiba, backing out of the room.

"In the meantime," Matsuda said, turning to Thatcher, "I am sure we would all be grateful for an overview of Lackawanna's financial position, from the creditors' point of view."

"I'll be happy to provide what general assistance I can," Thatcher replied. "But I don't have specific details at hand."

From across the table, Pamela Webb spoke up. "I have all the financials here," she announced. "I can supply any figures you want."

Subsequently Thatcher was amused to note that whenever Matsuda aimed a question at Lackawanna, Carl Kruger let Pamela do the talking.

Then Iwamoto spoke up.

"But is it prudent to permit a bankrupt corporation to make commitments in Japan that may be beyond its capacity?" he demanded hostilely.

During the subsequent exchange, Thatcher decided that Lackawanna was winning on points. Pamela Webb provided all the information requested and volunteered nothing. Yet somehow her replies lured Iwamoto into unwise rebuttal. The upshot was that despite the sniping, Miss Webb made a strong case to prove that Lackawanna's resources were adequate by anybody's standards.

But debates about capital reserve do not enthrall everybody. Ali Khan, with his own contribution postponed until the afternoon, bore up as long as he could, then excused himself and fled. A few minutes later, Bennet Alderman followed suit.

Iwamoto was still struggling to discredit Pamela's facts, figures, and projections when Fumitoshi Arai suddenly intervened. In a plaintive whisper, he requested clarification of a point he could not possibly have misunderstood. This gave Pamela the opportunity to reply with a glowing summation on behalf of Lackawanna.

Before Iwamoto could fire back, Matsuda stepped in. "And does that accord with the creditors' view?" he asked Thatcher.

Thatcher replied that the creditors knew of no undisclosed problems.

"Are there any further questions for Mr. Thatcher?"

Iwamoto had not given up. "At the moment, no," he said stubbornly. "But we have not yet seen your staff's analysis."

"Very true." Matsuda returned to Thatcher. "May we impose further on your time? We would be grateful if you could join our discussion this afternoon."

There was only one reply possible. Today the Sloan Guaranty Trust was a bystander. But if SloanCorp had a future in Japan, cooperating with MITI was essential.

"It will be a pleasure," said Thatcher.

"Then perhaps we might enter your affidavit into the formal record at this point."

More was required than a simple signature. Thatcher produced the customary swatch of documents. First there was the statement, duly notarized, that he was the official representative of the creditors of Lackawanna Electric Company. Then there was an imposing document from the State of New York, certifying that the notary in question was in fact authorized to perform this function. Finally there was a certificate bristling with the official seal of the United States of America, in which the secretary of state informed the Japanese government that the State of New York knew what it was doing and had the right to do it.

As every sheet of paper was handed to Matsuda, he studied it gravely. Only then did he produce the release, consulting his watch while Thatcher scrawled his signature.

"This will conclude our meeting this morning," said Matsuda. "I see we have run fifteen minutes overtime. So we will reconvene at two-fifteen — not two o'clock as originally announced."

Lunch, from John Thatcher's point of view, was neither comfortable nor uncomfortable. Now committed to returning to MITI, he accompanied the three remaining Lackawanna representatives to a nearby restaurant. Each gave evidence of being in his own internal holding pattern. Occasionally one of them emerged to make brief comments that never quite synchronized with anybody else's.

When Hodiak raised his glass to Pamela, congratulating her on her handling of Noriko Iwamoto, it was a moment before there was any response from Kruger.

"She was great, but it's still Yonezawa versus Shima," he said absently, before returning to his own thoughts.

As for Pamela herself, she produced an automatic smile of acknowledgment but showed no desire to expand the subject. Fiddling with her napkin, she continued some private calculation, until she suddenly said:

"I don't see how they can come up with anything else this afternoon."

Nobody inquired who *they* were, and nobody seemed to care. Battling the prevailing abstraction, Thatcher remarked that it had been interesting to observe Matsuda in his official role. Don Hodiak, jerking his attention back to the table, obligingly described his private meeting at MITI the previous morning.

"Matsuda isn't all that different when you've got him one-on-one."

He was giving his impression of Ushiba, when Kruger suddenly interrupted to say that he was eager to meet Arai's new supporters at the embassy reception.

Thatcher, recalling his first sight of the threesome at the Hilton, recognized that they were still united in a common purpose. But functionally they had split, with each of them withdrawing to his own concern. Presumably they were used to working this way, and it did not bother them.

It did, however, discourage general discussion. Abandoning the attempt, Thatcher ate his meal, wondering what the afternoon would bring.

After lunch they found that the conference room had been transformed. The long table remained, but panels had been moved and partitions rearranged. There were screens for graphics of every description.

"If Ali wanted to show his stuff with stereophonic sound, they've got the gimmicks," said Alderman, the room's solitary occupant. "It makes our setup back at Lackawanna look prehistoric. We really should upgrade, Carl."

"Join the club," said Don Hodiak with a grin.

"Holding down expenses at Lackawanna isn't the easiest job on earth," Kruger told Thatcher.

Thatcher thought a reminder was in order. "Nobody likes budget cuts," he commented.

"Except the banks and other creditors."

"Touché," Kruger replied.

"Say, I thought we were supposed to start at two," Alderman broke in. "I've been waiting for twenty minutes."

"You shouldn't have ducked out," said Hodiak. "Matsuda changed the time to two-fifteen. But here they come now."

There were familiar faces in the crowd that began filing in, and others Thatcher had never seen before. Mr. Matsuda, bringing up the rear, paused to explain that MITI had drafted technical experts to evaluate Ali Khan's claims.

Khan himself had slipped into the room with an armful of notebooks, accompanied by two men in coveralls who set about drawing shoji blinds across the vast expanse of glass. They had just finished when Pamela Webb arrived, hair and makeup in perfect repair.

"Sorry to be late," she said. "But I forgot how far away the women's lounge is."

Just then Ali Khan flicked off the light switch, plunging the room into darkness.

"Is that necessary?" Matsuda demanded.

"I need maximum definition," Khan replied. "You can all pull your chairs around to get a good view."

At the push of the button, his film began. The early footage illustrated, even to an ignoramus like Thatcher, a dramatic advance in the state of the art. What was more, an inspired photographer had caught sequences of precision and dexterity that rivaled the grace and fluidity of ballet. Alas, the entertainment did not last long. Now that he was dealing with peers instead of laymen, Ali Khan let loose. Freezing every other frame, he launched into a discourse that was incomprehensibly protracted.

Carl Kruger, sitting at Thatcher's side, muttered an excuse and left. Soon, under cover of darkness, other forms began drifting off. After half an hour, Thatcher reached his limits. He headed for the Western-style plumbing fixtures discreetly adjoining the coatroom.

Along the way he encountered Matsuda, trying to look as if he were hurrying back so as not to miss a single word. Thatcher, however, had no intention of hearing more of the lecture, and he was not alone. Outside the conference room, Don Hodiak and Rick Iwamoto were deep in conversation.

"Hi, Thatcher," Hodiak greeted him. "In case you're wondering, Ali's still going strong. I figure there's no point going back until he runs out of steam."

"I can't understand a word your man is saying," Noriko Iwamoto complained. "Furthermore, nobody doubts the value of his work. Shima is simply questioning how it's acquired. Matsuda should skip this."

Thatcher could not agree. "Even if there were no outside objection, I daresay Mr. Matsuda would want the ministry to be convinced."

"Sure, but his backroom boys could go over all this without wasting our time."

But somebody had not been wasting time. Carl Kruger emerged from a nearby office.

"Made a few calls while I had the chance," he explained. "I see Ali's still at it."

"You don't feel he needs any moral support?" Thatcher asked.

Kruger shrugged. "Not at the rate he's going. Besides, Bennet and Pamela are keeping an eye on him."

Finally the welcome sounds of general conversation emerged. The four men marched into a scene of confusion. Chairs were scattered all over the room, equipment was being dismantled, and models were being packed. Most experts were leaving, while a few had gathered around Ali with last-minute questions. An interpreter was leaning against the wall and smoking a cigarette, no doubt exhausted by his recent effort. But he roused himself quickly when Matsuda spoke.

"Go to the duplicating room and collect Mr.

Ushiba's report. If it is not ready, find out why."

Business out of the way, Matsuda rose.

"As it is now three-thirty and it will take several minutes to restore order, this seems the natural moment for our afternoon break," he announced. "Tea will be served in the reception room across the way."

He then marched to the door and began politely ushering his guests toward the refreshments. With both doors open, and people milling everywhere, the air was suddenly rent by one shrill scream after another.

For a moment Matsuda froze. Then he plunged toward the cries, with his guests at his heels. They pounded down the corridor, past the coatroom, to a small office around the corner. There, a young woman, her hands pressed to her temples, and her eyes glazed, stood shrieking uncontrollably.

Thatcher and Carl Kruger were almost abreast of Matsuda when he flung open the door. All three came to an abrupt halt.

Little Mr. Ushiba lay in a crumpled heap, the upper side of his head battered in, the lower side nestled in a giant, gleaming pool of blood. And standing over him, his cane splayed at a wide angle, his glance studying the dead man with clinical detachment, was Mr. Fumitoshi Arai.

Chapter 8

Mr. Matsuda, appalled by his discovery, acted with gallant efficiency to contain the crisis. The hysterical typist vanished as if by magic, the door to Mr. Ushiba's office was firmly closed upon a medical team, and everybody else was hustled into the reception room where tea and cakes appeared instantly.

By and large the gathering behaved admirably. Nobody went into shock, nobody had a heart attack, and nobody evinced a compulsive desire to discuss what they had just seen. But when Matsuda, after explaining that a police officer would appear in due course, tried to pretend that this was a social gathering, he did not receive support from either man or nature. In this room the shoji blinds had not been drawn, and wide windows afforded a view of the sodden gloom outside. Matsuda's face was shadowed by the prevailing murk, and his resolute commonplaces were accompanied by the sound of endless dripping.

His companions were no help. Mr. Arai, in a high-back chair behind which his aides hovered solicitously, sat with hands on knees, his eyes closed. As far as Thatcher could tell, he was engaged in Zen meditation. Carl Kruger and Pamela Webb, sitting apart from the others, paid no attention to Matsuda as they exchanged low-voiced comments. Noriko Iwamoto did not air his impatience, but it was manifest as he jerked his cup down, stubbed out a cigarette, and turned to the door at every noise. Hodiak, arms folded, stared into space, while Bennet Alderman wrote in a notebook. Most disruptive of all, Ali Khan roamed morosely around the room.

The arrival of an English-speaking police inspector was a relief. He introduced himself as Inspector Hayakawa, expressed a desire to minimize unavoidable inconvenience, and got down to work.

". . . and brief statements from you may be of immeasurable assistance to our investigation."

First he explained the relevant geography.

"As you will have observed, Mr. Ushiba's office is just around the corner from the visitors' coatroom. Unfortunately, on his own corridor, several maintenance areas intervene between him and the other workers. I am therefore interested in the possibility that someone using the coatroom may have heard or seen something."

He then proceeded to a discussion of time.

"At twelve-thirty Mr. Ushiba told a messenger from the duplicating department that he would be working through lunch. That was the last time he was seen alive. So we are tentatively concentrating on the period between one-thirty and three-thirty. As that coincides with your return from lunch, I ask if you noticed anything unusual."

There was a flurry of negatives in English and Japanese.

Undaunted, Hayakawa moved on. "Perhaps some of you may have visited the coatroom later in your session?" he suggested.

Thatcher was the first to answer.

"Yes," he said, "but I am afraid I saw and heard nothing."

"And were you alone in the coatroom?"

"I was."

Rick Iwamoto and Don Hodiak told virtually the same story, but it required laborious thought to determine the order of their visits.

"Yeah, I remember now," Hodiak decided at last. "Rick was already waiting outside the meeting room when I got back."

There was nothing uncertain at all about Mr. Arai's statement. In a thin, precise voice, he declared that he had been emerging from the coatroom when the typist began screaming in the hallway. Mr. Arai had entered the office to assure himself that the victim was beyond medical assistance.

After listening respectfully to this testimony, Hayakawa reverted to his earlier line of questioning and asked about the time of everyone's return to MITI.

"Let's see," said Kruger. "We came in a bunch — that is, Thatcher and Don Hodiak and Pamela Webb and myself. We were in the conference room one or two minutes before starting time."

Mr. Arai had been moving with his usual convoy of attendants. "I entered the coatroom with my staff as Mr. Kruger's party was leaving," he said impressively.

"That's when I came in — alone," said Iwamoto with gentle irony, as if to point the contrast.

Hayakawa's glance swept over the remaining guests. "And Miss Webb, you of course left your coat elsewhere."

"Yes," she agreed. "I used the women's coatroom at the other end of the floor."

Ali Khan had been frowning in thought. "I got back long before everyone else, because I didn't know Mr. Matsuda changed the time of the meeting. Then I had to help get the room set up. I was in and out, seeing about the projector and the models, but that was in the opposite direction. I never went back

101

to the coatroom."

During the silence that followed, Bennet Alderman seemed startled to find everyone looking at him.

"Oh, I got here early too," he said hastily. "I was in the conference room by five before two."

"And remained there for twenty minutes?" Hayakawa asked patiently.

"Well, I was in and out," Alderman explained. "I kept going into the hall to see if anyone else was coming, but not far enough to do you any good."

"Thank you. You have all been most responsive. We have taken care of the period after lunch. Now if we could be more precise about your later visits?"

This, of course, proved far more difficult, but the inspector, with impeccable courtesy, persisted. Ali Khan demonstrated total recall of the order in which he had presented his topics, but it soon became clear that this aide-mémoire was useless.

John Thatcher led the way to clarification by abandoning the text and referring to the pictures.

"There was a schematic for an electronic circuit being shown when I slipped out," he recalled.

Ali brushed this contribution aside.

"I showed a number of circuits."

"This was the first," said Thatcher, sinking the fact that one complex circuit had been quite enough to drive him from the room.

The others were prompt to follow his lead. Kruger had left when Khan started freezing frames, and Iwamoto had given up hope when three MITI technicians embroiled Ali in controversy.

Hayakawa was pleased with these results, particularly when Ali Khan agreed to produce a rough timetable.

"If Mr. Khan would stay behind, I see no need to detain the rest of you. I can only thank you all for your cooperation and regret the inconvenience you have endured."

The words were scarcely out of his mouth before he was sucked into a brisk skirmish with Matsuda. Rick Iwamoto, who had come to rest by Thatcher, was grimly amused.

"Poor Matsuda really is the perfect bureaucrat. He wants to go on with our session," he translated, "in spite of the fact that neither Khan nor the area will be available for some time."

"It's not surprising he's upset," Thatcher remarked. "This is scarcely the image that MITI is in the habit of projecting."

"No, it isn't. But then," Iwamoto said with a Mephistophelian smile, "I'm not at all sure it isn't in Shima's best interests to have MITI's routine shaken up a little. I wasn't all that crazy about the way things were going."

Noriko Iwamoto was absolutely right, Thatcher decided. Almost anything that interrupted Lackawanna's greased ride to victory was a good thing for Shima.

An hour later, the situation had improved, from Matsuda's point of view. Instead of dealing with a mere inspector, he was closeted with one of Hayakawa's loftier superiors.

"Nothing could be further from our wishes than to occasion the slightest unnecessary embarrassment to MITI," that experienced and tactful individual murmured.

Matsuda inclined his head graciously. "Thank you."

"It is of course unfortunate that your distinguished guests should have been allowed to see the body itself."

The commissioner waited for agreement.

"Extremely unfortunate," Matsuda conceded. "It is therefore doubly essential to minimize any further intrusion on their time."

"Certainly. We must, however, remember that they are all men acquainted with the workings of government. Given the distressing nature of events, they understand the need for official action."

"As does MITI," Matsuda responded stoutly. "Under no circumstances would we suggest any abridgment of your usual activities. We ask only that they be conducted with discretion."

They were in total accord. The prospect of headlines about these people and these issues made both men shudder.

"As to that, I am happy to say that Inspector Hayakawa, immediately upon being informed of the address to which he was called, acted responsibly and efficiently. Except for the first patrol car, all police entering the building were in plain clothes, and the ambulance attendants were instructed to say that there had been an accident."

Matsuda could think of a further improvement.

"It is of the utmost importance that this investigation be brought to a rapid conclusion."

"You may rest assured that we will bend every effort to do so. To that end, it would be helpful to know as much as possible about the victim."

"What is there to know? He was a junior clerk who seems to have brought his sordid affairs to the office." At this point Matsuda became almost human. "Why not someplace else? Anywhere else!"

The commissioner could think of a very

good reason, but he was master of the incremental approach.

"You believe he was involved in something discreditable?"

"I know nothing about Ushiba's personal life but obviously it had its faults," Matsuda rejoined. "Otherwise he would not have been murdered."

Soothingly the commissioner agreed. "But unfortunately your reception desk tells my men that no strangers were ushered to this floor, which would indicate that someone on the premises killed him — either a member of the staff or an official visitor."

Matsuda was perfectly capable of looking facts in the face.

"The only official guests on this floor were those participating in the Midland Research hearings. And we can surely eliminate Mr. Arai or Mr. Iwamoto, or even Mr. Kruger for that matter." In his zeal for the cause, he went too far. "Businessmen do not run around committing crimes."

Even as he spoke, he remembered Recruit.

"I was referring to crimes of violence," he amended.

"That goes without saying," the commissioner replied ambiguously.

"Besides, Ushiba was far too low-level to have any interaction with principals."

"That is exactly the kind of thing we wish to ascertain. I would be grateful for anything more you could tell us about him."

"Ushiba was a man with a slovenly mind!"

The commissioner had not expected much, but this was worse than useless. It was time to say what he had come to say.

"If Ushiba had no personal contact with your guests, it is unavoidably necessary to pursue his relationships with your other employees."

Again Matsuda bowed to logic.

"Naturally."

With a sigh of relief, the commissioner began his departure. "I am sure you will forgive me if I now leave these details to Inspector Hayakawa. It is necessary that I convey the latest intelligence of this situation to your minister and assure him of our diligence."

"I rather enjoy calling on ministers these days," the commissioner confessed later. "They are always so relieved that my appearance has nothing to do with their peccadilloes that they are abnormally reasonable. And how are things over at MITI? Are they really co-operating?"

"Oh, yes," Hayakawa reassured him. "We've been given free run of the staff and the whole floor."

The commissioner devoted a moment to silent appreciation of MITI's being turned upside down by his men.

"What have you found out?"

"Nothing much, I'm afraid. Ushiba had been in his present assignment only six months. The people in his section claim they didn't know much about him. If he was chasing somebody's wife, or running up gambling debts, he didn't talk about it."

"No matter how stupid, the man presumably had some sense."

"Yes, but it means the digging will take time."

The commissioner abandoned his relish for terrorizing the high and mighty. "Just what we don't have. The papers will find out about the murder within a day or two," he predicted. "That will not be a problem if we can announce an arrest at the same time. Have they finished the medical examination?"

"No, but the autopsy may not be decisive. If Ushiba was comatose for a while, the time of death will not coincide with the time of attack."

"And what about these exalted witnesses who do not traffic with mere mortals?"

Pessimistically, Hayakawa reported that they were too inexact to be much help.

"Then the most immediate task is to question the workers at Ushiba's last posting. They may know something about him."

"I have already assigned a man to that, but Ushiba was there only eight months."

The commissioner was beginning to find the late Mr. Ushiba as unsatisfactory as everyone else had. "The longer it takes to find an intimate, the longer it takes to make progress on the case. Our forty-eight hours are looking very inadequate."

A wise subordinate lets his superior run out of valuable suggestions before advancing his own. Hayakawa waited, then took the initiative.

"There is one promising area," he said diffidently. "Ushiba's desk was in disarray when we arrived. There were even papers on the floor. But the messenger who was there at twelve-thirty reports it was very orderly then."

"Ah, you think the killer was searching for something — love letters, IOUs, a list of gambling debts?"

"It's possible. And with all that activity nearby, the murderer would not have lingered. If Ushiba had any documents hidden away, they may still be there."

The commissioner was nodding approval. "And someone is searching now?"

"They have orders to tear the place apart.

It is possible," the inspector said, "we may find something that will produce results soon."

"If so," said the commissioner, brightening, "we may yet be spared undue publicity."

He was in for a rude surprise.

Chapter 9

When an American ambassador is scheduled to host the Prime Minister of Japan, it takes more than the death of a clerk to interrupt these plans. Furthermore, John Thatcher believed that nothing ever canceled an occasion requiring formal attire. In New York he could usually flit from his apartment into a taxi. Tonight he was doomed to expose himself to an entire hotel.

In the lobby, however, he found himself upstaged. The usual mob of businessmen and tourists had been transfixed by the spectacle of Pamela Webb and Ali Khan loping toward the elevators, just back from a jogging session. In a silver-and-blue running suit, Pamela was radiant from exercise, her blond hair now a disheveled aureole. Beside her, Khan was all glistening dark skin and rippling muscles in shorts and a T-shirt.

"They're a real showstopper, aren't they?" said a voice at Thatcher's side.

Don Hodiak, like everybody else, was watching his colleagues.

"Does this happen every day?" Thatcher

inquired. "How can I have missed them?"

"Pamela usually does her running before breakfast. This is just an extra she's squeezing in."

"Well, she's getting plenty of PR mileage out of it," said Bennet Alderman, who had drifted over. "Let's hope Carl does as well at the embassy."

After the apparition in the Hilton lobby, the embassy crowd seemed elderly and arthritic. Thatcher had to remind himself that these were men of achievement. Youth provides the vitality that starts a man along the road. By the time he arrives, the dewy look is usually gone.

Of course certain skills take its place. With experience comes the ability to display, not real feelings, but those that are useful.

Noriko Iwamoto was a prime example. Calling Thatcher over to his group, he acted like a man without a trouble in the world. Midland Research was never mentioned. Instead Iwamoto enlarged on his plans for Alaska.

Thatcher decided to make hay while the sun shone.

"It's a genuine pleasure for the Sloan to handle the arrangements when the interests of both parties mesh. Ridgeway's holdings of timberland made him a natural when

Shima started looking for a substantial supply of wood pulp."

Everybody agreed that Japan's need for pulp was increasing daily.

"I have not yet met Mr. Ridgeway," Iwamoto said, sticking to the theme, "but we have spoken on the phone frequently, and I'm sure there will be no difficulty with the final details."

His companions envied him the opportunity to see Alaska.

"I'm ashamed to say how often I've taken the polar route through Anchorage and never gone further than the airport," he confessed.

Thatcher was able to tell him that more than Anchorage lay in store for them.

"Ridgeway has planned a field trip to the proposed site in Bethel. It will give us a chance to see something of the country."

Without a break, the conversation flowed on smoothly to the outrage of oil spills and the need to protect Mother Nature's wonderful legacy.

Suppressing the thought that wilderness areas would be quite safe if it were not for the forces gathered here, Thatcher moved on.

Carl Kruger was also fine-tuning his public response to the MITI hearing. For once he and his Japanese partner were appearing together, and they were drawing a crowd. The combination of the reclusive Fumitoshi Arai and the much-publicized Kruger was hard to beat. What's more, the two inveterate actors were playing it just right. Mr. Arai, taking advantage of age and disability, occupied an entire settee. Kruger, at his side, remained standing.

Thatcher, when he joined them, was amused to hear the president of Lackawanna breaking new ground as an admirer of things Japanese.

"They've written a lot about the advantages both our companies could receive from this deal," Kruger was saying soberly, "but they've left one factor out. By having Yonezawa handle our distribution and servicing, Lackawanna can study your methods and incorporate them into our system back home."

Thatcher liked Carl Kruger as earnest student, itching for instruction.

And when the discussion turned to a speech just made before the Chamber of Commerce in Los Angeles, Kruger remained muted.

"I was sorry to read that but not very surprised," he said, shaking his head sadly. "But you've got to understand the senator's predicament. Ohio's filled with companies that are sore as hell at being barred from overseas markets. After all, an elected official can take just so much heat."

Nodding sagely, Arai took the lofty position that cooperation between Yonezawa and Lackawanna might be the first step in averting the calamity of an all-out trade war and then, turning courteously to the newcomer, asked his opinion.

As Thatcher had feared at Narita Airport, here he was simply one of the spear carriers in Kruger's little opera. In this capacity, he produced some bromides about open markets, then confirmed the creditors' enthusiasm for Lackawanna's plans. But bankers are adept at submitting bills for services rendered, and Thatcher was no exception. During the first pause in the conversation, he said artlessly:

"Isn't that Mr. Watanabe of the Izuma Bank over there? I've been hoping to have a word with him about one of our projects."

Mr. Arai was a prompt payer.

"Ah, yes," he murmured. "Shima has had the benefit of your bank's counsel for its latest joint venture. You must have much to discuss with Mr. Watanabe."

"Only a few final arrangements. Our Mr. Fleming has already done the important groundwork," Thatcher replied.

Under Arai's adroit direction, the next five minutes centered on Fleming's sympathetic understanding of the requirements of Japanese investors.

By the time Thatcher slipped away for the now-mandatory exchange with Watanabe, he felt his time had been well spent. But he soon discovered there was more work to be done.

"John, you remember Stan Zaretski," Fleming said, emerging with a companion. "We've been doing a rundown of who's here."

Thatcher's earlier meetings with the commercial attaché had taken place during office hours, so he regarded the burly figure with some appreciation. No tailoring in the world could make that barrel chest look as if it belonged to the diplomatic corps. Instead Zaretski's appearance suggested that the embassy had hired a private bouncer for the evening.

But Zaretski was all business. "You've probably already talked to most of the people you should meet."

After reviewing their list, Thatcher realized how much he had accomplished. The Sloan had already discharged two thirds of its obligations.

"Then let's get on with it," he suggested, foreseeing a brisk conclusion to this work.

Before they could proceed, however, an embassy aide materialized.

"The Prime Minister has expressed his interest in meeting you, Mr. Thatcher. He would be pleased if you could spare him some

116

time," he said impressively.

"It would be an honor."

Thatcher was obediently turning when the aide continued:

"And perhaps Mr. Fleming could accompany you to interpret?"

Thatcher privately wondered which one of them was actually being accorded the interview. This thought was immediately echoed by Stan Zaretski.

"Neat," he rumbled. "Gene's too low on the totem pole to rate an audience, but the PM's curious about him. This way he gets two for the price of one."

The Prime Minister was not the only one getting an unofficial bonus. Within the secluded alcove stood Tomaheko Matsuda, clearly basking in this sign of special favor. Displaying far more affability than had surfaced at MITI, he was delighted to see Thatcher again, delighted to meet Mr. Fleming . . . in fact, delighted about everything.

The formal conversation followed predictable lines. Fleming, as grave as a judge, went through his paces. The Prime Minister asked questions, to which Thatcher replied suitably. Then the exchange ended with a few recollections by the PM of his last visit to the United States.

As soon as they had retired from the Presence, Gene Fleming announced his conclusions.

"No wonder Matsuda is on top of the world! The PM must have made his decision."

"About what?"

"The permanent secretary of MITI is seriously ill and expected to resign soon. All the odds-makers in Tokyo have been wondering which deputy secretary will get the nod. That performance we just saw means Matsuda has the inside track. They must like the way he's handling the hearings."

One serious flaw in Matsuda's chairmanship occurred to Thatcher. "Having us stumble across a corpse doesn't make any difference?"

"Why should it? It's not his fault that some nonentity got himself killed."

Thatcher agreed, then reverted to his own schedule.

"Two more names to go, and we can leave," he said.

But Fleming shook his head. "Not a chance, John. Nobody goes home until the guest of honor does, and he's notorious for actually enjoying these shindigs. He always stays late."

In any event, it took longer than Thatcher had expected to reach their last two prospects. Everyone in the room seemed to know Fleming and welcome his appearance. As they moved from one group to another, Gene maintained a running commentary on figures of note.

"You see the guy next to the cultural attaché, just taking some champagne? He's the next one the prosecutor's expected to arrest."

And the portly gentleman surrounded by sycophants was also not to be envied.

"For three years he was in the running to be next head of the LDP. Now that's gone with the wind, poor fish!"

It was a relief to reach an industrialist whose world was still intact. Unfortunately he was so outraged by the U.S. budget deficit that he could talk of nothing else. Thatcher only hoped that the general irritation did not spill over onto U.S. banks.

Inconsequent thoughts were speedily banished, however, when they tracked down the last name on the list. Gene Fleming's fame had preceded him, and the prospect admitted that he had been thinking of making an appointment. After announcing that he planned some acquisitions in the Common Market, he produced a shopping list guaranteed to stop any banker in his tracks.

The conversation proceeded sedately through a joint automotive venture in Italy, a shipyard in Scandinavia, a pharmaceutical firm in Germany. It was a final item that was mystifying.

"A china manufacturer in France?" Thatcher repeated expressionlessly.

The small, tidy figure facing him vibrated with anticipation.

"A personal enthusiasm," he apologized. "This would be a small self-indulgence."

Thatcher sincerely hoped this meant something on a par with Arai's second-rate vineyard. If they were talking about Limoges, the result could be blood in the streets. National pride can set unpredictable limits.

"I would be delighted to have our people investigate the possibilities," he promised, wondering if the Sloan had an expert on porcelain.

Another shot in the arm followed this satisfactory interview, when Stan Zaretski stopped to say that the Prime Minister had left unexpectedly.

"Splendid!"

Gene Fleming, casting a knowledgeable eye over the salon, was not so enthusiastic. "Something must have happened. It's not just the PM. The whole damned government's gone."

"That's what I was going to tell you," Zaretski continued. "They've been slipping quietly away, one by one."

"What the hell can it be?"

Stan Zaretski was inclined to be playful.

"The public prosecutor strikes again?" he suggested.

"Or another of his key witnesses has committed suicide," Fleming said more seriously.

But Thatcher, with freedom in sight, saw no reason for idle speculation. "We aren't going to find out anything by bouncing possibilities off each other," he observed. "And even that we could do someplace else."

Fleming suggested adjourning to his house for a nightcap, but Zaretski declined.

After taking formal leave of the ambassador, the men from the Sloan were free to depart. Thatcher, pausing for a last glance at the gathering, discovered that Gene Fleming had overlooked one important Japanese official.

Conspicuously alone, Tomaheko Matsuda was almost obscured by a potted palm as he stared at the depleted scene with a puzzled frown.

Thatcher always enjoyed encountering his Tokyo manager's wife. Haru Fleming was as great an anomaly as her husband. On the street, in a fur coat, she looked like the wife of a Japanese businessman. At any gala function that she could be persuaded to attend, she seemed, in her dress kimono, like a charming survival from the past. She was, of course, neither. Haru had successfully bridged two cultures. She spoke both languages, was at home in the United States and Japan, and had spent years ensuring that her children reap the benefits, rather than the disadvantages, of their double inheritance.

A tiny, delicate woman, she was often silent in company for long stretches, content to occupy herself extending hospitality and listening. Then, weary of the labored pace of the conversation, she would suddenly produce swallowlike flights that soared far ahead of her guests.

Tonight, displaying no alarm at being surprised in slacks and a shirt, she welcomed Thatcher and automatically produced Scotch rather than sake. She did not come to life until Gene began a familiar refrain.

". . . yet still retaining their traditional way of life."

"Pooh!"

It was a soft puff of sound. Nonetheless it conveyed Haru Fleming's abundant contempt.

"You don't agree?" Thatcher turned expectantly to his hostess. She was, he knew, an indefatigable reader of the American and Japanese press. Were her articles different from his?

"Look at this room," she invited, pointing to the sofa and chairs. "When Gene and I first set up housekeeping in Tokyo, we had two main rooms, the Western one for Gene's friends and the normal one for my family. Now we still have two rooms, but my family comes here. The other one is for foreigners who want a touch of the old Japan. And as for food! When my parents go out, they wouldn't think of ordering anything but French or Italian."

"But that's just prosperity, Haru," her husband protested. "Like having a VCR or stereo. It doesn't change the fundamentals."

She swept on. "Every family with a child tries to give him a room of his own. And as it isn't public, it usually has a permanent bed. When people change the way they sit, sleep, and eat, you're introducing basic alterations."

Thatcher did not really believe that attacking a veal cutlet with a knife and fork radically altered one's orientation.

"Those can scarcely be called major social changes," he said.

"No?" she challenged. "When I grew up, the home was a place shielding its members from the outside. There was no such thing as privacy from each other. You don't think introducing a small child to that concept is a departure?"

"I can't begin to imagine the difference it would make," Thatcher confessed.

"Neither can I," she said cordially. "But I do know that the idea of family is changing daily and nobody wants to admit it."

Gene Fleming was frankly enjoying his wife's rigor about tribal custom.

"You're a fine one to talk," he teased. "After marrying me."

"I ceased to be Japanese that day," she said with dignity. "But I recognized the consequences of what I was doing. Apparently nobody else will —"

Before she could continue, there was a knock on the door, and within seconds Stan Zaretski was making perfunctory apologies.

"Sorry to barge in on you, but I thought you'd want to know right away."

In his rumpled penguin outfit, Zaretski loomed over them, filling the small room.

"That murder at MITI this afternoon has opened up a real can of worms," he said. "While the police were rummaging through the victim's papers, they found a lulu in his Midland Research file. There was an envelope containing part of a letter in German. That's what held things up."

"German?" Thatcher repeated blankly.

Zaretski's face was grim. "From Switzerland. A financial agent over there was certifying the arrival of one million dollars. It would be deposited in a numbered account for the letter's recipient as soon as the agreed-upon conditions were satisfied. And scrawled at the top, the initials *MR*."

There was a throbbing silence.

Finally Thatcher asked the most important question. "Any names?"

"Absolutely none. It was a middle sheet, you see. So it's anyone's guess who was bribing who. They don't even have the name of the agent."

"Jesus Christ!" Fleming breathed softly. "No wonder the Prime Minister skipped out. They'll have to burn the midnight oil on this one."

"I see what you mean," Thatcher agreed. "If Mr. Ushiba was killed because he found out somebody was getting a million dollars for the right Midland Research decision, then the murder has become a political hot potato."

Fleming looked at him with excitement. "It's a lot bigger than a simple murder. The LDP has been through enough pressure to bring down several cabinets, so they've learned how to live with scandal. But this is too damned blatant. MITI is the lodestar of the Japanese miracle, a sort of holy of holies. It's supposed to be above reproach."

"What steps do you think the government will take?" Thatcher asked.

Both the experts spoke at once, their answers colliding in midair. Fleming's higher pitch won out.

"They'll try to keep the lid on. Not that they can for long."

"They've already taken their first step," Zaretski announced impatiently. "How the hell do you think I know all this? The ambassador has been told informally that Carl Kruger is no longer *persona grata*."

Fleming nodded vigorously. "Of course. That's the natural line of defense. A foreign barbarian pulled this stunt, so it has nothing to do with the powers that be. A wonderful ploy, when you come to think about it."

"Wonderful for them, but not so hot for me." Zaretski was already foreseeing a difficult morning. "I'm the lucky one who gets to break the news to Kruger."

Haru Fleming, diligently refilling glasses, was bright-eyed with interest.

"I wonder how he'll take it," she mused.

John Thatcher bitterly resented the fact that he was the first one to find out. When he returned to the Hilton he made the mistake of detouring to the desk for his messages, only to discover Carl Kruger before him. For once the president of Lackawanna ignored appearances. He was reading and rereading a single sheet of paper.

Without replying to Thatcher's greeting, he lifted a frowning face and, after a moment's hesitation, extended the communication.

"This just came by special messenger. What the hell do you think it means?"

Thatcher rapidly scanned the formal language. With every circumlocution possible, MITI first congratulated Lackawanna on its splendid presentation, then brightly declared the nature of Mr. Ali Khan's work to be so unusual that only physical demonstration of the robots and their manufacture could establish the value of the technology. They were, therefore, suspending further evaluation and proposing a meeting two weeks from date in Birmingham, U.K. Given the shortness of the notice, they realized it would be necessary for Mr. Kruger and his staff to depart at once. With profound apologies for any inconvenience occasioned by this decision, they remained . . .

Kruger was hoarse with shock. "This is some kind of bullshit. Nobody's ever had any doubts about the value of the robotics. I'll bet Iwamoto's gotten himself a phony technical expert."

The path of duty was all too clear.

"No, that's not it." Thatcher took a deep breath. "You see, Carl, something has happened."

Chapter 10

When John Thatcher arrived in the international departure lounge at ten-thirty the next morning, the first thing he saw was a storm center around which most travelers were making a wide detour. At the heart of the turmoil stood Carl Kruger. Flushed and angry, he was snarling at the pack surrounding him, for all the world like the traditional stag at bay. Three or four men, whose placatory tones marked them as members of the American Embassy, were ranged against him. Behind them lurked the second string, ready to go into action if required. Bennet Alderman darted here and there, desperately trying to engage the attention of men who would not listen. Slightly removed from the conflict, Pamela Webb and Don Hodiak had slumped against a post, looking shell-shocked.

It was all a far cry from the many pictures of Kruger's arrival at this same airport. Apart from other differences, there was not a single Japanese in his vicinity. As far as the visuals went, Kruger was being ejected by his own countrymen.

One of the outriders, catching sight of Thatcher, detached himself from the controversy and lumbered across the hall.

"We've been at it all night, and it's been a real bitch," Stan Zaretski reported wearily. "Kruger started calling his pals back home as soon as he got MITI's letter. Then they called their pals in the State Department and the White House. After that the calls were going back and forth across the Pacific nonstop. It must have been four o'clock before the ambassador finally got his go-ahead."

"It's hard to believe the result was ever in doubt."

"Of course not. Kruger may be important, but American foreign policy still cuts some ice. If doomsday comes for the LDP, it's not going to be Washington that lights the fuse. But try telling Kruger that."

Thatcher pointed out the obvious.

"He doesn't care about foreign policy. He's thinking about his deal."

"So he's explained to us. Over and over again. At first his line was that the ambassador didn't have the guts to stand up to the Japanese. Now he's cursing the whole administration."

"It's characteristic of him to want to stay and protect his position."

Zaretski shrugged. "Oh, he's a smart

cookie. The ambassador can feed him that pap about giving the Japanese time to clean house, but Kruger knows damn well that they're hoping to load it all on him. And once he's branded, he can kiss his MITI approval goodbye."

At this point one of the men from the embassy incautiously reached for the suitcase at Kruger's feet. The ensuing burst of vituperation made Alderman grab Kruger's arm and start pleading. Kruger shook him off with one galvanic heave.

"If Alderman isn't careful, he's going to get swatted," Thatcher predicted.

Zaretski was tolerant. "That's a PR man for you. Alderman's scared how all this will look if some roving cameraman passes by. Nobody else gives a damn."

"Kruger certainly doesn't, and I'm afraid he isn't giving an inch."

"He'll be on that plane to San Francisco if I have to hoist him on bodily," Zaretski growled. "I plan to be in bed fifteen minutes after this flight leaves."

As the critical moment approached, Thatcher was privileged to observe the tactics of diplomats acting as riot police. The whole group shrank inward and began surging toward the departure desk. Kruger, in the middle, was inexorably hustled forward in spite of his protests. Ignored by everybody, Hodiak and Pamela Webb shouldered their belongings and trudged along.

The clerk at the counter took one look at what was headed his way and buried his head in his work. Stretching out a blind hand for documentation, he ripped and stamped at record speed while pretending not to notice the commotion.

Zaretski waited until the last suitcase had been thrust into airline custody. Then he uttered a hasty farewell and added his bulk to the compact mass that was slowly making its way to the departure gate.

Thatcher's last glimpse of Carl Kruger was confined to a clenched fist, extended over the surrounding heads.

Thatcher was on board his own plane before he realized that he would be traveling with another member of Lackawanna's delegation. There was a scurry near the entrance, and the stewardess's voice could be heard urging a last-minute passenger to take his seat. Then Ali Khan plumped down next to Thatcher and began strapping himself in.

"Good morning, Mr. Khan."

As Ali looked up, his eyes widened.

"Did they throw you out too?" he asked baldly.

"I was already scheduled to leave on this flight," Thatcher replied, stifling the sudden vision of himself on the receiving end of Stan Zaretski's muscular attentions. "But isn't the polar route the long way around for London?"

"It's worth the extra time not to travel with the others."

When the thrusters had done their work and they were airborne, Ali unbuckled his seat belt, stretched his long legs as far as he could, and sighed. "You wouldn't believe how they're carrying on," he continued. "Carl is so bloody mad he's flailing out at anybody within reach, and Alderman is yapping like a Pomeranian."

"What about Miss Webb and Hodiak?"

The young Pakistani's reply was tinged with contempt.

"I guess they just do as they're told."

Thatcher reminded himself that Ali Khan was not part of day-to-day life at Lackawanna. For the most part he ran his own show, far from the center of power.

"At least I didn't get shortchanged," Khan said, confirming Thatcher's impression. "It's my robotics that they want, and I did give the presentation."

This analysis, of course, omitted Lackawanna's role entirely. But from Ali's point of view, it was the higher realism, as he went on to demonstrate.

"I may not know much about business, but I do know that now they've seen what's available, they'll find some way to buy MR's technology." Then Ali remembered recent events. "I still don't understand why they threw us out. By the time I got up this morning, Carl was so busy fighting with your embassy people, he had no time to answer questions."

Thatcher could well believe that Kruger was not a source of rational information. Nonetheless some driblets must have percolated through the exchange of hostilities. "Surely you heard about the letter in Mr. Ushiba's files?" he asked.

"The police found something about a bribe at MITI, didn't they? But why pick on Lackawanna?"

Thatcher explained the legacy of the Recruit scandal.

"Even if some of their people have been taking payoffs, that still doesn't mean we're the villains," Ali said impatiently. "Shima has the most to lose, doesn't it? According to Carl, he was going to take a big slice of their business."

"Perhaps. But the last thing the government wants is a highly publicized bribe to MITI by any Japanese company. That could destabilize the entire political situation. If they

133

can blame this all on a foreigner, it makes things much easier for them."

Ali Khan was beginning to understand. "Now I see. Carl thinks that once they get rid of him, he won't stand a chance."

"Exactly. But the only way he could mount a real fight was with the backing of the American government. And they're not intervening in a criminal case."

Khan frowned, digesting the scope of interests involved. "Then who do the Japanese really think murdered that clerk?"

"I doubt if they care very much at this stage. But certainly, if Kruger is accepted as the briber, the implication will be that Lackawanna was trying to prevent exposure."

Satisfied, the Pakistani nodded. "No wonder Carl was wild. This morning it seemed crazy to me. If the government wants to throw you out, what's the point of staying?"

"Very true. Actually Kruger is in a cleft stick now that he's a source of embarrassment. It remains to be seen whether his ouster will serve the government's purpose."

"Well, if he's out of the country and the embassy is lying low, it has to, doesn't it?"

Thatcher was sorry to have to add further complexity.

"Not necessarily. The reason for the haste was that there still hasn't been any publicity.

But once the opposition smells bribery, there will be howls for a complete investigation."

"Good God!" Khan exclaimed. "Carrying out research is straightforward compared to all this. You just do your work and hope you come up with something."

This might be the ideal path of scientific inquiry. In view of headlines about fraudulent experimental results, Thatcher did not believe that scientists were immune to more sordid motivations. When he said as much, Khan was swift to make a distinction.

"They're the ones who joined the rat race. They're either working for a company or fighting for academic promotion. They have to produce results, and some of them don't care how they do it. I will say this for Carl. When he bought MR, he didn't understand beans about my research, but he did realize that it takes time."

"Well, your research has certainly been successful," Thatcher said agreeably.

The compliment was scarcely necessary.

"I always knew it would be, although I didn't realize how far I'd have to carry it. According to Lackawanna, there wasn't anything to sell until there were functioning robots. But at least that avoids the question of faked research. Anybody who wants can come in and see the bloody things work." Suddenly he smiled shyly. "I don't really feel that way about them. In fact, whenever we have a demonstration, I feel like Thomas Edison showing off his gramophone."

Thatcher could well believe it. The thrill of accomplishment always benefits from public recognition.

"And working out practical applications doesn't bother you?" he asked, aware that this process was anathema to some theoreticians.

"That's where the money is." A gleam of amusement lit the dark eyes. "I do understand that much about business. Besides, it's interesting. I like finding out about new things."

This enjoyment was not limited to the world of industrial applications. When the pilot announced their imminent arrival at Anchorage International Airport, Ali turned his attention to their destination.

"I want to see as much as I can. Do you know how long it takes to get to their zoo?"

Thatcher did not, but the stewardess did. She explained about the free people movers servicing downtown Anchorage and some of its outlying attractions.

"Good," Ali said, nodding. "That will give me a couple of hours there and time for lunch."

In the face of these plans, Thatcher drew a conclusion.

"You mean they wouldn't even let you wait for a through flight?"

"I didn't bother to ask," Ali replied. "With the Japanese creating, I wasn't going to be left alone there. Carl can get his ambassador by snapping his fingers when things get dicey. I doubt if mine has even heard what's going on."

"Good to see you, John," said the current Ridgeway that afternoon when Thatcher presented himself at Ridgeway, Ridgeway & Hall. "They fix you up all right over at the hotel?"

"They've given me a spectacular view," Thatcher said politely.

Len Ridgeway knew all about the Chugiak Inn; he had built it.

"We're going to have some time alone," Ridgeway announced with satisfaction. "Iwamoto called to say that he and his boys will be taking a later flight. In fact, they'll come to dinner at my place directly from the airport."

It was not hard to guess how Noriko Iwamoto was spending the day. Huddled with his supporters, he was no doubt driving the final nails into Carl Kruger's coffin.

"Tell me about him," Ridgeway concluded.

"From your point of view, he's ideal. He's very eager to get into production as rapidly as possible."

"Yes. In fact, he's so gung ho, I wonder why Shima didn't consider going it alone."

"There are two good reasons," Thatcher began. "First of all, starting from scratch is more time-consuming for the Japanese than for us. Secondly, they're sensitive about all-Japanese undertakings abroad. They can avoid resentment by taking a local partner."

Ridgeway still wanted more.

"And what kind of a guy is he?"

Given Iwamoto's chameleon characteristics, Thatcher found this a difficult question. Len Ridgeway would probably never see the Iwamoto who had been losing points to Pamela Webb or the one nervously jerking his way through the aftermath of Mr. Ushiba's murder. Even the good-time Rick who stage-managed golf games might never appear in Anchorage.

"I think you'll find Iwamoto easy to deal with," he said cautiously. "He's very Americanized and, at the same time, a member of the Japanese establishment. Of course I've only seen him in Japan. He may well be different here."

He was. From the moment that he arrived at Len Ridgeway's front door, Noriko Iwamoto was determined to please. Leaving his hapless aides to fend for themselves, he began working the crowd as if he were running for state office in Alaska.

As Thatcher moved through the cocktail hour, he overheard Iwamoto claiming a deep interest in the Native Peoples Rights Association, then expressing the intention to start a collection of Alaskan artifacts, and finally regretting the fact that he was not privileged to live the frontier life. All this could be credited to the desire to make a good impression. Thatcher, however, suspected a welling ebullience that had to be vented . . . which gave him a fair notion of current thinking in Tokyo.

Not surprisingly Iwamoto was the hit of the evening.

"If you ask me, one reason for the Japanese success is that they believe in facing facts," said a burly lawyer to Thatcher. "Take this Iwamoto, he understands that we're sitting on top of a lot of potential here in Alaska and the way to go is forward. You don't have to tell *him* that we're coming up on the twenty-first century."

The baleful look he directed at a group near the bar prepared Thatcher for the views of his neighbor at the dinner table. She was the publisher of a newspaper with a long track record opposing unregulated development.

"It was a relief to hear Mr. Iwamoto's

views," she said approvingly. "The Japanese are way ahead of us in understanding that you have to study the consequences of a project beforehand and in relation to an overall plan. God knows we've seen the havoc that uncontrolled expansion can cause. But some people act as if they're back in the gold rush days."

Her glance down the table could have peeled varnish.

If Iwamoto pursued his course of universal accommodation, Thatcher reflected, he might never be able to set foot in Anchorage again.

But Len Ridgeway had no complaints. When he cornered Thatcher after dinner, he was beaming.

"It's going great, isn't it? And Rick is the kind of guy it's a pleasure to do business with. He tells me he's really excited about our field trip tomorrow."

Thatcher had no intention of discussing the reasons for Iwamoto's well-being or explaining that a visit to the Anchorage dump would evoke the same enthusiasm. Instead he raised a question of his own.

"Several of your guests told me that they've been active opponents of the pipeline and similar developments. How have you managed to line them all up?"

This earned him a brisk lecture. When times are tough, people lose interest in saving the moose, Ridgeway declaimed.

"Of course new jobs would be desirable," Thatcher said. "Still I would have expected someone to be protesting."

Ridgeway first looked around for enemy ears, then lowered his voice. "These days the environmentalists are so busy being anti-oil, they don't have time for anything else. Besides, RR&H is Alaskan, which makes a big difference."

Thatcher could well see how it might. After Exxon, anything that did not sound like the casual arrogance of an occupying army would be welcome.

Bethel is five hundred miles from Anchorage. Situated on a broad delta, it is a fishing village, a transportation center, and an administrative hub. Some three thousand hardy inhabitants call it home.

RR&H's Cessna took one hour and twenty minutes to make the trip, giving Len Ridgeway ample time to relay this information. As the same facts had been pressed on Thatcher for over three months, he concentrated on the breathtaking scenery.

Noriko Iwamoto, however, had still not simmered down. Drinking in every word, he hailed each detail as if it provided him with new and powerful insights. Nonetheless,

Thatcher reflected, by yesterday's standards, Iwamoto's responses were almost muted.

". . . soon be touching down at the airport," droned Ridgeway. "Then we'll survey the ground."

The party that clambered aboard utility vehicles a few moments later was gunning for big profits. The giant high-tech pulp mill would be only the beginning. If Ridgeway, Shima, and their cohorts came to terms, Bethel would boast a new long-runway airport, the largest drydock in the world, and dredged channels in all directions.

All numbers mentioned were dizzying.

". . . fifteen thousand acres north of town."

"Within four years, the crew level stabilizes at six or seven thousand year round . . ."

". . . an easy two hundred million tons by year three . . ."

When the caravan returned to downtown Bethel, Thatcher was happy to see that the Sloan was not underwriting the desecration of an Alaska treasure. Bethel could use all the money it could get.

The climate, however, was something to boast about.

". . . and since we're on the ocean, the weather is better than it is inland."

"Sounds great to me," Iwamoto rejoined.

No one was labeling Bethel a gourmet's paradise. Lunch had been flown in with the inspection team and was served in the command post. Once they were seated at the groaning board, Rick Iwamoto relinquished his role as the voice of Shima. One of his associates was a structural engineer, the other a hydrologist. As RR&H had contributed a paper chemist and a metallurgist, Thatcher was not the only one to withdraw from the main conversation. Separated from his Japanese partner-to-be, Len Ridgeway relaxed.

"Say, John, Rick tells me you've been dealing with Carl Kruger in Tokyo," he began.

"That's right," said Thatcher cautiously, wondering how much Ridgeway knew about the MR debacle.

But Len was thinking along different lines.

"Down in Juneau there's been a lot of talk about him. Ever since he salvaged Lackawanna, there've been guys saying he'd make a great presidential candidate."

"Yes, that crops up every now and then."

"I guess it's happening often enough to start worrying some of the party regulars." Ridgeway frowned. "I know Jake's concerned about what would happen to party structure if an outsider blew the primaries open. And I hear that some of the heavyweights in Washington are thinking the same way."

Thatcher detected an underlying note of

perplexity. "You don't agree?"

"I don't know. Like I was telling Jake, if we don't get a real winner on the ticket pretty soon, there won't be much party to worry about. And you can't deny that Kruger's got a lot going for him."

Thatcher was spared the necessity of replying. Unheard by him, Rick Iwamoto had padded over to their end of the table.

"I can take just so much when the experts get going," he said lightly.

"Pull up a chair," Ridgeway invited. "Hey, Ben, can we have some more coffee over here?"

Iwamoto let him bustle, then said, "Did I hear you talking about Carl Kruger?"

Unsuspecting, Ridgeway expanded. "Yep. I was just telling John that some of the local pols are beginning to wonder if he's got the makings of a serious presidential candidate."

"That's interesting."

"Like it or not, you have to admit his strong points. God, just the exposure on his trip to Japan was worth millions. I hear his PR guy used to be a political hardballer."

"Bennet Alderman," Iwamoto provided. "He did several of your senatorial campaigns. Very successfully."

Thatcher was surprised to hear Iwamoto reveal this much knowledge, but Rick turned

144

to him with a smile.

"Shima is always thorough."

"So I see," said Thatcher, refusing to be drawn.

Ignoring this byplay, Ridgeway began to worry a different bone. "Of course Kruger's got drawbacks too. For one thing, there's that woman he carts around with him."

Iwamoto was only too happy to extend the list. "And then he's run into some hitches in Japan," he said with considerable tact. "At the very least, he's stubbed his toe."

Thatcher's earlier question was now answered. Ridgeway's reply made it clear he had still not heard the details.

"Oh, I don't know," he said judiciously. "Although I'm crossing my fingers when I say this, a lot of business deals fall through. It's still not a crime."

"No," Iwamoto agreed calmly. "It's still not a crime."

But Carl Kruger's political future was not why they were in Bethel. Before the last drop of coffee was downed, time came for the nitty-gritty.

"Now about production quotas . . . ," Ridgeway began.

Within ten minutes Thatcher had every reason to congratulate himself on the Sloan's acumen in arranging this partnership. Ridgeway and Iwamoto shared far more than might have been expected from their surface differences. They were both capable of projecting the full sweep of their ultimate goal while staying on top of the details.

"And housing for the start-up labor force?" Iwamoto asked.

"We'll ship in kits so as not to waste time," Ridgeway replied. "They sell them in a big way down on the West Coast."

"I know. We've even got a couple of dealers in Japan planning to import them."

He sounded almost distracted, as if contemplating a world in which a Toyota car, a Sony television, a Canon computer, would all be adjuncts of a Shima house. But instantly he got back on track in an impressive display of concentration. Nothing existed for him except reaching agreement with RR&H. For over three hours he matched Len Ridgeway's intensity, then announced himself satisfied.

"It looks good to me," he said finally, shuffling his notes into order. "I'll have my people look at these shipping schedules and insurance costs. I still think we can do better on the transportation, but we'll be back to you before the week's out."

As he rose, Thatcher could almost hear the changing of gears. Rick had done what he had come to do and was now moving on.

★ ★ ★

By the time that Thatcher shared an airport limousine with Rick Iwamoto the next morning, the calls from Tokyo had been coming thick and fast.

"Shima's people are breaking out the champagne," Gene Fleming had reported.

"And how is Mr. Arai reacting?"

"Who knows? But he's never wasted his time on lost causes. And my guess is that Kruger's application is deader than a doornail. If it weren't for the clerk's murder, I'd begin to smell a setup. But that isn't the way they do things here, even by accident."

Thatcher thought of other reasons for rejecting Fleming's theory out of hand. "Without Ushiba dead, Kruger wouldn't have been thrown out. Nobody could have planned on one without the other."

Rick Iwamoto had been on the phone too.

"I've been talking with my office," he began, "and they tell me the news blackout on MITI is about to end."

Thatcher agreed that he had heard the same thing.

"Of course from my point of view that's welcome," Iwamoto continued, with a parade of frankness. "Now that the Lackawanna threat is a thing of the past, Shima can look forward again. Given the world economy, this is no time to sit still.''

"You assume that Lackawanna will not resurface?" Thatcher asked. "I realize that Kruger's timing was dependent on the cabinet's desire to project a new image."

Iwamoto radiated confidence.

"That was just a fluke," he announced. "Kruger was clever to recognize the moment, but it won't occur again. On the contrary, it is now in everyone's interest to shelve the entire proposal."

Leaning forward, he embarked on an analysis of the political situation in Tokyo with the same single-minded intensity he had brought to his discussion with Len Ridgeway. There was no doubt that Noriko Iwamoto had a formidable ability to exclude from his mind everything irrelevant to the work at hand.

Chapter 11

Getting back to Lackawanna always invigorated Carl Kruger. After the ambiguities of Japan, the clank of machinery came as a relief.

Not that his office was anywhere near the assembly lines. Kruger worked in the usual comfort, and after an evening at home, his sense of priorities was restored. Japan would have to go on hold.

He was in for a nasty surprise.

"Hi, Sally. I'm back," he announced.

"Oh, hello, Mr. Kruger," she said. Nearby a telephone rang unanswered. "I think everything's clear on your desk, but I'll come along and see if you have any questions. Oh, and Mr. Alderman just called; he wants to see you soonest. . . ."

Every phone in the place seemed to be ringing. The one on his own desk was blinking frantically.

"What's going on around here?" he demanded, snatching it up. "Yeah?"

"So you haven't heard the bad news," said his wife. "Everybody else has."

"Shoot," he ordered.

"It was all over the *Morning* show. Oh, they covered themselves by saying it was a rumor. But apparently there's an article in the *New York Times* too. . . ."

Bennet Alderman, like Sally and half the rest of the population, always switched on television before he brushed his teeth. So this morning he had taken the blow unprepared. Nobody had called Alderman to warn him. But there was an emergency to deal with, and Alderman swung into action. He reached the office an hour early.

". . . absolutely no foundation in fact," he was saying when Kruger sought him out. "That's why Lackawanna doesn't want to dignify the story with a comment."

Shouldering the telephone, he raised two hands for silence when Kruger strode in. Then he resumed: "Well, naturally the Japanese authorities aren't corroborating garbage like this. Look, all the parties agreed to change the negotiation format. That's the only thing that happened —"

The telephone interrupted.

"You're stringing a lot of coincidences together and coming up with nothing," Alderman shot back. "Somebody got knocked off at MITI, which is somebody's bad luck. That had absolutely nothing to do with Lackawanna's talks with Yonezawa. . . .

Sure I'm sure. . . ."

Alderman went on for several minutes before he could get to Kruger. Even then he was almost curt.

"I've got a million calls to make, Carl," he said. Then, shouting to make himself heard, he yelled: "Norma, hold everything for five minutes — unless Reuters gets back."

He swiveled back, to find Kruger studying him. Flushing slightly, Alderman said: "Sorry, Carl, but I want to squelch this brushfire before it roars out of control."

Kruger was wry. "After it's all over the networks, don't you think you're a little late?"

Alderman shook his head. "No! They're just saying that there are rumors in Tokyo about something rotten at MITI. No details, no sources — and above all, no footage. Garbled hearsay isn't enough to keep a story hot. That's how we should play it."

"Okay," said Kruger. "But I'm not going into hiding. There's too much I've got to do. And, Bennet, don't forget that I'm used to doing my talking for myself. I can tell anybody that he's full of bullshit."

Before Alderman could protest, Kruger continued nonchalantly: "Still, it's kind of funny. Nothing got out over there, and now, all of a sudden, somebody plants a story. Doesn't make much sense, does it?"

Alderman was thinking as he spoke. "You're probably jumping to conclusions — about a deliberate leak. It's more likely that some reporter got wind of what happened at MITI — or even at the airport. When there are that many people involved, it's pretty hard to keep things secret."

"In other words" — Kruger cut in with off-hand brutality — "you don't know any more than I do. Oh, well, what the hell. The Japanese authorities are probably digging into it."

This produced a frown. Alderman leaned forward earnestly. "Carl, the Japanese authorities aren't Lackawanna's problem. Lousy publicity like this is. I want to tamp it down before somebody gets the idea of using Carl Kruger to win the Pulitzer Prize."

Kruger suddenly lost interest. "Okay, you do your work. But don't get overexcited. This isn't anything to worry about. By tomorrow it'll all blow over."

At the door, he turned for a parting shot.

"But you don't want to underestimate the Japanese authorities," he said. "I know that I don't."

Alderman was still wondering exactly what Kruger meant when Norma announced Reuters.

". . . the reason they don't name sources in Tokyo is because there aren't any," he said when he belatedly remembered another call he should make. Reuters detained him for ten minutes. Then Bennet Alderman dialed Washington, D.C.

Kruger, meanwhile, was looking for Pamela Webb. In the last office on his rounds, he learned she was a quarter of a mile away, in a meeting of district managers.

"Hell no," he said emphatically. "Don't call her out. It's nothing important. But tell her I'd like to see her when she gets back."

Ironically, it was Don Hodiak who turned up to provide a sympathetic ear.

Returning from an early-morning inspection tour, he presented a glowing report. "Everything's shipshape," he said. "They're finally getting a handle on the inventory over at Number Four. Things are looking up, Carl."

Kruger and Hodiak had their differences, but Hodiak was never devious.

"I guess that means you don't know that the shit has hit the fan," Kruger said.

When Hodiak remained blank, Kruger went on to sketch in the details.

"Oh, Jesus!" said Hodiak unguardedly. Then he pulled himself together. "Look, you know my stand about the Midland deal. But now that's on the back burner, I don't see that gossip about Tokyo makes a helluva lot of difference to us here at Lackawanna."

Kruger's expression made him add hurriedly: "Not that it's pleasant for you personally."

But Kruger was not looking for special handling. "Hell, that doesn't worry me at all," he said stoutly. "Facts are what break bones, Don. I learned that early on."

Hodiak did not know whether to believe him. Bravado was second nature to Carl Kruger, and so was carelessness about detail.

Hodiak proceeded cautiously. "Well, unless you're feeling thin-skinned all of a sudden, I'd forget it. Hell, Carl, there have been stories about Lackawanna before. And in the end they didn't make any difference. Talk is cheap."

"That's true as far as it goes," said Kruger impatiently. "But this situation's special."

"It's a lot less important. We've got to keep things in perspective around here."

"You've got me there, Don. I'm getting as bad as Bennet. Loose talk on TV doesn't matter one damn. This is just another little blip. Otherwise it's full steam ahead."

Before Hodiak could respond, Sally entered with the *New York Times*.

"You caught me red-handed," said Kruger with a shame-faced grin. "I want to see how black they're painting me."

What he saw was only the beginning.

★ ★ ★

By the time John Thatcher got back to the Sloan, Miss Corsa had a folder bulging with rumors about Kruger.

"You'd better arrange a conference call with the Creditors Committee," Thatcher said. "And make it for this afternoon, when I've found out what's going on."

As he spoke, the homecoming parade began. One by one his immediate assistants appeared. Everett Gabler was the first to cross the wire.

"Any serious problems, Everett?" Thatcher inquired.

When Gabler reported that conditions throughout the Sloan were satisfactory, Thatcher knew that they were clearing the decks.

"Hi, John," Charlie Trinkam hailed him. "You sure had fun and games in Japan!"

The research department also turned out to greet Thatcher. "Thanks for the memo, John," said Walter Bowman. "Did anything else happen besides murder and bribery?"

Watching her plans for a productive morning crumble, Miss Corsa pursed her lips and departed.

"I know Kruger's supposed to be a can-do kind of guy," Charlie observed, starting the ball rolling, "but personally I don't think shooting up MITI is the way to go."

"Actually the victim had his head bashed

in," Thatcher corrected.

Gabler, normally a stickler for accuracy, waved aside this hairsplitting.

"It amounts to the same thing," he said severely. "Just what did go on, John?"

After Thatcher had finished his account, there was a long silence.

"But, John, according to you there is not one single jot of evidence against Kruger," Gabler said at last. "Any one of the parties to those hearings could be guilty."

"They certainly all had motives," Thatcher agreed. "But it's obvious why the Japanese government prefers a foreign culprit."

Walter Bowman, in his own way as much of an expert on the press as Bennet Alderman, was frowning. "Not just the Japanese. Everybody over here wants to hang him too."

"You'll have to fill me in. I've been out of touch for twenty-four hours," Thatcher reminded them.

"That puts you behind the times," Charlie Trinkam said. "Yesterday everybody was buzzing about MITI. Now, somehow, they're all rehashing the old Lockheed scandal — another American company bribing the Japanese government."

"The suggestion is that all Lackawanna's international dealings could bear scrutiny," Everett said.

156

"That sale to Australia came in the nick of time, didn't it?" mused Walter Bowman. "One of the columnists mentioned it this morning."

During the darkest days of the reorganization, a major hydroelectric installation in New South Wales had gone on line with Lackawanna generators.

"Kruger was shaking hands in Canberra just when Washington was voting on the bailout package," Bowman continued.

Thatcher shifted impatiently. "And trumpets were provided by that PR man of his. I don't understand this tidal wave of suspicion when there seems to be no supporting evidence."

"Maybe it's the price of being a personality," Charlie suggested. "Kruger has made himself into a Hollywood star, and you know what happens when they get caught taking drugs or socking a traffic cop."

Thatcher was still pursuing his own line of reasoning.

"Ordinarily I'd suspect there were some fragments of evidence insufficient to protect against a libel action. But if the Japanese government has any proof, why don't they substantiate their case?"

Bowman never strayed far from essentials. "If this goes on much longer, it could hurt Lackawanna."

Thatcher thought about all those calls from the Creditors Committee. "So long as it hurts Lackawanna and not the repayment schedule."

Charlie Trinkam and Walter Bowman were inclined to scoff at this possibility, but they were both born optimists. It was more reassuring when Everett Gabler delivered his verdict.

"I see no immediate cause for alarm, John," he said soberly. "As long as the rumors are restricted to international dealings, Lackawanna's chief operations are unthreatened."

The restriction ended the next morning when a business weekly hit the stands.

Chapter 12

The cover boasted a vivid kaleidoscope of military hardware. Boldly plastered across one corner, the black-and-white legend asked: ANOTHER PENTAGON SCANDAL?

The text inside was less dramatic, but it was nonetheless lethal. Back to back were two articles. The first treated Kruger's ill-fated trip to Japan. The second addressed DOD's chronic problem with corruptible procurement officers. Even more damning, there was a boxed list of Lackawanna's contracts with the Department of Defense. It was impossible to miss the connection.

All across the nation people were spurred to response.

In Seattle, a camera enthusiast busy processing the film from his summer vacation stared incredulously at one picture floating in the tray. When he had pressed the shutter release in Narita Airport, he had been unexpectedly jostled. Now he saw a thin slice of his intended subject at the left of the frame, while the field showed Carl Kruger at bay amid embassy personnel. When the lucky photographer returned home the next day, he was exultant.

"I'm not an amateur anymore, Marge. I just sold my first picture," he announced. "Wait until I tell them at the Camera Club."

In Ohio, a senator on a fence-mending trip reached impulsively for the phone, then withdrew his hand. If Carl wanted to talk, he knew the number. Under the circumstances, it was all too likely that Carl did not want to talk.

In New York, Leonard Solletti and John Thatcher were having their deferred luncheon.

"The creditors are all worried, John. A lot of them want you to call a meeting," Solletti reported.

The time for optimism was past.

"I'm just as concerned as they are, but what good will a meeting be?" Thatcher replied. "Of course we have to keep a close eye on the situation, but there's nothing we can do."

"The place they should do something is Lackawanna."

But in Pennsylvania, constructive suggestions for action were few and far between. Don Hodiak had overflowed to Kruger and to anyone else who would listen with despairing predictions and undefined threats. Bennet Alderman had been even less helpful, apparently unable to comprehend the magnitude of the disaster.

"This is a fine time for Benny to fold on me," Kruger raged. "Instead of finding out who's in back of this smear campaign, he babbles about releasing a denial."

Pamela Webb had been a silent witness to the encounter.

"He's probably shell-shocked," she said wearily. "Bennet thinks he controls the press. When somebody else takes over, he goes to pieces."

"And somebody sure has. They didn't hop from a bribe at MITI to columns about Lockheed to a cover story on Lackawanna's defense contracts just by accident. This is becoming an all-out attempt to destroy us."

Pamela, close to exhaustion, struggled to be analytic. "That doesn't make sense. Who could it be? Do you think the Japanese —"

"It's too late for a lot of guesswork," Kruger interrupted with a snap. "The important thing is to stop it in its tracks."

"And how can you do that without knowing what's going on?" she retorted, her voice brittle with tension.

Unlike Pamela, Kruger had fallen back on instinct.

"Sitting around here moaning won't get us anywhere. It's time to come out fighting. Everybody's saying, 'Where there's smoke, there's got to be fire.' Well, the only fire around was in Tokyo. If I stamp that out, there's nothing for the rest of this junk to tie into. I'm taking the next plane to Washington."

As a result, Carl Kruger descended on the nation's capital like a steam engine. For forty-eight hours he made his pitch at the White House, the Senate, the Pentagon. Between rousting out old friends and confronting new critics, he was hard at it from early breakfasts to midnight drinks. Throughout he was photographed, pelted with questions, and packaged for the evening news. Seemingly indifferent to the mob at his heels, he deliberately chose to forgo his usual broad smiles and airy waves. He was reminding everyone that in a fight for Lackawanna's life, he could still deal out punishing blows.

So in Washington they watched and speculated.

In a very private club, in an even more private room, a small, wizened man crowed with jubilation.

"That takes care of the Kruger threat. I said we had to neutralize him before he got off the ground, and now it's done. He can't come riding in from left field anymore."

His companions were worriers.

162

"Don't leap to conclusions, Harvey," said one of them. "What if there's a backlash from this Tokyo business? There could be a sympathy vote out there."

Harvey was exasperated. "Kruger's knee-deep in murder and bribery. For God's sake, people are saying that the embassy saved him from being arrested. They can't run him for dogcatcher now."

The second pessimist demurred. "Don't get carried away. This could be a temporary glitch, Harvey. Kruger's working his tail off all over Washington; he could pull the fat out of the fire. If no hard news comes out of Tokyo, if Kruger gets a whopping big contract out of DOD, we'll be back to square one. He could still gallop into the convention and upset the whole damned applecart."

Harvey bared his teeth. "You want to bet?"

Five blocks away, other power brokers were huddling.

"Kruger's got a can tied to his tail," said the bald one. "He sure can't help us now."

"From long shot to albatross," said a colleague. "Does anybody know what really happened in Tokyo?"

The answer came in a soft Texas accent. "Not yet."

"I say we scrap Kruger," said Baldie, sticking to the point at issue.

"That means Paul walks away with the nomination," said the Texan. "Which guarantees losing the election. And if by any fluke Paul wins, we're out in the rain."

"There must be other people we could run against him."

"Who?"

A depressed silence ensued until the Texan said: "Kruger's the only one who's got a hope in hell of waltzing in and snatching the convention from Paul's grubby paws."

"Like hell! We need Mr. Clean, not somebody getting accused of everything but pimping."

But the Texan still had hopes.

"Look, maybe we'll have to dump Kruger. I'm just saying it's too early to tell. Sure, it looks like a big stink now. But it could pass. And you've got to admit, Kruger's making the effort."

"How do you think he's doing?"

"Who knows?"

The well-connected lawyer in a small office in downtown Alexandria delivered his opinion.

"So far it looks like a draw. Kruger's taken plenty of punishment, but he hasn't been knocked out. We can live with that — temporarily."

Alderman resented this heavy-handed prompting.

"I know the rules, Sam," he said. "Why do you think I dragged Carl up to see Will Trowbridge?"

"I figure we've got two months — maximum!" Sam continued.

Alderman did not indicate much respect for the deadline.

"Look, in two months anything can happen," he said. "I don't care what they're saying now; nobody can foretell what the Japs will come out with."

Without changing expression, Sam contemplated the future.

"That could be good — or bad," he agreed. "But do you think it's smart, sitting around waiting for the ax to fall?"

"Who's just sitting around?"

Kindly Sam studied him through the haze of blue cigar smoke.

"I hope that means you've got some more useful ideas, Benny."

Alderman met his eyes.

"I've always got useful ideas."

At the State Department, the response to Carl Kruger took concrete form. A polite request was dispatched to Tokyo for an official progress report. If the police investigation had produced no specific evidence against Kruger, surely it would be advisable for the Japanese government to issue a statement clarifying certain misconceptions.

"Specific evidence? We have no evidence at all!" Hayakawa said bitterly. "Have the Swiss told us anything?"

"No. And they justify their usual reluctance by pointing out that without knowing where the funds originated, they have no place to start," his assistant replied.

Hayakawa had expected this. The Swiss were certainly not going to rummage through every numbered account in the country. "Then unless we receive later information from them, all we know is that there was some sort of payoff, presumably to affect the Midland Research hearings. Ushiba learned about it. Do we know how he got his hands on that letter?"

The assistant broke off to cough delicately. "Ushiba requested material to prepare his synopsis. Files came in from everywhere. Including Mr. Matsuda's office — and that of the minister."

"Just what we need," Hayakawa grunted. "All right. A page could have been carelessly left in somebody's file."

"No matter how Ushiba found that German letter, it is puzzling he could read it. Wouldn't he need a translation?"

Hayakawa had already considered the point. "Not necessarily. The page consisted largely of standard transfer terms. Ushiba was familiar enough with financial documents to suspect that he was holding dynamite. He could have deciphered the rest with a dictionary. But all this is peripheral. The major question is what Ushiba intended to do with it."

"He had already put it into an envelope." The assistant looked pious. "No doubt he was going to report his discovery to the proper authorities."

The doubt was palpable.

"But even if you are correct, how did anybody learn what Ushiba was up to? And above all, why go to the extreme of murdering him?"

Japan's scandals had all been free of bloodshed so far.

"Furthermore," the assistant said, "we are talking about businessmen. When they are thwarted, they do not seek vengeance or fly into blind rages. They simply try to make money some other way."

"However," said Hayakawa, "one man there had everything to lose. Mr. Matsuda is neither an industrialist nor a powerful politician. For him exposure could mean personal disgrace, possibly even jail. What's more, Matsuda knew where his files had gone. If he had lost that page, he would know exactly where to look for it."

The assistant advanced cautiously. "There is another way Matsuda could have learned where his letter was. Ushiba might have told him. Perhaps Ushiba was planning to use the information to avoid transfer."

"That would imply that Ushiba's wants were very modest, considering the sums involved in these MR hearings," said Hayakawa. "No, I think it is more realistic to assume that Ushiba was demanding money."

"Then he wouldn't have approached Matsuda; he would have gone straight to the source," the assistant objected.

Hayakawa shook his head. "Ushiba was a stupid man. He seems to have made a mistake."

As a consequence of this discussion, the inspector forwarded a confidential report that left no room for misunderstanding. The police thought they knew who had taken the bribe and who had murdered Mr. Ushiba, but they were in no position to proceed against him. Furthermore, they could not single out which company, by suborning Matsuda, had tried to destroy the integrity of MITI. There were three equally likely contenders. . . .

The minister stopped reading when he came to the only sentence that mattered. Hayakawa's report gave him no alternative. Some statement to placate the Americans was now necessary. But it was going to be very carefully crafted.

Accordingly the next morning his spokesman read expressionlessly:

". . . no grounds implicating Lackawanna Electric Industries. The same is true of Yonezawa Trading Company and Shima Trading Company. The ministry wishes to go on record as affirming that in our many years of experience with these two distinguished firms, there has never been the slightest suggestion of impropriety."

Taking a deep breath, he continued. "The ministry has every confidence that Yonezawa and Shima are maintaining the highest ethical standards."

Chapter 13

Politicians may work day and night, but that is not the way of the normal world. At six-thirty that Friday afternoon, the offices of Shima Computers, U.S.A., located in a San Francisco high-rise, were approaching total somnolence. Most of the personnel had escaped to the pleasures of a summer weekend, leaving behind only isolated spots of activity.

It was a clerk crossing the deserted reception area who took the initial brunt of the invasion. Without warning the elevator doors slid open and an army of strange men trampled forward. While the clerk goggled, the leader waved his troops to strategic points before turning to her.

"Federal marshals," he announced.

When the only response was a blank stare, he made a suggestion.

"Maybe you'd better tell someone."

By the time the clerk fled back to her employer, she was incoherent.

"There are a bunch of police out there," she stammered.

The service manager, who was itching to

finish his last letter and depart, was not sympathetic.

"What are you babbling about?"

"I think they want to arrest someone," she continued wildly. "You've got to come."

Still dubious, he rose and followed her. Before turning the corner, he saw intruders seeping into every corner of the company.

"What the hell do you people think you're doing?" he demanded as he advanced into the reception room.

"We have a search warrant," the marshal explained, offering a document.

For this there was only one answer.

"Jenny, get someone from the law department up here," the service manager ordered, then stalked off with an air of finality.

But the law department valued its weekends too. Only a young specialist in patent law was available to pound upstairs and read the search warrant.

"This seems to be in order," he said gravely, sinking the fact that he had no way of knowing.

"Then we'll need keys to everything — drawers, file cabinets, safes."

Scowling in furious thought, the young man merely said: "You'll have to talk to the man in charge. Jenny, call Mr. Reese down here."

Nobody on the payroll doubted that Fred

Reese was the man in charge. When he had been hired as executive vice-president of the new organization, he had been pleased with the salary and the responsibility. It had taken only three weeks for the fly in his ointment to materialize, in the shape of Mr. Yasuhiro Kawate.

The president sent over from Tokyo had not been designed by nature to be a work-aholic. For over twenty years with Shima Trading Company he had pretended to relish long hours and sustained endeavor. Now he was ready to enjoy the fruits of an overseas assignment. From the moment of arrival, Kawate and his wife had become joyful captives of the California style. She abandoned domestic chores in favor of socializing, and he took to the sea. His pride and joy was a forty-two-foot sloop, and his most cherished achievement was membership in a select yacht club.

This was bad enough, but what really fueled Reese's resentment was that Kawate was not content to stay away. At unpredictable intervals he would descend, alighting at random anywhere in the company. Determined to maintain himself in Tokyo's good graces, he detected imperfections in Reese's system, instituted dazzling improvements, and then departed, leaving havoc and confusion in his wake.

Inevitably Reese's first thought as he confronted the marshals was irritation at Kawate's absence. Nonetheless he was mindful of his duty to give battle.

"So you've got some kind of summons," he snapped. "Then you're supposed to mail it. This isn't the way to do things."

"There's also the matter of the search warrant. I'm still waiting for those keys," the marshal replied.

For some time the young lawyer had been plucking at his employer's sleeve. He finally succeeded in drawing Reese into a corner.

"Look," he said in a lowered voice, "I don't know what's going on, but this has got to be a show of force. They don't send out half the marshals in the district simply to serve a summons. The feds must be mad at us."

"Or it's one of their colossal foul-ups," Reese growled, having hastily reviewed all corporate delinquencies known to him. "You know the way their drug people are always coming down on the wrong house."

"But they've got a grand jury indictment."

Frowning, Reese marched over to the marshal. "What's the underlying complaint supposed to be?" he asked.

"Export control violations."

"Ah ha! That proves it's a mistake. We're

a sales and service outfit for the U.S. and Canada."

Unmoved, the marshal began to intone: "Regarding shipments to Tokyo on January 7 of this year, February 11, February 27, March 14, and so on."

"You have got to be out of your mind. We import from Japan, we don't —"

Reese broke off abruptly as he recalled an almost forgotten instance of Kawate's officious intermeddling. The president had set up a small office, under his own supervision, for occasional sales of technical items to Japan.

The marshal, misconstruing Reese's silence, thought the time was ripe for action.

"And now I have to serve this summons, as well as several subpoenas for your staff," he said, producing a fresh sheaf.

Unlike the young lawyer, Reese did not pretend to read the entire document with which he was supplied.

"I'm afraid I'm only the vice-president. The man you want is our chief executive, Mr. Yasuhiro Kawate," he explained, the light of unholy glee dawning on his countenance. "Jenny, give these men the address of that yacht club."

There is a limit to both the viciousness and the omniscience of the federal government.

174

The young lawyer had been correct in scenting a show of force. The masterminds in the Department of Justice had deliberately staged their raid so as to demoralize a fragmentary staff. But never had they contemplated swinging the iron fist of naked power at the season's most gala wedding.

As luck would have it, however, eight hundred guests had arrived at the Hebrides Point Yacht Club that afternoon, together with a host of society reporters and photographers from every life-style magazine on the West Coast. Under a cloudless blue sky, the middle-aged were doing honor to the occasion with floating chiffons and impeccable mess jackets. The young, lithe and tanned, were making bolder fashion statements. Circulating through the crowd were bridesmaids in Victorian costume and ushers sporting Beau Brummell shirts complete with foaming jabots. Even the club members going about their usual pastimes had been inspired to do their bit. Every craft at the boat slips was flying colored pennants.

It had been a picture-perfect wedding for hours. A lieutenant governor kissed the bride, the commodore of the club danced with her, the wedding cake struck an appropriate nautical note. By seven o'clock the reception was beginning to wind down, as the guests waited for the bride to appear in her going-away out-fit. Many of them were stationed on the portico of the clubhouse, and the usual wedding prattle was flowing freely.

". . . of course they've been living together for two years."

"The lobster was great. I'm going to ask Gloria why ours never tastes that way."

"Did you see the brother's wife? I wonder where he found her."

"Myself, I think Baccarat is a mistake. I never give breakables now that they move around so much. Silver is always safe."

Several hundred people observed a cavalcade of cars sweeping into the driveway. When a squad of obvious officials alighted, rumors were happily bandied from one group to another. The groom's father was being arrested for insider trading. The brother's wife had jumped bail. The commodore's past had finally caught up with him.

It was something of a disappointment when the action moved out of earshot. Nonetheless cameras were hoisted to record a scene that would enliven Saturday's front pages.

An inner circle of dark business suits was surrounded by a sea of decorative wedding guests. At the exact center of attention stood Mr. Yasuhiro Kawate. Tumbling ashore from a canopied deck chair, he had been caught in his full glory as an old salt. His tidy little head was crowned by a snowy yachting cap, his meager shanks protruded from crisp Bermuda shorts, and his hand still clutched one of his famous margaritas.

Even without pictures, there would have been banner headlines.

According to the indictment, Shima Computers had shipped sensitive military technology behind the Iron Curtain. And it had done this, not once, not twice, but seven times over a course of six months. There had been forged invoices, fraudulent claims of end-user, and systematic bribery to customs officials in Tokyo. Shima had violated the export-control regulations of the United States, the trading laws of Japan, and the rules of the Paris-based Coordinating Committee for Multilateral Export Controls (COCOM), which governs exports to Communist countries.

The investigation had been started by the Pentagon, which had already alerted Tokyo. While federal marshals were making merry in San Francisco, Japanese police had been searching thirteen offices of the Shima Trading Company.

Nothing is more calculated to make the average congressman see red than security lapses by a purported ally. On Saturday night many elected officials were letting fly. The suggested reprisals covered a wide range of penalties, starting with the obvious.

"Let's throw the buggers in jail," said one of them.

Others, however, had learned to hit where it hurts.

"Take away Shima's corporate charter, and toss them out of the country."

"To hell with that. They're just a subsidiary." The speaker's eyes brightened. "Let's ban Shima Trading from selling in the U.S. I'm talking Shima cars, Shima motorcycles, Shima TVs."

When someone discovered that Shima Power Tools had had the effrontery to bid on a U.S. contract, his wrath boiled over. "And they can't be a federal supplier for the next ten years."

"Why stop at selling?" demanded a big thinker. "Make it so they can't sell, they can't manufacture, they can't invest."

The mathematicians on the Hill had numbers at their fingertips.

"Did you know that Shima does one billion annually in the U.S.?"

"We do it my way, and we can close down ten thousand jobs over there. After what they've done to my district, it'll be a pleasure."

The torrent of threats naturally reflected the grievances of the speakers. But one of them, Carl Kruger's old friend Mike, was keeping his eye firmly on the ball.

Poised on the steps of the Capitol, he responded gravely and calmly to television's questions.

"As you know, I have nothing but admiration for the achievements of most Japanese trading companies. However, when there's a rotten apple in the barrel, you have to take action. You can't do business with a company that systematically bribes its own country's civil servants."

This was not the aspect of the situation capturing most American viewers, but then Mike was not speaking to them.

Chapter 14

For Lackawanna, the Shima indictment was the biggest miracle since the parting of the Red Sea. Carl Kruger had been busy late into the evening. By the next morning he was triumphant.

"I cabled MITI an invitation to a demonstration in Birmingham next Monday. They're going to have a hell of a time trying to duck it."

"That testimonial to Shima's integrity has backfired beautifully," Pamela Webb chortled. "Without it, things wouldn't be half as good."

Kruger grinned. "That'll teach them to point the finger at me. And now Yonezawa can start using a little muscle. I just hope Arai doesn't want a pound of flesh for his efforts."

The thought disturbed Kruger, but it set Pamela's eyes dancing.

"Then let's disabuse him of that notion right away," she said blithely. "You're not the only one who's been thinking. Remember the last time I was in England there were some Koreans sniffing around MR? And I told them you weren't interested?"

It took Kruger a moment to realize where she was heading. Then he sat upright so suddenly his chair thumped.

"Wait a minute!"

But Pamela was rushing on. "By now the whole world knows that MR is on the auction block."

"And they know the price I'm asking is the Japanese market."

"After our troubles in Tokyo, the Koreans can't be sure that's the only offer you'll take. What if I zip over to England and suggest showing them around the facility? I can make such a splash that Yonezawa's London office will pick up the rumor within hours."

Kruger was nodding like a wound-up toy.

"I like it, I like it a lot," he breathed. "It dovetails beautifully."

"You want to bet on Arai's reaction?" she asked smugly.

Kruger chuckled. "He'll go after the whole damn Diet."

"And they'll like the idea of the Koreans getting steel robotics even less than he does."

"It'll knock on the head any thought about squeezing the price."

They were chanting rhythmically back and forth.

"And between your invitation and Arai's pressure . . ."

Kruger spread his hands a foot apart, then snapped them together with a crack.

"We get them on both flanks in a classic pincers," he finished for her. "In a way, Pamela, it's a shame you got hooked on business. You could have taught them a lot at West Point about diversionary tactics."

"The tactics are great," she agreed without false modesty. "So long as Arai has clean hands."

"I know."

For a moment their eyes locked.

"I got a rundown on the Japanese press from Benny's people," Kruger said.

She had no difficulty following him. "So did I," she admitted. "I even called Stan Zaretski in Osaka. According to him, Matsuda took the bribe but the police don't have a clue about who gave it. With luck there won't be any unpleasant surprises."

"Unless the police are keeping something under their hats. We just have to take the chance that they don't know more than they're saying."

Bennet Alderman's first reaction to the news about Shima was a vast sigh of relief. He knew just how to capitalize on it.

182

Kruger was less enthusiastic. "We're not trying to sway the man in the street, Benny," he said. "The only two groups that count now are the procurement boys at DOD and the cabinet in Japan."

"So? They follow public opinion too," Alderman replied confidently. "Now you've got a chance to tell your side of the story while everybody in the world wants to grab you for some airtime."

Today Kruger was willing to be persuaded.

"Not a bad idea," he said cheerfully. "But Pamela's come up with a real wingding. She's going to make overtures to the Korean competition."

Bennet Alderman had not fought his way to the top by admiring other people's achievements. "That can't do any harm," he said perfunctorily. "But let's finish off this business of your TV appearances. How about a one-two shot on Tuesday and Wednesday? I could put you on a breakfast show and a talk show."

After two years of the Alderman treatment, Kruger was a paraprofessional about the distinctions.

"I'll go with the morning show," he decided almost instantly. "That way I won't get stuck batting around the history of Japanese corruption with some professor. I'll be one-on-one with the host, and I can give it the old personal touch."

"That would be good timing," Alderman approved. "My sources say Shima is taking out full-page ads tomorrow in all the big papers. You know the sort of thing — black borders, profuse apologies, and so forth."

"Great!" Kruger was looking into the future. "After the show we'll be in a countdown for England, if all goes well. I've given MITI the date for a demo in Birmingham, and I don't see how they can get out of it."

Shocked, Alderman reared back.

"Now wait a minute, Carl, you haven't thought this thing through. I wish you'd talked to me first. We're presenting you as a clean-cut American businessman who is being victimized and exploited by the Japanese. How the hell can we do that if you're willing to climb right back into bed with them?"

Growing heated, he failed to notice the half-smile on Kruger's face until he had finished.

"My God, what's funny?"

"Benny," Kruger asked curiously, "have you ever looked at what's out there?"

Turning in his chair, he waved at the plate glass behind him.

"It's the same view I've got," Alderman muttered, without joining the inspection of smokestacks and grimy brickwork.

"That's where we make things to sell," Kruger continued gently. "The more things we sell, the better for Lackawanna. And Japan has a lot of people with a lot of money to buy things. That's why we're going through with the Birmingham demo."

The ABC instruction might have offended some people, but Alderman continued his attempts at dissuasion.

"You've missed my point. You're like a wife who moves back in with her husband just as she's filing for divorce," he insisted. "At the very least we lose momentum. If we don't watch out, we lose credibility too. I say we hold off."

"And I say we don't," Kruger retorted in a voice that brooked no argument.

Bennet Alderman was taken aback. He was always casual about the fundamentals of Lackawanna's existence. This time he had almost forgotten them.

Don Hodiak, of course, knew all about those fundamentals. His face, which had been sinking into deeper and deeper lines with every passing day, had shed years overnight.

"I just got off the phone with DOD," he announced buoyantly. "They've stopped acting as if I've got leprosy."

"Did they say anything about this Shima

business?" Kruger asked.

Hodiak preened himself.

"Hell no! They pretended they were asking about our delivery to Redstone Arsenal. So I told them we'll be shipping two days before due."

"Attaboy!"

They grinned at each other.

"When I got in this morning, I was afraid for a minute that Bennet was going to kiss me," Hodiak recalled.

"You should have come straight here. Then you would have gotten Pamela. She's feeling pretty good too."

Overflowing with energy, Hodiak had flung himself into a chair. Now he picked up a ruler from the desk and began flexing it.

"Well, I'm all for celebrating. This one has been a lot too close for comfort."

"You can say that again. But everything's beginning to fall into place now. Even that lousy trip to Washington is paying off."

Hodiak produced his own corroboration. "The boys at DOD sounded downright chummy."

"Oh, them. They were just scared of being sucked into the swamp. By the way, Pamela's doing an end run on Arai with the Koreans. He may not fall for it, but he'll damn well use it."

186

"Who cares about Arai now?"

When Kruger explained his invitation to MITI, Hodiak's expression turned to dismay.

"What's gotten into you, Carl? Two days ago you agreed that this whole idea of going to Japan was a loser. We've squeaked through by the skin of our teeth. For God's sake, let's get out while the getting is good."

"Oh, no we don't. How often does somebody hand you a second chance like this?"

"A second chance to throw ourselves into a meat chopper," Hodiak retorted.

But Kruger was impervious to barbs. "There isn't going to be any trouble this time around, now that everyone knows Shima was trying to fix the race."

"Nobody knows that. Bennet fed me the same line, but you and I know better. All we've seen is a lot of PR hype. First Tokyo was trying to twist things to make us the goat. Now Shima's getting the same treatment over here. But what does it all boil down to? Somebody in Shima's San Francisco office thought they could slip a few microchips to Russia. Big deal!"

"There was bribery, wasn't there? It shows how Shima does things."

Hearing the weakness of his own argument, Kruger looked almost sulky.

"Somebody spilled that poor guy's brains

all over the floor at MITI," Hodiak reminded him. "That's a long way from passing a few bucks to a customs clerk. Or have you forgotten what really went on back there?"

"I saw the body too," Kruger said shortly. "I don't know what the hell you're getting at, Don."

With a visible effort at control, Hodiak laid down his ruler and spaced his words.

"They could be turning over some rocks in Tokyo."

"Let them. It's got nothing to do with Lackawanna."

"So you think this was all a piece of wonderful luck?" Hodiak asked sardonically.

"I'm not exactly saying that. I'm just not looking a gift horse in the mouth."

"There's a lot you're not exactly saying, Carl."

Kruger shifted uneasily. "Come on, Don, you know how these things work. The feds have probably been digging into Shima's exports for months. I happened to talk to a few people in Washington, and it paid off. Someone decided to move things up the calendar."

"And they were ready to go to the grand jury in days? Who do you think you're kidding?"

Hodiak caught himself, then began again on a more conciliatory note.

"Carl, why don't you listen to yourself? You didn't know what was going on in Tokyo. You didn't know what was going on in San Francisco. And you sure as hell don't know what's going to break next week. Ever since this whole business started, it's been one rocket after another whizzing over our heads. The sooner we put distance between Lackawanna and Japan, the better."

Carl Kruger tried to be patient.

"I suppose you think I'm going too fast and we ought to delay the next round."

"To hell with delays. We ought to scrap the whole idea."

This was worse than Kruger had expected.

"Now? When I'll have Arai with his tongue hanging out?"

"If he wants MR's technology, we could make a bundle licensing it to him."

"MR has always been just bait," Kruger snapped. "Our goal is to sell generators to Japan. And I shouldn't have to explain it to you as if you were poor Benny."

Since entering, Hodiak had been on an emotional nosedive, passing from elation to despair. Without pausing to think, he spoke his mind.

"You know what's really happening? Somebody out there is pulling a lot of strings, and they've got you jerking around like a puppet."

It was a serious error. Instead of flicking his adversary, Hodiak had hit a nerve.

"We're going ahead, and that's final!" Kruger snapped in a cold fury.

They were both sitting upright, rigid as ramrods. Suddenly Hodiak's doubts congealed into determination.

"Then I want to take this to the board," he declared.

Kruger's eyebrows lifted arrogantly. "And what's that in aid of? By the time the board meets, I'll be back from England with the deal of a lifetime."

"Somebody's got to keep you from wrecking Lackawanna," said Hodiak, unyielding as stone.

"That's my board you're talking about. You won't get one vote."

Having crossed his Rubicon, Hodiak relaxed. "Maybe not," he admitted. "But you've forgotten how much can happen in a week."

"You want to make a fool of yourself in public, that's your lookout."

Everybody in the building soon learned about the quarrel, including Bennet Alderman.

"I just heard. So you think you're going to shiv Carl with the board," he said, storming into Hodiak's office an hour later.

Hodiak barely acknowledged his presence. "That's what we do in those meetings — discuss policy."

"Don't give me that bullshit! You think you can use the Tokyo mess to score points for yourself. Well, forget it. You're either with us or against us on this one."

"Will you stop sounding as if this is D-day, Bennet?" said Hodiak, looking bored.

Alderman, stung by the lack of response, was hanging menacingly over the desk.

"I don't give a damn what parlor games you play when it doesn't count. Right now the important thing is showing the world that Carl is on top of things."

"You don't know how funny that sounds. Besides, I got the idea you weren't so hot about this plan yourself, Bennet."

Alderman's eyes narrowed into slits. "My job is keeping Carl in the saddle, and I'm not sitting still for any sabotage."

With a sigh, Hodiak marked his place with a pencil and faced the man hovering over him. "You're going to have to, and call it what you like."

"I'm warning you, Don, I've taken out bigger threats than you."

"Sure," said Hodiak indifferently. "Now will you get out of here so I can go back to work."

Alderman marched stiffly to the door, where he turned for a final shot.

"You're going to regret this," he promised.

Chapter 15

Pamela Webb had not wasted any time. By the next morning she was instructing a hotel clerk in Birmingham.

"Mr. Dong is a Korean guest of Midland Research," she explained. "He will need a room for the one night, and we will appreciate any courtesies shown to him."

The Albany was suitably impressed. During the last five years, Lackawanna and Miss Webb had become valued customers.

"Oh, you can rely on us. We'll take good care of Mr. Dong."

Indeed, the Korean's discomforts were going to come from a different quarter.

"Welcome to Midland Research, Mr. Dong," Ali Khan greeted him. "We're very pleased with the way our work is going, and I hope you will be too. We thought we'd begin by having Miss Webb show you the extent of our operation, and then you can get down to the real business with the head of our test laboratory."

Several hours later, Mr. Dong was warmly expressing his appreciation to the crew that had put the prototypes through their paces.

"That was very satisfactory, and my principals will be extremely interested in my report." He beamed as he glanced at his watch.

Pamela had more in mind.

"Mr. Khan has arranged a dinner in your honor, which will also give you an opportunity to meet key management personnel at Midland."

Mr. Dong's face fell as he absorbed the fact that his working day was going to stretch well into the evening.

"How gracious of Mr. Khan," he said unenthusiastically.

At eight o'clock Mr. Dong was put on view in Birmingham's flossiest restaurant. Not one single diner there could possibly have missed the fact that the front office of Midland Research was wining and dining a distinguished Korean guest. And Ali Khan, in the role of host, would have been an eye-opener to Bennet Alderman. Here on his own turf, he was not a technical genius at loose ends; he was a man of substance summoning the best for his guest.

But restaurants were only part of the great plan for public display of Kwai Dong. Ali Khan had also been busy setting up appointments with Birmingham authorities.

As Mr. Dong worked his way through

breakfast the next morning, he found that Pamela Webb was taking an expansive reading of what would interest his clients.

"Naturally they will be concerned with conditions in the area — which couldn't be better from their point of view. Any substantial expansion of MR will receive a good deal of governmental assistance."

"There has been no discussion as yet of expansion."

"Nonetheless the economic climate is very important," she replied with brutal common sense. "I think you'll find that your people are very impressed by the possibilities here. And while primary attention has to be focused on the labor force, I'm sure you'll agree that we also have to consider . . ."

Within the hour Mr. Dong had begun a dizzying round of municipal offices. He was lectured about availability of labor, subsidies for training programs, building codes, environmental restrictions, and proposed industrial parks. Everywhere he went he met friendly faces and persuasive tongues. In Birmingham, the mere hint that a modest R&D company might launch into production was enough to bring out the troops in full force.

But every expert at the hard sell knows there is a time to put away graphs and statistics and introduce the warm personal touch. Mr.

Dong was only human. After he had been battered all morning with information he did not want, his spirits lifted at the introduction of two city councillors who suggested that they put their cares aside in favor of a long, relaxing lunch.

And they were as good as their word. Not one syllable fell from their lips about grants-in-aid or the possibility of building variances. Instead they discussed the amenities of English life.

"A very enjoyable luncheon," Dong said to Pamela in parting, scrubbing all reference to the morning that had preceded it.

"I thought the whole trip went well. Thank you for giving us so much of your time. I hope we didn't waste any of it."

"Quite the contrary," he said feelingly. "I have more than enough material to satisfy my clients."

Pamela, however, was already thinking about her own report. She had done all that was possible at her end. Now it was up to Mr. Arai.

Ever since the Shima indictment, Mr. Fumitoshi Arai had been waiting for the ideal moment to make his move. The time had now come. After sympathizing with the minister, he moved decorously on to muted encouragement.

"Perhaps the event will be less unfortunate than you anticipate," he suggested. "An accusation has been made, but an adroit defense can do much to mitigate the consequences."

Sato shook his head sadly. "Shima Computer has decided to plead guilty and accept whatever penalty is imposed. They hope thereby to avoid the legacy of bad feeling that would be engendered by a protracted — and futile — resistance."

"Ah!" Arai breathed softly. He then addressed himself to his teacup and waited to see if Sato could resist the theme.

"Shima has much to reproach itself with," Sato continued censoriously. "The passage of the microchips could have been treated as a piece of carelessness. Deplorable to be sure, but not entirely avoidable in a large firm. The existence of the bribe, unfortunately, renders that interpretation impossible. And of course it encourages the continued slander of our business practices."

Arai shook his head.

"We all have a great deal to lose by such an image. I, for one, would be dismayed at the suggestion that one of our national industries routinely employs bribery," he said sedately, sinking his shaft into the bull's-eye.

The minister's teacup became stationary at the implications of this statement.

"As you say, an appalling consequence," he murmured at last, "and one which we need not consider at the moment."

Arai indicated token agreement, then moved on to less sensitive areas.

"It is regrettable that these disclosures have emerged this week. Even if we are spared a major political crisis, it will make an awkward situation for those of us attending the Midland Research meeting in Great Britain."

Awkwardness, particularly for others, was something Sato could view with composure.

"We only proposed a meeting in Birmingham as a means of terminating an impossible situation here. There should be no insuperable difficulty in delaying the date Mr. Kruger suggested. He can scarcely object."

"On the contrary, Kruger is seizing the opportunity to sound out other potential buyers for MR."

In order to underline this news, Mr. Arai paused to inspect the pastry tray and make a careful selection.

"I had not realized there were other firms in contention," Sato said with a puzzled frown. "Do you know who they are?"

"My people in London tell me that the agent of several Korean interests has just spent two days at Midland Research."

There was a long, appreciative silence. Korea's economic miracle was a sore spot.

Arai, delicately licking his fingers, had said all that he had come to say. First the minister had been forced to consider the possibility that Shima's criminal acts might well have extended to MITI. Then, with Shima's claims to public support neatly undermined, Arai had delivered the real body blow. Could Sato, already fighting for his political life, afford to become the minister who had handed MR's robotics to Korean steel?

On the whole, not a bad morning's work.

The Shima indictment even affected Tomaheko Matsuda. For all practical purposes he had been a pariah since Ushiba's murder. His superiors dropped him from their conferences, his peers shunned him like the plague, and his subordinates approached only in response to a direct command. At first incredulous, Matsuda slowly realized that his guilt was silently and universally assumed. Without a single colleague available for consultation, he shouldered the burden of his problems alone. After a week's miserable silence, he was reduced to discussing the matter with his son.

"It was bad enough before," Matsuda lamented out of the agony of his soul. "But since the Shima admission, it is even worse. Because of a violation that has absolutely nothing to do with me, they assume there is evidence of corruption in my office."

"They are embarrassed by the Shima news. As soon as the initial reaction has worn off, they will realize there is no connection between the two incidents. You must be patient, Father."

The son was a levelheaded young man of thirty, but Matsuda still regarded him as a giddy youth.

"Don't you understand what I'm saying? They are comparing me to a wretched customs clerk!"

The son tried again.

"It is certainly an unfortunate coincidence. If the timing had not been so close, nobody would dream of such a comparison."

Old habits die hard.

"Don't be so silly," Matsuda snapped with all the vigor he usually brought to these exchanges. "The Japanese government discovers a bribe and ejects a party of Americans with the clear implication that they are at fault. Within a week the American government indicts a Japanese firm for an offense that centers around a bribe. And you call that a coincidence. How can you be so innocent? That timing was no accident."

Chapter 16

The Shima scandal was a topic of conversation in suburban New York as well.

". . . so it's a hell of a time to be on vacation," said Gene Fleming. "I'll be stuck with the IFMA in London till Thursday. But the minute that's through, I'll grab a flight back to Tokyo."

The Flemings' brief stopover in New York entailed dinner with Haru's married niece. An additional guest was John Thatcher, who had been invited to observe the growing Japanese community in Westchester.

"Are you talking about motorcycles?" he guessed, hazily aware that Gene had some official capacity in that world.

"The International Federation of Motorcycle Associations," Fleming explained absently. "But you see, the ramifications from Shima may start a chain reaction that blows everything sky-high. I should be there with my ear to the ground."

Before Thatcher could comment, Fleming continued his lament.

"And now that they're stuck with sending

Mr. Matsuda to the MR demonstration in Birmingham, anything can happen."

"You mean Matsuda's still in charge?" Thatcher demanded.

"They can't help themselves," Fleming replied. "They wanted to put him on the sick list, but he wouldn't oblige."

Remembering Matsuda in triumph at the Prime Minister's side, Thatcher said, "The man must be desperate."

This did not accord with the nephew's view of deputy secretaries, so he was relieved to interrupt: "Dinner, I believe, is ready."

Thatcher expected a dinner conversation centering on Japanese impressions of America. Instead he got a pitched battle, with Haru Fleming taking on all comers.

"Japanese society is about as stable as a rocket immediately before blast-off," she announced defiantly.

After a hissing intake of breath, the nephew regained his composure. "How can you possibly say that? We have maintained our traditional coupling of family, community, and workplace."

"That simply isn't so," she retorted. "We are no longer a bunch of rice farmers in rural villages."

"Naturally there have been changes due to modernization. But as Japanese, we have replaced the requirements of the farm with those of industry. Every individual still has his sense of *uchi* and —"

"*Uchi?*" Thatcher interrupted.

"It refers to one's place of belonging," Haru hastily explained. "One's place of primary affiliation."

Undeterred, the nephew continued: "All over the world it is recognized that our achievements are due to establishing the company as a source of *uchi*."

Haru disagreed again.

"I know that. What's more, every mother is told that the *uchi* of her children comes from the school, while her own comes from the home. In fact, you are making my point. On that famous rice farm, everybody shared the same *uchi*. Now the husband, the wife, the child, all have different ones. It may be wonderful for industrial production, but it's terrible for the family."

The introduction of the family threw the nephew into disarray, but to Thatcher's pleasure, Haru's niece moved onto the field.

"Now, Aunt," she said soothingly, "I know, when you were a girl, Grandfather walked to his works and came home for meals. All that has gone. But unlike the Americans, we've encouraged the schools to play an important part in socializing the children. That's where they learn about responsibility and diligence and cooperation."

"That's also where they learn about role playing," Gene remarked to Thatcher. "They learn the formal courtesies expected of them."

"It is not role playing," the nephew said huffily. "It is an acknowledgment of the fact of authority, whether it's child with parent, student with teacher, or employee with employer."

Gene was more than agreeable. "Actually, once you cotton on to the rules, things are a lot simpler."

This admission unleashed the floodgates, as they all related their shock upon first encountering the American system.

"I laughed and laughed," Haru confessed. "Everybody calling each other by first names and pretending to be equals, when they aren't."

"The lady next door is twenty-five years older than I am, and she wants to be friends," the niece said indignantly.

"They even do it in the office," the nephew marveled.

Across the table, Gene Fleming solemnly winked at Thatcher, then added fuel to the flames.

"The Japanese always think it's comic," he said tolerantly, "and after all these years, it seems pretty weird to me too. But it's not entirely divorced from reality. With job relocation what it is in the States, many employees can regard themselves as free agents. So they're not the only ones who have to measure up. The employer has to as well. And under those circumstances, you get less of the *yes, sir, no, sir* routine."

"As a matter of fact, on this last trip over, I thought I noticed some slight movement in that direction even in Japan," Thatcher observed.

The nephew was lofty.

"Certain formalities may be abbreviated," he pontificated, "but the system is unchanged."

"I'm not so sure," Gene ruminated. "It was easy to create company loyalty when half the university graduates couldn't find jobs. Now that the labor pool is becoming tight, you have a lot of pressure building up."

"But no one seriously anticipates Japanese employees starting to adopt American attitudes," the nephew insisted.

Gently Fleming refused the bait.

"The change isn't starting with them but with Mr. Arai and his ilk. He hasn't made any bones about stealing personnel from other companies. It wasn't difficult, since he offered young family men more money and the prospect of faster advancement. Arai has slipped the notion of job mobility into the labor market. That's certainly new and probably asking for trouble."

"But nobody will admit it," Haru sailed in. "Any more than they'll admit the change in the schools."

This time the nephew counterattacked too quickly for his own comfort.

"Naturally you feel that way —" he began, before coming to an abrupt halt.

His wife, however, bravely advanced where angels feared to tread. "But, Aunt, you're a special situation," she said, her small hands fluttering in decorative apology. "Of course you had problems."

"And handled them magnificently," her husband chimed in, determined to retrieve his lapse. "You got your son into Tokyo University."

Unfortunately his tone said that he would never understand how she had managed it.

"I'm not talking about mixed marriage," Haru said, calmly dismissing all this sensitivity. "I'm talking about the two-tier system."

"Oh, Lord, now we're in for it," Gene groaned in mock dismay. "This is Haru's hobbyhorse. Just because, like all the other children, our kids spent half their day at the regular school and the other half at a cram school."

"I'll do the same thing you did, Aunt," the niece said earnestly. "After all, the crammer is necessary to get into the right high school and the right university."

"And then the right job," the nephew said gravely.

Haru was not retreating one inch.

"That's just it. The point of the whole system is continuing, relentless competition. But because that's not acknowledged, the child is expected to pretend in the regular school that he's only interested in team results. Then he goes straight to an environment that emphasizes individual results. That's a heavy burden of pretense to lay on small children."

Gene was more relaxed. "But the Japanese are used to that sort of thing, Haru. They've been doing it a long time."

Haru had heard this before.

"That's the answer we get whenever any kind of social service program is proposed. They say it isn't needed because the Japanese family is organized to take care of its own. But we're already seeing grown children unable or unwilling to take in their elderly parents. And what is the suggested remedy? Building old-age colonies abroad to take advantage of the strong yen!" Her voice vibrated with scorn. "They want us to throw the elderly out of the country. We'd be worse than the Americans, and you say Japanese society is stable."

The niece and nephew were silent. Thatcher could appreciate their quandary. They disagreed with what they were hearing and disapproved of its being said. But while the Flemings might talk revolution, their track record was above reproach. Even Gene had been a model Japanese employee, loyal to his company until its last gasp of existence. Haru, while sighing for the serenity of a lost Japan, had racked up over twenty years as ideal wife and mother. Could the young people guarantee a comparable performance? Earlier in the evening the nephew had indicated a flicker of interest at the suggestion that his services might be valued by a more generous employer. The niece, with a year of graduate study at UCLA, was an unknown quantity. This couple might provide contradictions of their own. They might end up espousing conservatism while in fact they heeded the call of personal ambition.

Unlikely as it seemed, it was Thatcher who became the champion of the new order.

"You're not being entirely fair either to Japan or to the United States," he began.

Haru was in no mood to mince words.

"America treats its old people like garbage."

It was rare for Thatcher to hear this kind of candor from a Sloan wife, but few of them were in the position of knowing that the bank needed them more than they needed the bank.

"Very true," he agreed temperately. "But we didn't always. Once, people in their sixties were taken care of by people in their forties. Now the near-old are being asked to maintain the very old. It's happened here first, but life expectancy in Japan has jumped twenty years. Demographics are creating an entirely new problem for all of us."

He had played right into Haru's hands. "Then why aren't we doing something about it? The schools should spend a little less time turning out dedicated employees and a little more turning out responsible family members. If they don't, we'll end up with a generation that isn't properly socialized — not in my definition of the term."

"And what is your definition?" he asked curiously.

The indignation of her earlier remarks evaporated as she frowned over the problem of translating her concept into an idiom comprehensible to a foreigner.

"The child has to understand that he's part of a web that is connected to everyone with whom he has a social relationship," she said slowly. "Sometimes he gives to that web and sometimes he takes from it, but his actions always have to maintain the web. He can't rush off to gratify his own wishes when it means ripping the web to pieces."

Silently Thatcher wondered how her own extraordinary marriage fitted into these precepts, but all he said was:

"It's the ideal at which the individual should arrive, but it can take decades to get there."

"It does if he's left to figure it out for himself," she rejoined tartly. "But isn't that the whole point of raising children? In America it sometimes seems as if each infant is expected to start from scratch. That's an awful waste of experience."

Nobody could possibly quarrel with this conclusion, and the young couple had lost their appetite for jousting with Haru. Dinner ended with a catalog of the surprising services offered by the Scarsdale Public Library.

Driving down from Westchester, Fleming reiterated his intention to hurry back to Tokyo.

"Yes, I'm afraid you'll have to curtail your vacation," Thatcher said. "But you'll be doing your work in England."

Haru was delighted to retain her London holiday, but Gene wanted details.

"Ever since MITI accepted Kruger's date

for the Birmingham demonstration, the creditors have been in an uproar," Thatcher said. "They're afraid of a chain reaction too. Solletti couldn't calm them down until I agreed to monitor what Lackawanna is up to. If I'm there keeping an eye on Kruger, I'll need you to watch the others."

Chapter 17

The Carl Kruger that America saw over its coffee and cornflakes was the Carl Kruger it had come to know and love — sturdily optimistic no matter what the problem.

"You've got to realize that these are complicated situations, Helen," he was saying to the program's hostess. "There were reasons why some Japanese would favor our proposal and reasons why others would oppose it. We knew all that, and we expected a dogfight, but that was no excuse to back off. Where would Lackawanna be today if we folded whenever the going got tough?"

"You may have expected a fight, but did you expect bribery and murder?" the hostess pressed, bringing them down to earth.

"Of course not. Who would? And we didn't like being thrown out of the country on the grounds that we were the ones responsible. When you set off for a business negotiation, you don't think you're being set up for a murder rap."

Bennet Alderman, following one of the monitors offstage, nodded approvingly. Carl was not only getting his message across; he was making it look as if Helen had forced it out of him.

The previous day, Alderman had spent over two hours on the phone with one of the program's researchers, whose function was to prime Helen about Kruger's background, personal style, and newsworthiness. This exchange was an opportunity to skew the program in a favorable direction. But Alderman knew perfectly well that the final result depended on Carl Kruger's performance, and Carl was doing a brilliant job.

The hostess was making it easy.

"But, Carl," she objected, "how can you hope to do business in that kind of environment when everything we hear suggests that it's rotten with corruption and crime?"

"Now come on, Helen, you don't want to generalize from one incident."

"I'm not talking about one incident," she said, falling into the trap. "They themselves admit that there's bribery and worse involved in your application for Lackawanna. Then Shima has just confessed to payoffs in its export operation. And on top of that, we have the scandals about Recruit."

Kruger was at his most benevolent.

"I'm not denying all that. But look at the other side of the coin. Sure, somebody tried to keep me out of Japan by bribery, but it was the Japanese who found out about it and moved to investigate. I grant you that they lost their heads at first," he said magnanimously, "but they're on the right track now."

"You're saying that there are corrupt Japanese and honest Japanese in the business world over there," she said, conscientiously boiling it down for her audience.

If she had been listening more carefully, she would have realized that he was saying — not surprisingly — that the bad Japanese were his opponents and the good ones were his supporters.

"That's right," he agreed. "In fact, it's the same over there as it is here. In the past few years we've had plenty of our cabinet members called on their business dealings, and as for insider trading . . ." He spread his hands disarmingly. "I don't have to tell *you* about that, Helen."

Helen was finding Carl Kruger the ideal guest. He accepted her knowledgeability without ever putting it to any embarrassing test. It is, after all, the business of a talk show host to assume a stance midway between the expertise of the guest and the ignorance of the viewers. Helen gratefully nodded appreciation of Kruger's tribute and pushed on.

"Well, if people had practically accused me

of murder and thrown me out of the country without a chance to say a word in my defense, I don't think I'd be that forgiving."

Kruger shrugged his shoulders. "Look, I'm no saint. I was threatening a lot of things at the time. But I've cooled down, and so have they. I'm willing to bet they realize they did the wrong thing by now."

Involuntarily Bennet Alderman sucked in his breath, but he need not have worried. Carl Kruger did not explain why the Japanese were being forced to reconsider.

"All right, we'll be charitable and say it was a momentary lapse." By now Helen sounded as if she were urging an admirer of all things Japanese to modify his position! "But Shima didn't slip those microchips abroad during a fit of absence of mind. What do you say about that?"

"Naturally I don't like to see American technology stolen." It is not only questions that are prepared prior to broadcast. Carl Kruger had a very important answer ready for delivery. But he was enough of a gambler to wait for a better cue.

Fortunately Helen, like all good interrogators, had the instincts of a terrier. Faced with a brief, indifferent reply, she immediately began to dig.

"Isn't that just lip service? After all, you're

an advocate of free trade with all restrictions lifted."

Now it was the program's research team holding its breath, as Helen toppled on the brink of exposing ignorance. The grunt that came from Kruger, however, could equally have signaled earnest preparation for a more complete reply or sheer satisfaction at a risk paying off.

"Look, I deal in technology myself. I'm saying that when you've developed technology, you have the right to decide on the conditions or the forms in which you'll dispose of it. And if people won't abide by your terms, then it's only sense to look for customers who will."

Some people make their living by flicking red capes in front of fighting bulls. Kruger, who knew his words would be rebroadcast in Tokyo, was willing to dangle Korea before select members of that audience.

Helen, of course, thought he was answering her question.

"Then you think we shouldn't sell export-control items to Shima anymore?"

"I say the United States government has got the right to do whatever it thinks is in its own best interest. I don't know what they'll decide that is. And let's not forget there could be extenuating circumstances. Maybe it was just a case of some Shima employee trying to make his sales record look good. I certainly hope so."

"But the problem's a lot bigger than Shima," she said, pursuing her objective. "Your proposal to enter the Japanese market has to be approved by officials we know take payments under the table."

"Now hold your horses just one little minute. You've cleverly gotten around the fact that those handouts were not illegal in Japan."

Helen was glad to hear him accuse her of diabolical cunning. Because the little red light that had come on at her reference to free trade was once again blinking. Twice in one interview was below her normal standard. Happily Carl Kruger was busy towing her out of whatever depths she had floated into.

"If you want to compete on the international scene, you can't run around applying your own laws or even your own morality. Different cultures have different usages. Come on, Helen, you've read all that stuff about how the Japanese, when they come over here, bend over backward to accommodate themselves to local custom. I admire that, and I plan to act the same way when I start doing business in Japan. It's the only way to go. That's why I'm so pleased that Yonezawa Trading Company will be handling our warehousing and distribution over there, and I suppose that's why Shima has taken an American partner to help with its plans for Alaska."

Helen glided gracefully away from the sudden intrusion of Alaska. She was taking no chances on a red-light score of three.

"All right, I agree that technically it's not illegal. So is it one of those local customs you're prepared to adopt?" she challenged, giving her audience a glimpse of the feisty Helen they admired.

Smiling, Kruger shook his head. "Unlike Recruit, we're not issuing stock — I'm glad to say."

On a roll, she continued her counterattack. "And if issuing stock way below its value to politicians is so much in accord with local usage, why is the story the year's biggest exposé over there?"

With the end in sight, he could afford to abandon the expert-to-expert approach. Grinning broadly, Kruger became a man of the world, explaining the facts of life.

"Oh, now that they've found out what was going on, they're going to have to make it illegal."

Helen might be weak on Japan's criminal code, but she knew exactly how to handle men of the world.

With an infectious gurgle of laughter, she

threw up her hand in the classic gesture of one duelist acknowledging a tricky touch by the other and immediately began thanking Kruger for his appearance.

When the commercial break began and Carl Kruger surrendered his chair to the representative of the Harlem Glee Club School (currently sending over ninety-five percent of its graduates on to college), Bennet Alderman added up the tally on his clipboard. The results were not quite what he had hoped for. True, Carl had managed, on five separate occasions, to admit that his opponents had bribed a ministry representative. By now nobody in the audience was likely to remember that the identity was still very much an open question. He had also made it abundantly clear that he was ready to forgive and forget. So far Alderman was with him.

"But why all the other stuff?" he protested as the two men were leaving the studio.

"Just punching it home that the forgiveness is conditional on getting my way. Otherwise . . . all hell breaks loose."

Kruger was moving along so buoyantly that Alderman had to scurry to keep up.

"But the idea was to paint yourself as a victim — a guy who went over there with good intentions and got burned by a bunch of crooks. Why drag Alaska into it? Why waste time on export control? It just dilutes the impact."

Tolerantly Kruger explained: "You've got to broaden your horizons, Bennet. I wasn't just talking to Americans. The guys in Japan are sitting on a tinderbox. The minister is wondering whether he'll keep his seat in the cabinet. The rest of the cabinet is wondering whether the Prime Minister will be bounced. They were all edgy about trade agreements even before we went over. Now they're afraid it'll all blow up in their faces. On top of that, Iwamoto has laid himself wide open just as he's planning a new operation on American soil, and Arai should already have heard from his people in London. That's a lot of heat going on, and I want to keep it boiling."

Alderman, still mutinous, could see one objection.

"Does it ever occur to you, Carl, that it's possible to think too big?"

Carl Kruger only had to mount one response to the Shima scandal. John Thatcher, however, was wearing two hats. As a creditor of Lackawanna, he applauded Kruger's opportunism and hoped to benefit from it. But many incoming telephone calls reminded him that the Sloan Guaranty Trust had other obligations.

From Anchorage, Alaska, Len Ridgeway had been bellowing down the long-distance lines on a nonstop basis. What penalties were going to be assessed against Shima? Would they just ban sales, or would they hit capital investments too? And if the joint venture were allowed, could its offspring sell to Japan? The idiots in his legal department had been unable to come up with a definite answer.

"Well, the idiots in our law department can't say, either," Thatcher replied soothingly. "The fact is, nobody knows. Every time this sort of thing happens, the pressure for major sanctions increases."

If the newspapers in Alaska were anything like those in the effete south, Thatcher reflected, there were editorials galore comparing Japanese industry, cosseted by its government at every turn, to the lonely, shivering American company, naked to the blast.

Ridgeway was feeling the chill.

"Look," he said, "I like the deal with Shima, but I can live without it. All I want to know is where I stand. Is that too much to ask?"

"You'll know when they go to court."

"That's the problem. Haven't you heard?" Ridgeway yelped, outraged at Thatcher's ignorance. "They've just announced the date, and it's not for two weeks."

The other party to the Alaskan deal was

even more unhappy, as Thatcher learned within fifteen minutes.

Failing to recognize the voice, Thatcher at first thought that Miss Corsa had slipped up in her iron policy of demanding a principal on the line. The dead monotone did not sound like Rick Iwamoto in either of his previous incarnations — the scrappy underdog in Tokyo or the jubilant guest glad-handing the VIPs of Anchorage.

"John, have you heard that they've set the court date?"

Even under stress, Iwamoto silently conceded that the Sloan might have other concerns. This put him way ahead of Len Ridgeway.

"Yes, Rick; it's in two weeks."

"I want to know if this is a squeeze play," Iwamoto said bluntly. "Yonezawa and the ministry people are leaving for England tomorrow. I get the feeling that you people over there are saying that if the MR deal falls through, Shima is going to pay through the nose."

A marriage broker has many duties. The Sloan had brought Shima and Ridgeway together. And normally its role would have ended when the two parties reached agreement. But when unforeseen problems arise before the happy couple has marched down the aisle, work begins anew. The more the match-maker knows, the wiser his advice.

"The sooner I know, the better."

Thatcher controlled the temptation to say that this went double for Len Ridgeway.

Chapter 18

Among those planning to fly to Heathrow because of the renewed Midland Research hearings, Fumitoshi Arai was the first to set forth. As word of his departure spread, it caused astonishment in many quarters. Although Arai was not as immobile as he led the world to believe, he rarely left Japan, and it had been many years since he had strayed as far as Europe. His reluctance to travel had less to do with his increasing years than with Yonezawa's managerial structure. All important decisions received the personal scrutiny of Mr. Arai. As the company's activities multiplied, the need for his presence increased.

"You're kidding," Stan Zaretski said upon hearing the news.

"What's more, he left a couple of days early," the embassy aide continued.

"Then who's minding the store? He sure as hell isn't letting his vice-presidents call the shots."

His crony was enjoying the role of informant.

"Arai's taken a whole office staff with him.

I figure they keep in touch with home base while the old man rests up from the trip. That way he'll be in fighting trim by the time MITI and Lackawanna show up. What puzzles me is why he's going at all. Do you think it could be simple human curiosity?"

Zaretski refused to believe there was anything simple about Arai. "No, that's not it. But he knows we've already had two wild pitches thrown from these MR hearings. The first one landed on Lackawanna, and the second one hit Shima. Just on probability alone, he could be worried that Yonezawa will be beaned next."

"Or mathematics has nothing to do with it. Maybe," the crony reasoned, "Arai knows exactly what's coming."

"If he did, he could instruct a subordinate. It's more likely he doesn't have a clue." Zaretski plucked his lower lip thoughtfully as he pondered Arai's motivation. "When MITI found itself landed with a corpse, everybody was shook up. The Japanese knew nothing like it had ever happened over here. Now they've had time to discover it never happened in the States, either. That means there's a real loony running around, and logic is out the window. Nobody can foresee the next act. Matsuda may bare his breast and tell the world who bribed him. Rick Iwamoto may decide to commit hara-kiri in front of the whole pack."

It made sense to the crony.

"No wonder Arai wants to be on the spot."

Fumitoshi Arai was carrying out his program of rest and rehabilitation in the same hotel that housed Gene Fleming. But while the Yonezawa staff maintained a constant vigil over doings back in Tokyo, Gene had been immersed in different concerns.

For three long days and nights he had labored, together with the other governing members of the IFMA, over the inevitable problems of a worldwide sport. They could now look back on a satisfactory array of achievements. The schedule for next year's competition contained no major conflicts. An appeal against the suspension of an Italian rider had been finally disallowed. The new regulations for cross-country rallies were in final form. And they had even found time to gossip about the new racing models several manufacturers planned to launch.

When the meetings came to a formal close, Fleming felt as if he were breaking the surface of the water after a particularly long dive.

"As long as I'm here, I think I'll stay on for the All Midland Rally," a member from Australia said chattily. "What about you,

Gene? Will I see you there?"

Still gulping for air, Gene studied a pocket diary in disbelief. "Not a chance," he said regretfully. "I've just got time to take my wife to Stratford tomorrow, and then it's back to work."

"Good Lord, has she been here all this time? Doesn't she find it dull?"

In common with most husbands, Gene believed that all was well with his wife until the air was rent by shrieks of discontent.

"Oh, she always finds plenty to do," he said comfortably.

Haru Fleming was not the only woman who could occupy herself in London.

"I've been thinking, and I've decided I'd like to come with you," Audrey Kruger announced at the dinner table, the evening before Lackawanna was due to depart.

Carl looked up from his jellied consommé in surprise. "But you hate business trips. You never want to come."

"The last time I said that, you were going to Omaha," she retorted. "This is different."

Audrey was a pretty, slightly plump woman who had experienced no difficulty shinning up the economic pole along with her husband. Carl, grateful to have an old-fashioned wife who busied herself with home and children, had always been tolerant of the mink coats and designer gowns.

"You may have the wrong idea about Birmingham," he said. "It's not really your kind of town."

"Oh, I'll stay in London," she said instantly. "After all, you'll be there for the first couple of days."

Now he eyed her with growing suspicion. "I'll be tied up most of the time," he warned.

"So? I'll see some friends. You know Margaret Bentwood has been living there since she remarried."

Mildly puzzled, Kruger was running out of objections. Audrey, he knew, never interfered in business or complained about his long hours. And her decision to remain in London removed the possibility of distractions in Birmingham. Listening to her prattle about her need for a change, he decided that she was simply succumbing to the call of bright lights.

Audrey was relieved to see his brow clear. She neither knew nor cared about the ins and outs of Lackawanna's plans for Japan. But she had been dismayed by the condition in which her husband had returned from Tokyo and Washington and feared that England might generate the same stresses. As the only person in the world really adept at bringing down Carl Kruger's blood pressure, she had no intention of being three thousand miles away.

Fortunately there was one sure method to dispel any lingering doubts.

"Besides, if I'm really at loose ends," she said bravely, "I have a little shopping I can do."

Kruger's lips twitched.

"That's big of you, honey," he acknowledged.

The amenities of London might not have existed, for all the pull they were exercising on Pamela Webb. Apart from one dash south to parade Mr. Kwai Dong through the financial district, she had spent her time at Midland Research. No longer able to prolong her stay, she was giving Ali Khan a final pep talk.

"I don't see what you're worried about, Ali. The demonstration will be great."

"Of course it will," he said impatiently. "But I'm not looking forward to meeting with the bunch again. Look what happened last time."

"But this will be different," she insisted. "Everybody will pretend that last time never happened. Not only that; they won't be discussing the business aspect of the proposal. Nobody wants to emphasize how much they stand to gain or lose."

Khan erupted into a short bark of laughter.

"That doesn't leave much for them to talk about."

Shaking her head at his density, Pamela said meaningfully: "Just robotics."

She had managed to fix his attention.

"If I can only get them to stay in the room," he half groaned.

"Oh, come on, Ali. You practically drove them away with your equations and your schematics. But a demonstration is different. You saw how fascinated Dong was. They can actually see what it is you've done. Besides," she continued on a more sober note, "nobody's going to be tempted to wander off. Don Hodiak doesn't want to end up as Iwamoto's alibi again. And poor Carl isn't going alone anywhere. I'll bet they stick together in a clump."

Khan was grinning broadly. "It would serve them right if I gave them the equations."

"Control yourself. Let's not forget what this is in aid of," she directed. "You give them a wow of a demo and let Carl pitch his sales talk, and we'll all be happy."

By the time Ali left, Pamela knew that her work had been effective.

"Now if only someone would reassure me," she muttered to herself.

Don Hodiak, for one, was willing to defer the clump policy.

"Look, if you're having trouble getting space for Audrey, I could take another flight," he offered the next morning.

"Thanks, Don, but the travel department already has her seat."

The two men had come to terms with their fundamental disagreement. Hodiak, having openly declared his opposition, had become easygoing and helpful. If the heavens now fell, his stance seemed to say, he had done all that was possible to avert the calamity. Kruger, as usual, had put the past behind him. After an initial spurt of fury, he had dismissed Hodiak's threats as meaningless. Either Lackawanna would return from England with an agreement too attractive to be denied or there would be nothing to argue about at the forthcoming board meeting. As a result of these responses, Kruger and Hodiak were working together more harmoniously than when their differences had been relatively minor.

"Then we're still on the same schedule?" Hodiak asked.

"Yes, the limo will be here at one-thirty."

"Fine; I'll be ready."

By now time was running out, but Bennet Alderman still hoped to clean up some unfinished business before he left for England.

His instructions, given four days ago, had been explicit.

"Make it a rush job, and spend as much as you have to. I want anything you can dig up on Don Hodiak. That's Donald P. Hodiak. He lives at 329 Countway . . ."

At Lackawanna, eyebrows would have been raised, but Tony Cella's one-man office was a long way from the company. Cella was a specialist in asking only necessary questions.

"What about Hodiak's family?"

"Look into every damn thing you can find," Alderman had replied revealingly. "I want results I can use."

Both of them approached other people's secrets with professional detachment. As far as Alderman was concerned, Don Hodiak had been a marked man ever since he threatened to go over Carl Kruger's head. Tony Cella's assignment was to provide the ammunition.

"I'll call you as soon as I have anything," Cella had promised.

He was as good as his word.

"For starters, there's the wife," Cella said, consulting a thick dossier. "Maiden name, Mary Ellen Carmody. Born in Trenton, attended Oberlin. Married when she was twenty-four. Two sons, one daughter. They attend First Presbyterian Church of Meadowview . . ."

Alderman restrained his impatience. Dull preliminaries were the price Cella always exacted for his pay dirt.

". . . and she was pregnant when she married Hodiak," Cella continued.

"Oh, for God's sake," Alderman interjected. "These days that just sounds quaint."

Cella shrugged, then went on to more promising material.

"Since then she's had a string of drunk-driving convictions. And for the past five years she's been a regular at the Henley Institute for Substance Abuse. Right now she's getting psychiatric treatment on an outpatient basis."

Alderman blinked at this revelation, but after thinking for a moment, he said: "So he doesn't have a happy home life. I can't do a helluva lot with that, Tony."

Cella's clients got information, not counseling.

"You never can tell," he said. "But you may be in luck. I've dug up something a little better."

"Don't tell me Hodiak's going to a shrink too," said Alderman.

The blots on Don Hodiak's record were depressingly normal. His dreary love affair with a suburban neighbor was long past, but his occasional fishing trips to Florida seemed to include feminine companionship.

233

"I've got a man looking for photographs, but maybe there aren't any," Cella reported. "That kind of solid citizen is usually extra careful, if you know what I mean."

"Sure," said Alderman, somewhat taken aback by the contours of Don Hodiak's life. "But put a little muscle into that search. If there aren't any pictures, I could use a hotel registration."

What Cella did have to offer was a fully documented survey of Don Hodiak's finances.

". . . and even with those hospital bills for the wife, Hodiak seems to live pretty much within his means," he said, providing details about insurance premiums, tuition payments, retirement packages, and mutual funds. "He hasn't had to borrow on the house, for example."

This kind of recital was calculated to tow Bennet Alderman well beyond his depth. Money as a form of power was something he understood completely, but the economic underpinnings of middle-class life were totally alien to him. He was beginning to suspect that Cella had fallen down on the job, when the investigator said:

"There are just two other things."

Hoping that Cella was saving the best for last, Alderman said:

"Go on."

"Japan," said Cella. "Apart from these little quickies in Florida, Hodiak usually takes vacations with the whole family. You know: Cape Cod, Europe. But twice in the last three years, the Hodiaks visited Tokyo. Didn't you tell me that trip with you and Kruger was his first?"

Alderman was almost surprised into sharing his thoughts with Cella. "Well, I'll be damned," he exclaimed. "Do you suppose . . . I mean, I wonder if Carl knows. Or Pamela."

"I'll tell you who does," Cella told him firmly. "The Japanese police. That's why I can't tell you who Hodiak met or talked to. I make it a point not to step on police toes unless I have to. And in a murder case, I don't have to."

"What I'm after doesn't have a damn thing to do with murder," Alderman protested angrily.

"If you say so," said Cella levelly.

Alderman was still trying to factor murder into his thinking, when Cella continued:

"Then there's the stock that Hodiak owns."

The anticlimax roused Alderman. "What about the stock he owns?" he said irritably.

Cella explained that Don Hodiak owned no shares in the company for which he worked. From other sources Cella had ascertained that

Hodiak's modest portfolio contained Coca-Cola, AT&T, and some utilities.

". . . but no Lackawanna," he concluded.

Alderman did not see why this was particularly significant.

"Lackawanna's got a stock option plan," Cella said patiently.

During his years with the company, Hodiak had participated in the program that provided incentives for key executives. He had purchased stock below market price.

". . . Then, all of a sudden, he began selling. He got out just in time, and he hasn't touched the stock since. It's all there on the public record."

"Where anybody can see it," Alderman said with disgust. "Hell, Tony, I'm not paying you big bucks for something people already know."

Cella was unresentful. "That's the best way to hide things sometimes." He paused to let this sink in, then added: "It looks to me as if you can make a good case that Hodiak has been betting against Kruger for a long time."

"Maybe," said Alderman, not altogether convinced.

Nevertheless he was quite satisfied to sign a large check for the first course. Cella had provided a tempting appetizer to lay on Carl Kruger's desk.

Chapter 19

Shortly after arriving in London, John Thatcher found himself in a taxi headed for the Sloan's local office. His mission was to introduce Gene Fleming.

"I've just arrived, but Gene's been here several days on personal business," he told Toby Lemieux.

After the usual polite preliminaries, Fleming remarked: "I feel right at home. Half my hotel seems to be Japanese."

"They're pouring in for the opening of the Japanese Trade Show that we'll be attending tomorrow night. But they've been coming in waves for months. It's a mobilization for European economic unification. All the Japanese are shopping for acquisitions, and big ones at that."

Thatcher seized the moment. "Thanks to Gene's efforts in Tokyo, some of them will be handled by the Sloan," he said. "You'll have seen the list we sent over."

"Certainly, and made good progress with it. The pharmaceuticals still need winnowing, but we're ready to make a preliminary recommendation to the client on the shipyard," Lemieux announced before continuing less confidently. "It's a shame he isn't interested in English china. However, we'll do the best we can to find something in France."

"I'm sure you will."

Lemieux remembered his obligations to the new boy in the Sloan family. "All in all, that list was a magnificent effort."

"We're beginning to take off," said Fleming without false modesty. "To the point where the Japanese banks are pretty sour."

Lemieux countered with a résumé of his own accomplishments, before saying: "You mustn't be misled because we've been around longer than you have. For years we were merely providing standard services for American corporations with a U.K. presence. We didn't start investment banking for quite a while — not till after we brought Lackawanna and Midland Research together."

Thatcher straightened. "I didn't know we had."

"I thought perhaps you might not." On his mettle before a rival branch manager, Lemieux welcomed any opportunity to detail London's triumphs. "Of course it was quite informal and took place only because of an earlier visit by Ali Khan."

"Tell us about it," Thatcher invited.

"Ali had some bright ideas about robotics when he was finishing his stint at Cambridge. So he went back north and began work in a makeshift lab with a few employees. He had some insane notion that MR would start paying its way in a year or two."

The rate of small-business failure was, in Thatcher's opinion, largely attributable to this line of reasoning.

"What in the world did Khan think he was going to sell?"

"That's just the point. He was still living in a world of university research, where you're a big hit if you develop the possibility of a breakthrough. He didn't start learning the facts of life until he ran out of funds. The investors had already kissed their money good-bye and the suppliers had cut off credit when he sallied forth to get financing. The local authorities and the banks laughed him out the door. Finally he tried some industrial firms, and that's when the vultures began to gather. They all figured that once he was out on the street, he'd be desperate."

"Poor kid," said Fleming. "How old was he when the roof fell in?"

Lemieux shook his head at the recollection of the youthful Ali. "He was twenty-five and had taken quite a mauling. When he wandered in here, you could practically see his exposed nerve endings. He assumed that everybody was saying his work was no good, and he was actually brandishing a tattered evaluation from a couple of Cambridge professors. The whole thing was pathetic. So I explained that the banks thought he was a bad risk because he was proposing an undertaking much more expensive than he realized. Asking people to bail him out of his immediate problems was ridiculous. He wouldn't make a sale until he attacked the specifics of a particular application, constructed working prototypes, and designed cost-effective production methods."

"You mean to say he listened?" Thatcher asked.

Toby laughed.

"Not a bit. Ali was nodding in dumb despair until I told him one of his problems was asking for too little."

As all bankers know, one of the hardest things to explain to budding entrepreneurs is that a financial plan viable on its face is more attractive than a much less expensive program doomed to failure by its very modesty.

"Although," Thatcher admitted, "it doesn't sound as if either approach would have done him much good."

"Exactly. I let Ali blow off steam, because that was about all I could do for him. Then I forgot MR until two days later, when Carl

Kruger strolled in."

Gene Fleming's eyes were gleaming with interest. "Two days? This Khan must live right."

"That's the luck of the draw," Lemieux said philosophically. "Lackawanna U.K. was in a tax jam which made purchasing and financing a small undertaking attractive. Kruger was considering various options when I mentioned MR. He liked the sound of robotics, and I arranged the most disastrous meeting of my career."

"They didn't hit it off?"

"There wasn't enough contact for even that. Carl explained that money would have to be poured into MR for at least four or five years before payback. Ali treated Kruger as if he were a backward student and hurled technical details at him. Neither of them listened to a word the other one was saying."

Thinking back to Tokyo, Thatcher realized that nothing had changed. When Lackawanna presented financials to MITI, Ali left the room. When Ali unfurled his projector, Kruger walked.

"I'm surprised they ever got off the ground."

"You can thank Carl's refusal to be diverted from his goal. He actually read those recommendations from Cambridge and agreed to fund MR for a month while the experts took a look. Then he came back with an offer to buy MR's stock and give Ali a very handsome five-year contract. So the investors back in Birmingham actually made a profit, and Ali had found himself a backer."

Gene Fleming had seen other backyard operations taken over by giant, soulless corporations.

"He'd found a little more than that. It must have been a shock when Lackawanna sent its troops over."

"Ali's pretty good at refusing to be diverted too. In fact, Pamela Webb was quite funny describing his amazed pleasure when she started giving him bigger labs and a crowd of technicians and computer people to do a lot of his dog work."

It was just as well that Ali Khan had been receptive, Thatcher reflected. Once Carl Kruger had set up a schedule, it was unlikely that the cool, efficient Miss Webb would have allowed Ali to waste time on dog work even if he had wanted to.

"This must have been quite early in her career," he observed.

"That's right. Her first assignment was to overhaul the financial controls at Lackawanna U.K., and while she was at it, she set some up at MR. Since then she's climbed to the top at Lackawanna." Lemieux paused to smile with deliberate provocation. "Now her time is far too valuable for that little charade this week. She brought a Korean in here — to meet MR's bankers, she said."

This was news to Thatcher. "But Kruger is still hoping to break into the Japanese market. It's scarcely the ideal time for covert negotiations with a Korean."

"Covert!" Lemieux snorted. "Pamela would have had to meet him at the changing of the guard to be any more public. At least five different persons have told me they saw her lunching with Kwai Dong."

Kruger's tactics were now clear to everyone, but Gene Fleming had the keenest appreciation of their impact where it counted.

"Oh, that's very nice," he said approvingly. "Kruger made it possible for Arai to invoke the national interest."

"Why do they keep telling us Kruger doesn't know anything about Japan?" Thatcher asked the world at large. "He seems to be much more sophisticated about their political situation than we've been led to believe."

Fleming was a notorious bottom-line man. "Even if he isn't, he's got the right instincts. So it boils down to the same thing."

"Pamela Webb even took Kwai Dong up

to Birmingham," Lemieux continued his tale. "Ali must really be enjoying this. By now every big company that turned him down knows he's become a prize on the international market."

Thatcher agreed that it was only human to relish that kind of triumph. "It was hard to tell how he felt in Tokyo. He stayed in the background except when he expanded to the Japanese experts."

"Would you like a shot at Ali without the Lackawanna people?" Lemieux suggested. "He's coming south for a symposium at Cambridge today, and I'm having a quick drink with him."

"You still keep up with him?"

Lemieux's smile was almost a smirk. "Thanks to me, Ali invests a portion of his salary. I was so appalled at his attitude to money when he sold MR that I read him a lecture."

Fleming knew all about high-spending young rock stars and sports figures. "You mean he wanted to go on a spree?"

"Quite the contrary. He was planning to shove the proceeds into his current account and forget about them. Thank heavens he's become a little more normal — he doesn't work every single waking moment. But basically he's a very frugal young man."

★ ★ ★

Any bystander watching from afar that morning as Ali Khan departed for Cambridge would have been inclined to endorse this assessment. Unlike the rest of Midland Research's senior staff, Ali did not live in a modern development within easy distance of the company. He had chosen a longer commute and more traditional housing. Seen from the road, his small, out-of-the-way dwelling was unpretentious, to say the least. England is filled with workmen's cottages, originally two-up and two-down, that have been enlarged and modernized into choice residences. Ali's home had been subjected to no such process. It was only in the rear that the raison d'être for his establishment became apparent. Here, a scruffy, patchy lawn sloped down to the river. From boyhood Ali had been an enthusiastic member of the Birmingham Rowing Club. Still a loyal participant, he was no longer dependent on communal facilities. His modern boathouse with its professional shell was worth more than the rest of the property.

To Ali it all made sense. He was prepared to put time and money into the few things he really cared about. Everything else suffered from benign neglect. His ancient, battered car was a disgrace to the number-one parking slot at Midland Research. His cleaning woman had long since relaxed her efforts to the point where they were almost nonexistent. Fortunately Ali's meals were not the solitary outings of most bachelors. When he ate dinner in downtown Birmingham, he did so at his father's modest Pakistani restaurant. When he wanted grander surroundings, he could drive out to the new gourmet establishment over which his sister and brother-in-law presided.

Like the restaurants of Birmingham, Cambridge University was filled with familiar faces. Ali was hailed before he had finished signing the register.

"Ali!"

"Geoffrey!"

They had known each other since grammar school.

"I was back home visiting my people two weeks ago, Ali. And when I tried to call you, they told me you were in Tokyo, of all places!"

Geoffrey's booming tones carried to the far corners of the room, and Ali could have hugged him.

"The Japanese are interested in some of our developments."

At these magic words, a circle formed around Ali, composed of fellow toilers in his field.

"The steel industry!" a young woman exclaimed. "Did you hear that, Victor?"

As Ali was careful to tell them, his work was attracting the attention of more than one industrial power.

"Koreans too?"

"They're just displaying interest. Nothing has been decided yet."

"That doesn't matter. With two of them in the field, you've got an international auction under way."

"I suppose so," Ali agreed.

He was more forthcoming after arriving to meet the Sloan contingent.

"Koreans, Japanese — what's the difference? They're all a bunch of outsiders."

Lemieux was reproving. "That's what you said when Kruger made his offer, and you haven't regretted that, have you?"

"It's not the same thing," Ali said stubbornly. "Lackawanna has never interfered. They're an electrical company. They didn't have anybody in my field. But these big trading companies all have armies of electronics and computer people. They'll send over some big brother who thinks he knows more about my research than I do."

Fleming was appalled at how little Ali had noticed in Tokyo. "That's crazy," he protested. "Yonezawa is willing to throw half the Japanese industrial community into convulsions in order to get your work. Believe me, they know you're ahead of them."

Ali shrugged. "All I can do is wait and see. But I keep reminding myself that there's just a year to go on my contract. Anybody bugs me too much, and I'm gone after that."

Thatcher could see how this unexpected sensitivity might create land mines for Mr. Arai.

In the meantime, Ali had handed over to Lemieux a list of stock trades, which was greeted with grave approval.

"You're beginning to get the hang of it, my boy. I'll put in your orders for market opening tomorrow. On the whole, you've done very well for yourself these past couple of years."

"I suppose so."

This indifference grated.

"Don't you care?"

"Of course I do. That's why I'm doing it. But you said I needed financial advice," Ali defended himself. "I figure I've done my part and the rest is up to you."

"We could have handled this on the phone," Lemieux said. "But I suppose you had to come to London to meet with your Lackawanna people."

"No, I'm not seeing them until tomorrow night. I had to drop by Colmer & Bradshaw to tell them we were finding a new supplier."

"And you couldn't resist doing that in person?" Lemieux said severely.

Ali's teeth showed white in a broad smile. "It was worth the trip."

Lemieux explained the private joke. "Colmer & Bradshaw turned Ali down when he was looking for backing."

Ali was still delighted with his day's activities.

"When I left Cambridge for MR, nobody talked about the risks I was willing to take," he told them. "Instead I was reminded of the superiority of academic research. You should have heard them today. All they could talk about was the money. And I drove them wild when I played the innocent who didn't really care as long as I had perfect freedom to do my thing. They were explaining to me the value of having the Japanese and the Koreans bidding against each other."

"I can see how you might enjoy that, but Colmer & Bradshaw is a different matter."

Ali remained unrepentant. "I gave them quite a show too. I acted as if I didn't remember a thing from the past, not when I was so busy with the present."

"You can't hold these grudges forever."

"Maybe not," Ali said merrily. "But when an opportunity to draw blood comes along, you can't expect me to let it pass by."

Late that evening Ali slipped into the back booth of his father's restaurant, where he was strategically placed for the convenience of any family member who could snatch a few moments from work. As always, his mother was the first to arrive, with inquiries about his trip to Cambridge.

"Nobody's right on my heels, that's the important thing," Ali reported. "Incidentally, I ran into Geoffrey Osborne. You remember him, Mum. He went to university with me, and we used to come in here at night."

Within minutes he was regretting his mention of Geoffrey. Under his mother's merciless cross-examination he admitted that there was not only a Mrs. Osborne but two little Osbornes.

"And look at you," she accused. "Just wasting your time."

Her husband's arrival took most of the fire out of her.

"Ali's not wasting his time. He'll have a fine position when he does start a family. Be satisfied with one wedding at a time."

Thereafter the conversation veered to Ali's younger sister, who had first startled her family by training as a veterinarian and had now found a young man with whom she proposed to exploit the adoring pet owners of Kensington.

"Smart," said Papa approvingly.

"Too far away!" wailed Mum.

Chapter 20

As Fleming had reported, the lobby of London's newest deluxe caravanserai was filled with Japanese briskly going about their business.

"Some of them are your old friends," Gene pointed out. "The Yonezawa people have the biggest suite in the place. And Matsuda moved into the MITI quarters today."

Here, as at the embassy in Tokyo, many people had greeted Fleming. Now he slipped off to have a word with a passerby. When he came back, he was grinning.

"Matsuda is here all right, but so are a pack of cops. Two of them are right behind him wherever he goes."

"So we can look forward to having them with us at MR."

"More than that. They'll be parading around the trade show tomorrow night." Fleming evinced a certain admiration. "You've got to hand it to Matsuda. He's really hanging in there."

The dynamics were familiar to Thatcher. "In fact, Matsuda is in the same position as

Kruger was. If he agrees to disappear, he's afraid the decision will go by default."

"It's bigger than that. Now, with this Shima mess, the government is trying to cast itself as the exposer of corrupt practices. So it's no longer worth Matsuda's while to do whatever they want to keep things quiet. To protect himself, he figures he has to write his own lines."

Thatcher nodded. "What about your friend Rick Iwamoto? Is he going to be present? I gather he isn't staying at Tudor House."

"Of course he'll be coming," said Fleming, shocked at any other suggestion.

Fleming, Thatcher noticed, made a sharp distinction between Matsuda and Iwamoto. The employee was seen as a pawn; the industrialist was recognized as a power in his own right.

"At least there's one stabilizing factor," Thatcher remarked. "With Tokyo waiting for the U.S. decision on the export violation, we should complete the MR hearings before the Japanese take any punitive action."

"Yes, and with any luck, Shima will get through the Midland rally as well."

Before Thatcher could reply, a parting in the crowd revealed Carl Kruger and Don Hodiak sitting resignedly in a corner, with the look of men waiting for female companions.

Kruger wasted no time on niceties.

"Hello, Thatcher. Do you know that they've sent Matsuda over? How do you like that? They kick me out of the country, and they let him manage important business."

The opportunity was too good for Hodiak to miss. "Well, Carl, I warned you that doing business with them was going to have a lot of new wrinkles." He went on to expand his theme. "At least they're keeping him on a tight rein."

"I hear Matsuda has police watchdogs with him," Thatcher agreed.

"And some pretty high-powered ones. You remember that inspector who questioned us at MITI? They've sent him over too. He stays in the background, but you see him keeping an eye on things."

Kruger admitted that the situation was unusual but, with bulldog tenacity, claimed that the only important thing was that MITI was here. Before he could press his point, Mrs. Carl Kruger, in a whirl of chiffon, joined them, beaming her way through the introductions.

"I absolutely insisted Carl take tonight off," she announced. "I know what it will be like once the avalanche starts."

"Well, honey, you're the one who wanted to come along," Kruger said good-naturedly.

"Don't blame me if you're bored."

"Two of those suitcases I brought are empty," she replied on a note of triumph, "and I intend to fill them."

There is much to be said for a shopping lady, Thatcher decided. Armed with the Kruger credit cards, Audrey would be no problem to her companions.

She might have been reading his thoughts. "And I gave Margaret Bentwood a ring. So I'll be out of Carl's hair tomorrow night too."

She was still prattling when Thatcher saw her eyes narrow in critical appraisal. Turning, he found that Pamela Webb was approaching. For a moment he wondered if they were all about to be plunged into embarrassment.

He discovered that he was doing Audrey an injustice.

"Pamela," she announced with vehemence, "I *like* that outfit."

The outfit was a dashing red jacket atop harem pants, with a long silk scarf floating in the breeze.

"You should wear that kind of thing more often," Audrey continued judiciously. "All those grays and blues of yours are so blah!"

"If I wore this outfit to the office, we'd all be in the *National Enquirer*," Pamela teased.

It seemed to Thatcher that she was straying

perilously close to dangerous ground, but if so, she was quick to retreat.

"Carl, did you know that Arai has been here for two days?"

"You too?" Audrey protested. "Oh, I know this bunch" — a sweeping gesture encompassed the male contingent — "likes to pretend that work is more fun than fun. But, Pamela, women have more sense."

As Pamela greeted this sally with a giggle, Thatcher concluded that the ladies were too skilled for a mere man to understand. One thing, however, was clear. They were both determined to create a holiday spirit, and Pamela underlined this intention by linking her arm through Hodiak's.

"Isn't it time for us to leave, Don? When does the curtain go up?" Turning to Thatcher, she amplified. "We're all on our way to the ballet."

"Are you a ballet fan?" he inquired.

"Far from it," she disclaimed. "This is my first time. Don's the one who never misses a performance."

Smiling, Hodiak assured her she was in for a treat.

"Yes, it's time we all got going," Kruger agreed, picking up his wife's stole.

They began drifting toward the point where Thatcher and Fleming would peel off, when fate brought them directly into the path of a party emerging from an elevator.

At its head was Tomaheko Matsuda. Behind him was a considerable entourage. To Thatcher's eye the MITI aides were indistinguishable from the police escort.

Kruger nodded abruptly and would have passed on, but Matsuda launched into courtesies that embroiled them all in a string of introductions.

". . . and Mr. Fleming too. I hope we will have the pleasure of seeing you all at the trade show."

With Matsuda donning the mantle of official host, it was now impossible to avoid expressions of anticipation. Settled firmly on his heels, Matsuda then responded with similar high hopes for his trip to Birmingham.

"As you see, I have brought with me a full complement of technical advisers," he said with a wave, "so that the excellences which I am unqualified to understand may be properly appreciated."

Unfortunately Matsuda was inspired to conclude with expressions of regret for the necessary curtailment of the proceedings in Tokyo.

"The nerve of that bastard!" Kruger fumed as soon as they were out of earshot. "Where the hell does he get off talking about unavoidable discontinuities? He gets me branded as a criminal, and then he acts as if he's above the battle."

For once Gene Fleming's explication of Japanese attitudes was ill-timed.

"The poor guy was simply embarrassed because we caught him with the police at his elbow," he said. "That's why he went into the pompous act. He was trying to pretend that it's business as usual."

"Poor guy!" Kruger mimicked savagely. "None of this would have happened if he didn't have itchy fingers."

"Now, honey," Audrey protested. "We agreed that this was going to be a night off. Why don't you just forget about Tokyo for a couple of hours."

Thatcher feared that Gene Fleming's maladroit remark had made this impossible, but he was reckoning without Pamela Webb.

"Besides, Carl," she said, hurling herself into the fray, "a man with presidential ambitions has to shed this sort of thing like water off a duck's back."

"What the hell is that supposed to mean?"

"That's what I'm trying to tell you. I picked up a nice little item when I had lunch with one of my old buddies from Wharton. He works for Beaver, Day & Collins now."

"So?" Kruger said impatiently.

Pamela let him simmer for a moment before continuing. "They conduct opinion polls all the time. That's why Milo asked me when you're going to announce that you're running."

"Not that old chestnut again?" He sounded bored. "Honest to God, I don't know what's wrong with these politicians. I've said flat out I'm not interested, but there's no such thing as the plain unvarnished truth in their vocabulary."

Clever Pamela! thought Thatcher. She had broadened Kruger's irritation from one government official to the entire tribe.

"I thought it was the same old story too," Pamela confessed. "But then Milo really woke me up."

Kruger was now listening attentively. "Go on."

"Some big shot in Washington has been ordering full-scale weekly polls about you for almost six months."

"What!"

Kruger's bellow came from the heart, halting them in their tracks. He was immobilized long enough for Audrey to capitalize on the news.

"Why, honey," she cooed. "Only one little thing bothers me. When you made up your mind, why didn't you tell me?"

"It's not a joke," he snarled.

"Oh, no," she said piously. "It's the most important decision you could make."

His mouth began to spread reluctantly.

"If you don't behave yourself, I really will run," he threatened. "Then where will you be?"

"No more Bergdorf's, Audrey," Pamela predicted gaily. "Instead you'll have to find a disease to adopt."

Even Don Hodiak joined in. "Not to mention beautifying America," he reminded her.

By the time the foursome swept out to the taxi rank, they sounded as if they did not have a care in the world.

John Thatcher and Gene Fleming were not left alone very long.

"There is a restaurant in Pimlico that serves authentic English dishes," Haru announced, joining them with her research findings. "It may be odd, but it will be good for us."

At The Tankard, Fleming gave his order, then said:

"That was quite a reaction from Kruger, wasn't it? Do you think he was faking?"

"Oh, I thought he was sincere," said Thatcher.

Haru, unlike Audrey Kruger, countenanced

shoptalk. But she insisted on being brought into the picture, so her husband obliged.

". . . Then Pamela Webb told him about these polls, and he hit the roof. I wondered if he was putting on an act, but apparently John didn't."

Thatcher defended his position.

"Kruger is probably affronted to discover that somebody is initiating action about him without consultation. That would certainly be in character."

Haru, who had been listening and eating with quiet contentment, spoke up.

"So Pamela Webb really stirred up a rumpus," she remarked. "Funny, that doesn't sound like what I've read about her."

"It was partly my fault," Fleming told her. "I set Kruger off about Tokyo, and she was just trying to distract him. But she picked a sore subject. Besides, she was probably nervous."

"Why should she be nervous?" Haru inquired.

"Well, everybody says she's Kruger's mistress," Fleming argued. "And he's got his wife with him this time. For God's sake, Haru, I don't care how civilized everybody's being — it can't be easy, can it?"

Thatcher had no intention of discussing eternal triangles. But one aspect of Kruger's immediate plight was irresistible.

"One can only hope that they all enjoy the ballet."

Chapter 21

They gave every appearance of doing so during the performance at Covent Garden. Afterward, during supper at the Villa Romana, Carl Kruger joined the lively banter caused by Hodiak's encyclopedic knowledge of every other rendition of *Giselle*. But Audrey was not deceived. She had seen Carl bide his time during too many weddings, funerals, and United Way dinners. He had a gift for putting his real concerns on hold during social delays.

Later that night, when she bustled in from the bathroom, she was not surprised to find him cradling the phone with a half-guilty expression.

"I'm expecting someone to call back," he apologized. "But it shouldn't be too late."

"It won't bother me," she assured him, heading for the dressing table.

As she searched for her tweezers, Kruger stripped off his jacket and tie. When he next spoke, he was half submerged in the closet.

"I suppose you noticed Benny wasn't with us tonight," he said over his shoulder.

"Yes. I thought he probably had work to do."

"Actually I got rid of him. I wanted time to cool off. Do you remember how, when Don said he wanted to go to the board, I was annoyed?"

She raised her head to watch him in the mirror.

"Of course I do. I heard all the things you said," she replied, wishing that Carl would not always back into his late-night confidences.

"The thing is, I overflowed to Benny too. And damn if he didn't hire some kind of detective to dig up dirt about Don. An hour before we took off from Lackawanna, he dumped a pile of garbage on my desk, as pleased as punch with himself."

Critically examining her right eyebrow, Audrey decided to speed things up.

"I suppose you found out about Mary Ellen?"

"I thought you might know about that," he grunted triumphantly. "If you didn't come running to me with that tidbit, why the hell does Bennet have to? And if poor Don finds himself a playmate for an occasional weekend, that's his business."

Having reduced her eyebrow to perfection, Audrey said idly: "What were you supposed to do about it?"

"God knows! Bennet was even talking about getting some pictures. He had some crazy notion about smearing Don with the board — as if they give a damn about his sex life."

Audrey could believe that her husband had been initially disgusted by Bennet Alderman's malice, but she did not accept it as the cause of the symptoms she had observed during supper. Don Hodiak was simply serving as introduction to whatever was really nagging at Carl. Which meant that all her good work in providing an evening of relaxation had gone to waste.

"Bennet has a habit of rushing in where he has no place being," she said deliberately.

Kruger knew that she had never liked Alderman. "I admit he needs direction, but that's the way we work. I formulate the plans, and he implements them."

"Is that right?" she said, crossing over to her bed.

"So this time he went off the track," Kruger admitted. "Usually Bennet knows better than to go beyond his brief."

She switched on the bedside lamp and began rummaging in a drawer. "If you say so. But I've been wondering, ever since he took me to lunch in order to suggest that I pressure you into firing Pamela."

There was a moment of dead silence.

Then Kruger began to bluster. "Come on, honey. You know better than to listen to all that talk. It's just —"

Retrieving her reading glasses, she ignored his interjection. "I told Bennet to mind his own business. And I said that if he ever intruded in my personal affairs again, I'd make him very, very sorry. That was six months ago, and he hasn't tried anything since."

"The little twerp," Kruger snarled before moving on hastily. "He wouldn't have time to bother you if he paid more attention to his work. Take those polls, for instance. They don't make sense."

With all her experience, Audrey could not tell if Carl was at last coming to his real problem or simply skedaddling away from a sensitive topic.

"But you've had reporters ask if you were planning to run," she reminded him. "I suppose the poll was to see what kind of popular support is out there."

"That would explain a one-shot deal. Somebody could be deciding whether or not to approach me. But every week? That kind of tracking is way beyond the undecided stage."

Unerringly Audrey put her finger on the sore spot. "And you never knew?"

"I didn't, but you can bet the farm that

a whole lot of other people did. That's what really sticks in my craw. By the time Pamela is picking this up over a casual lunch, that means it's common talk — at least in some circles. So how come Bennet wasn't onto this?"

She sniffed. "He likes to act as if he's an insider, but it's a long time since he's been in politics."

"That's not it," Kruger said stubbornly. "Bennet keeps up; he has to. One of the reasons I hired him was because Lackawanna needed someone with that kind of know-how. And you should have seen him when we went to Washington. He was real buddy-buddy with everybody. Hell, even the new secretaries know who he is. I'm beginning to think Benny needs more supervision than I bargained for. He should be busy bringing me the kind of information I really need instead of trying to make a stink out of Don's going on one of those four-city tours of the Orient."

Audrey, who had armed herself with *Walks Through Dickens' London,* laid the book aside.

"You mean that vacation they went on when they brought back all that stuff from Hong Kong?" she asked with a puzzled frown. "What does that have to do with anything?"

"Oh, Bennet was hot on the fact that Don had been in Tokyo a year ago. For Chrissake, it was long before I decided to tie up with Yonezawa, and Don was only there for three days."

"Then it's simply ridiculous."

"Bennet was reaching." But now that Kruger had begun to examine Alderman's deficiencies, he was finding them on all sides. "Bennet wasn't worth beans while Lackawanna was getting all that bad press. He just sat around in a state of shock until the Shima business turned things around. And he sure as hell isn't going to be able to tell me who's behind these polls when he hasn't even heard about them."

It was no part of her plan to encourage unnecessary tension.

"I'm sure you'll find out somehow," she said soothingly.

"Of course I will. Why do you think I'm sitting up for this call? But I shouldn't have to," he snapped as if she were the enemy. "If my contacts are more useful than Benny's, what good is he?"

Audrey Kruger expected to be asleep before the end of the first chapter. But she was doggedly trudging from Doughty Street to Devonshire Terrace when the phone rang an hour later. After the initial acknowledgment, Carl's side of the conversation was easy enough to follow.

"Trowbridge?" he repeated in blank astonishment. "Are we talking about Senator Will Trowbridge?"

When Kruger went in search of his subordinate the next morning, there was no trace of his famous hot temper. Even when it developed that Bennet Alderman was spending most of the day at Lackawanna U.K., Kruger put the time to good advantage. Waking one of Lackawanna's lawyers at home, he telephoned some drastic instructions.

"Go through Alderman's files. All the drafts of our press releases are there. Tabulate the changes he's made, Johnson. And I don't just mean the technicalities. I want to see what kind of spin he put on those stories that we didn't catch at the time."

"It'll be a pleasure," said Johnson grimly.

"And fax it over here as fast as you can," Kruger told him.

With every passing moment he was becoming colder and colder. In this mood he was a far less familiar figure, and a far more dangerous one.

Surprisingly, Bennet Alderman missed all the warning signals. When he began to report about his trip, Kruger listened attentively, made a few suggestions, and let the subject wind down to a natural conclusion. Then:

"Pamela brought me some interesting news yesterday. She picked it up from one of her old Wharton buddies. He works for Beaver, Day & Collins. It seems they've been running polls on me for the last six months."

After a fractional pause, Alderman said: "Well, I guess that proves we really have made you a household name. When they take polls on you, you've really arrived, Carl."

"Sure," said Kruger blandly. "Only I like to be the one who decides where I'm going."

Alderman still saw no threat.

"So what's the problem? Somebody's impressed by your recognition value. It was bound to happen."

"The somebody was Will Trowbridge."

This time there was a perceptible delay.

"Will?" Alderman repeated.

"That's right. The big gun in Washington you're supposed to be so close to. So how come it's Pamela who's telling me this instead of you?"

By now Alderman had caught his breath. "Because I didn't know, that's why," he said resoundingly. "You don't think Will tells me everything, do you? He plays things pretty close to his chest."

"Oh, yeah? Then how about that little romp in Washington? How come it was so important to see Trowbridge?"

"Will wanted to meet you. I figured we'd do him a favor and someday he'd do one for us." Alderman shrugged. "That's how things work."

Kruger did not relax the pressure.

"You should have told me."

"My God, what's the big deal? If Will's interested in your political potential, it's no skin off your nose."

"I'll tell you what the big deal is. People who work for me don't get their orders from Will Trowbridge."

"Come on, Carl. All I did was take you to meet him. Maybe I should have told you —"

"That better be all," Kruger interrupted. "I never did figure out why Lackawanna got all that bad press. It never occurred to me somebody might be trying to stop a political campaign I didn't even know about. If your fun and games with Trowbridge practically cost us our defense contracts, I wouldn't like that at all."

"You can't be serious," Alderman protested. "Maybe I made a mistake trying to oblige Will Trowbridge. Be sore about that if you want. But it's no reason to listen to somebody trying to spread poison about me, particularly somebody who's always had it in for me."

Alderman's fluency, usually his strongest

weapon, was bouncing off his opponent.

"I admit she doesn't like you and probably with good reason," said Kruger, who had no intention of discussing Audrey. "But just to be on the safe side, I'm having Johnson double-check your press releases."

"You can't do that," Alderman said involuntarily.

"Oh, no?"

Alderman's shoulders hunched defensively. "That's the same as throwing me to the wolves. You know damn well Johnson would like to hang me out to dry."

"That's tough," Kruger retorted. "But I'm the one who makes the judgment calls. And if you've been pulling any tricks, you're out on your ear. I play by straight rules."

"Straight rules?" Alderman shot back. "What about Shima?"

"You've lost me," Kruger said quietly. "What about Shima, Benny?"

Alderman was floundering. "I just meant that when Shima got caught in the chopper, you were willing to finagle to put pressure on the Japanese."

Kruger let a moment pass before he replied. Lounging against the wall, he was studying his subordinate with sleepy eyes.

"Now, that was a mistake," he said at last. "The minute you say Shima, I start thinking about Tokyo. I had everything set for a clean, quick decision there. Then somebody had a bright idea about bribing MITI, and I leave Japan with egg on my face. I'd hate to think all that happened because you're hooked on the idea of riding into the White House on my coattails."

White-faced, Alderman instinctively offered other scapegoats. "That could have been anybody. It could have been your pal Arai that you're so damned anxious to protect. Or Iwamoto, who'd do anything to keep you out. Or his good friend Don Hodiak, who tried to shaft you just last week."

The wilder Alderman became, the calmer Kruger became.

"Let's hope so. Because if you had anything to do with it, I'm not just going to throw you out, Benny," he said pleasantly. "I'm going to have your balls."

Chapter 22

Trade shows were no novelty to John Thatcher, and he avoided them when possible.

"But you can't skip tonight," Fleming said. "Not when the Japanese know you're here."

The Sloan did not retain Gene Fleming in order to ignore his expertise. Bowing to the inevitable, Thatcher asked:

"What's the agenda?"

Dinner and speeches, he was told, would precede the main event.

"Then transport out to White Palace for the exhibition. And that's where we'll score points."

"If we still have the strength."

Certainly everybody breathed a sigh of relief upon arrival at White Palace. Now they could walk about and chat freely. What's more, this was the part of the evening they had all come for.

The first order of business for Thatcher himself was to examine the scope of the competition. It went without saying that the London fraternity was out in force. But within an hour Thatcher spotted colleagues from

274

Switzerland, West Germany, and France.

The high point of the evening, however — and the one that proved the value of Gene Fleming's insistence — was Thatcher's encounter with the Sloan client who had signed on during the embassy reception in Tokyo. Thatcher was able to introduce Toby Lemieux as a man who had the ideal Scandinavian shipyard in his pocket.

"We're not the only ones putting in some good work," Toby remarked, pocketing his engagement diary after this refreshing interlude. "You see that man with Carl Kruger? That's Kwai Dong."

Thatcher examined the twosome at the bar. Kruger appeared to be deeply absorbed in his discussion with his companion. But it was surely no accident that they had taken up their position at such a strategic spot. Lackawanna was still trailing the Korean threat before as many Japanese eyes as possible.

Any trade show flushes a diversity of interests. As the evening progressed, Thatcher met Japanese who were there to sell as well as Japanese there to buy. He heard about agricultural equipment and oil tankers, about high-definition television and about more cars than seemed humanly possible.

There were even people looking at the exhibits, as he discovered when he came face to face with an unexpectedly elegant Ali Khan.

"Have you seen the computer display?" the young Pakistani asked before launching into an enthusiastic and incomprehensible description.

"It sounds splendid," Thatcher said at the first opportunity. "I expect there's a good deal here you wish to see."

"I was on my way to the electronic guidance section when I was nabbed by that Mr. Arai. Now I'll have to do it tomorrow morning."

Thatcher blinked at the vision of the stately, immobile Arai interrupting anybody's progress. Of course it was not difficult to understand the motivation.

Ali, obscurely amused, was thinking along the same lines. "He seemed to think I was the one to tell him all about Kwai Dong's trip to Birmingham."

"And did you?"

Khan's face was a study in innocence. "Oh, absolutely. I overflowed with simple gratification that the Koreans are so interested in my work."

Recalling the Pakistani's account of his own duplicity at Cambridge, Thatcher realized how much Ali must have enjoyed the encounter.

"You seem to have finished what Kruger started," he remarked.

"It's what Arai wants, isn't it?" Khan said. "Ammunition for his battle back home?"

"That is certainly one way of looking at it," Thatcher said diplomatically. Arai probably wanted to know whether the Koreans were in serious contention for his own purposes, but he was unlikely to find out from this young man. "And you're spending tomorrow looking at exhibits, even though we're all transferring to Birmingham the day after?"

"Why not? Everything at Midland Research is fine." Ali's gaze drifted around the multinational throng. "The problems are all here."

Fifteen minutes later, Thatcher acknowledged the full justice of this remark. Rather than search for Fleming and Lemieux with an eye to departure, he had decided to wait in one of the sitting areas until they surfaced. There he had been hailed by Don Hodiak and found too late that he was responding to an S.O.S.

Bennet Alderman was very drunk.

"I've had it up to here with the Japs," he announced with a graphic gesture.

Hodiak winced. "For God's sake, will you keep your voice down?" he hissed.

"Afraid that I'll screw up the Yonezawa deal?" Alderman retorted mockingly. "Hell, you've been dead set against it from the beginning."

Hodiak made the mistake of trying to humor him. "Now, Bennet, that's no way to —"

"In fact," Alderman interrupted reflectively, "you make a great pair. You and Pamela the Bitch."

Hodiak's jaw dropped while Alderman, sprawled lazily in his chair, continued:

". . . And if she thinks she can knife me in the back, little Pamela's got another think coming. She's going to regret the day she went running to Carl. This is going to be the end of little Miss Wonderful."

With dismay, Hodiak spoke sharply to him. "What do you mean, running to Carl? Did Carl have you on the carpet today?"

"We had a few words," Alderman muttered. Then, as if regretting this admission, he went on: "It was a misunderstanding, that's all."

By now Thatcher was certain that drink was the crutch Alderman was using to get through a personal crisis.

"Well, take my advice and forget it," Hodiak said. "Carl's always chewing somebody out — you know that. And while you're at it, you can forget Pamela too."

Alderman's reply was a bitter and knowing smile. "I'm not a big one at forgetting," he announced. "You'll find out."

Hodiak turned to Thatcher with an unconvincing laugh. "You probably won't believe me, but we all got along just fine at Lackawanna before this bloody Japanese deal. Since then it's been an albatross around our neck, and as you can see, the pressure's beginning to tell."

"Yes, of course," Thatcher murmured meaninglessly.

"Maybe I'm prejudiced," Hodiak continued with nervous determination, "but the only thing I can see coming from this sale is bad luck for everybody concerned. And I mean the Japanese, as well as Lackawanna."

Thatcher could not agree. The Japanese were past masters at taking the rough with the smooth.

"Look at the Shima scandal," he said. "If the Japanese can live with that, they can live with anything. Bad luck doesn't enter their calculations."

Bennet Alderman shoved back his chair and leaped to his feet.

"Are you insinuating that Lackawanna's got anything in common with Shima?" he shouted.

Thatcher did not bother to reply.

"Sit down and stop making a spectacle of yourself," Hodiak ordered.

"Okay," Alderman said sullenly. "But there's

been too much talk like that going around. The Japanese are trying to shovel all their dirt on Lackawanna and Carl — and I don't like it. Understand?"

Thatcher did not know the reason for Alderman's reaction and did not care.

"I was using Shima as an example," he said, keeping any hint of apology from his voice.

"Oh, yeah?" Alderman retorted rudely. "Well, it sounds like the Japanese line to me. They're so busy covering up, they don't care who gets hurt. If I have to, I'll beat the truth out of Matsuda, so help me God. That squinty-eyed bastard isn't going to wreck everything I've worked for."

Hodiak was frankly horrified.

"Thatcher, I hope you'll accept my apologies. As you can see, Alderman here has had one too many."

Before Thatcher could reply, Alderman spoke up.

"Like hell!" he said. "I'm sober as a judge."

"You are not," said Hodiak, still concentrating on Thatcher. "I'll get him back to the hotel, then first thing tomorrow morning —"

"Of course, you're the big expert, aren't you?" Alderman drawled.

The words, which meant nothing to Thatcher, froze Don Hodiak.

"You've had all that experience hustling

Mary Ellen home too," Alderman crooned. "That is —"

In a fury, Hodiak launched himself at Alderman.

Alderman, stiff-arming instinctively, held him off. "Have you gone crazy?" he panted.

Hodiak finally managed to land a blow.

"Dammit, will you cool off!" Alderman cried, aiming a punch at Hodiak's midriff.

A crowd was watching the antagonists grapple clumsily with each other when security guards hurried up to stop the conflict.

"They ought to be ashamed of themselves," said one of Thatcher's neighbors.

"Perhaps they are," Thatcher replied thoughtfully.

Suddenly he realized that he was talking with the CEO of Shima Trading Company. Among those observing Don Hodiak and Bennet Alderman claw at each other was Rick Iwamoto. And if Thatcher was any judge, Iwamoto liked what he was seeing.

Chapter 23

When two businessmen engage in a brawl that requires forcible intervention, the news spreads. By the next morning it had, in one form or another, reached virtually all interested parties.

"Honestly, Don," said Pamela Webb, encountering Hodiak in the hallway. "What got into you? Bennet can give you twenty years."

Hodiak, his right cheek sporting a large purple bruise, was abashed.

"That occurred to me as I hit the floor. But when he started in on Mary Ellen, I saw red, and in a way, I'm glad I did it."

"Oh, for heaven's sake, you're all alike," she snapped.

She was turning to go, when Hodiak caught her elbow. "Wait a minute. I've been wanting a word with you."

Misinterpreting his reference to his wife, she spoke before he could continue. "Carl didn't know what Bennet was up to. It would never occur to him to set detectives on you, and he was furious at that report."

"I know, I know. I've already seen Carl,"

Hodiak said impatiently. "I guess you haven't heard that Bennet tied one on because he's in big trouble. Carl suspects his white-haired boy has been working for somebody else all along, somebody who wants Carl Kruger waiting in the wings as a presidential candidate."

"And he might just be right!" Pamela exclaimed. Then, her wide brow furrowing in thought, she continued: "You know how Bennet is always trying to feed Carl lines. And how excited he gets when he's left out of decisions. Those polls are just a drop in the bucket. Everything fits."

Hodiak was not finished.

"It's a lot more serious than that. Carl is beginning to wonder if Bennet tried to turn Tokyo into a sure thing by getting together with the Yonezawa boys to grease Matsuda."

Taken aback, Pamela could only stare for a moment.

"What a mess!" she finally gasped. "If it's true, the fat's really in the fire."

Having finally arrived at his point, Hodiak underlined his next words. "And Bennet is convinced you're the mastermind who's blown the whistle on him."

"Me?" she said indignantly. "This is the first I've heard of it."

"You're the one who told Carl about those polls."

Pamela was looking baffled. "Yes, you're right there. But it was just a joke. It never dawned on me that Bennet had anything to do with them."

"Try telling Bennet that. He's got his knife into you now, and you've got to remember he doesn't know a thing about business."

"Of course not," she said. "He thinks those bits of fluff he produces can make or break Lackawanna. He's never figured out our only important release is the quarterly earnings statement. So what?"

Hodiak had set himself the task of warning Pamela, and he was determined to carry it through. "The point is, Bennet's never understood your role at Lackawanna. He doesn't realize you're tops in your field. He thinks . . ."

As his voice died away, Pamela became exasperated. They could both waste a lot of time searching for a delicate rendition of what Bennet thought.

"He thinks I've hooked a rich older man and I'm taking him for all he's worth," she offered crisply.

Relieved to have that out of the way, Hodiak continued: "So he'll try to dig up personal dirt."

"Oh, no!" she cried in involuntary dismay, before catching herself and saying grimly:

"And from the job he did on you, Bennet will go all the way back to when I was twenty-one. I really don't want my past to be an open book."

Hodiak had been thinking of the present, but he suddenly realized that Pamela must have had a life before Lackawanna. And twenty-one was not an age notorious for good sense and balanced judgment.

"Carl isn't likely to hold it against you," he pointed out.

"No, he'll just roar with laughter and never let me forget it." She produced a wry grimace. "Oh, well, I suppose I'll have to grin and bear it. Unless, of course, Bennet's getting the boot right away."

"No such luck. The evidence isn't all in yet. Carl's waiting for Johnson to fax some material over here."

Meanwhile Pamela had rearranged her thinking.

"I take back what I said earlier, Don. It's high time somebody did deck Bennet."

The designers of Tudor House, when allocating interior space, had badly miscalculated the requirements of the fax station. Intent on creating an atmosphere of opulent leisure, they had relegated the installation to a small, out-of-the-way cubbyhole, camouflaged by a jungle growth of potted trees. Unfortunately the love affair between business and instantaneous transmission was just flowering as Tudor House opened its doors. Within six weeks the facility was dealing with ten times the volume of work anticipated. The modest floor space was first crowded, then overcrowded, with personnel, equipment, and soaring mountains of paper.

"What's more," complained the manager after a particularly trying encounter with some Venezuelans, "they don't seem to realize it's only the transmission that's faster. If they ask their home office to prepare a report, it takes the same time as always to do it."

"And they won't wait for us to call their rooms," the billing clerk lamented. "They all —"

He broke off as swaying green fronds warned of the approach of a customer.

"Good morning, Miss Webb," the manager chirped. "If it's that material Mr. Kruger is waiting for, I'm afraid it hasn't arrived. But we'd be happy to phone your room when it does."

Pamela grinned cheerfully. "I suppose we're being pests," she acknowledged. "But we were hoping it showed up while we were out."

She was turning to leave, when a machine operator in the farthest corner of the room suddenly yelped: "There's something coming in from Lackawanna now."

He snatched up the first deposit in the delivery tray and carried it to the counter. "Would this be it?"

But Pamela, after a cursory glance, shook her head. "No, this transmission is for Mr. Alderman."

The manager, conscious of overflowing storage shelves, was reluctant to see her go empty-handed.

"I expect he's waiting for it right now," he said brightly.

Pamela, however, ignored the hint.

"Oh, no; he's out for most of the day."

She had no intention of playing messenger boy for Bennet Alderman. In fact, the less she saw of him right now, the better.

Not everyone associated with the Midland Research controversy was being subjected to the claustrophobic atmosphere of Tudor House. Ali Khan was happily touring exhibits at White Palace. Until his guests arrived in Birmingham, they were somebody else's responsibility. Rick Iwamoto, doing even better, had actually managed to get outdoors. Clad in mud-spattered coveralls emblazoned with the Shima logo, he was watching a motorcycle roar around a dirt track. When it finally coasted to a halt, he advanced eagerly to question the padded figure in a black helmet.

"Well, what did you think?"

Gene Fleming pushed back his grimy visor.

"You know, we ought to do what the jockeys do. Wear about eight pairs of goggles and throw away the top ones as we go."

"Come on, Gene," Iwamoto pleaded. "How did you like it?"

"It's more like driving a Cadillac than being on a bike," Fleming complained.

Iwamoto was delighted. "That's the whole idea. You can't sell the upscale, middle-aged market with a bone-crusher."

Fleming, who harbored a nostalgic attachment to the motorcycles of his youth, was disparaging. "If you're planning to line the streets of Beverly Hills with this thing, I'm surprised you haven't put a muffler on it."

"Not on your life. The one thing they do want is the sound of that *varoom!*"

Gene Fleming gave a valedictory pat to the flank of his steed as he dismounted.

"Actually it's a real honey, Rick."

"We expect to be shipping it by next May."

"If you bring it in at the right price, you should make a splash," Fleming predicted, surrendering the machine to two Shima mechanics, who tenderly trundled it away.

"We'll need a winner by then," Iwamoto

said frankly. "Shima Computers isn't helping our worldwide image, and our day in court may cost us the wood pulp deal too."

These days motorcycles were merely a hobby with Gene Fleming. Cocking his head thoughtfully, he considered the implications of that last remark.

"Len Ridgeway is still hanging in," he said noncommittally.

"But for how long? Especially if things snowball. They're already trying to make a connection between the export violation and that bribe to Matsuda. Who knows what else they'll come up with?"

Iwamoto's voice was casual, and he had half turned to watch a competitor's motorcycle taking to the track. But Gene Fleming knew perfectly well that he was being prepared for the possibility of further damaging revelations about Shima. Abiding by the rules of the game, he pretended he was answering the question as it had been phrased.

"Len likes the deal you've both worked out, but the Japanese demand for wood pulp is cresting. He can't afford to wait too long."

Iwamoto did not have to be told that there were other potential partners for Ridgeway, Ridgeway & Hall.

"I suppose I'll have to see how things develop. You win some, you lose some," he said fatalistically. "But you know what really burns me up, Gene? It's the fact that one word from Matsuda could straighten it all out. Everybody knows he's the one who had to be getting the bribe. The only question is, who was handing it to him? If he'd just open up, Shima would be off the hook."

Gene Fleming could not be encouraging.

"Don't hold your breath," he advised. "It's a long way from being a universal suspect to making an open confession, and Matsuda's an expert at riding out trouble."

"I know all that. He's not going to spill anything unless someone makes it worth his while. In the meantime I have to take it." Iwamoto shrugged the subject aside and took one last look at the track before turning away. "At least that model is no threat to anybody. Do you want to see them strip down my baby?"

Fleming realized that no additional disclosures would be forthcoming.

"I thought you'd never ask."

Gene Fleming had only his instincts and his long acquaintance with Rick Iwamoto to suggest new troubles lurking on the horizon for Shima. Mr. Fumitoshi Arai was getting information direct from the horse's mouth.

Ensconced in ducal splendor, he scarcely

stirred from his suite after the ritual pre-breakfast stroll through Green Park. Countless minions, however, were picking up every tremor of activity from the City, while his secretary fielded calls from around the world. Mr. Arai's meditations were rarely interrupted by this activity, but there were exceptions.

"It is Minister Sato on the line," the secretary announced.

Arai lifted the receiver and punctiliously exchanged formal greetings.

"I trust that all is well."

"Far from it. The opposition is planning a test vote, and they have decided to use the Civil Service Reform Bill."

"How very intelligent of them," Arai murmured.

By starting with the civil service, the opposition could use every sordid detail of the Lackawanna hearings as its springboard. And a vote of no confidence would bring down the government.

"The Prime Minister has told us he will allow the bill to come to the floor in two weeks," Sato continued.

"No doubt he has excellent reasons for the delay."

"Prior to the debate, the Prime Minister will demand certain sacrifices from leading party members."

The scenario was now clear. The government's action against its own was intended to create an aura of sweeping reform. At the moment, Arai was more interested in how other issues, more closely affecting him, would be handled.

"Shima's penalty will have been assessed by then," he remarked.

"The penalty for the export-control violation," Sato specified. "We have been hearing some disturbing rumors that there may be additional charges arising from the files seized in California."

"That would certainly be most distressing."

"I believe that we would have to consider withdrawing our support," Sato said on a magisterial note. "That would, however, change our position in one respect."

Arai was as humble as if he were a stranger to the intricacies of policymaking. "Naturally you have many aspects of the situation to consider."

"Until now Secretary Matsuda's silence has been acceptable. If, however, a general clarification has become desirable, then it would seem to be time for him to speak. That is, if what he says is in conformity with our overall program."

Decoding this message was child's play for Arai. If the government was going to spend the next two weeks on a heroic housecleaning, then it would like to get rid of as many problems as possible. And a public disassociation from the Shima Trading Company would be more than justified if Deputy Secretary Matsuda announced that he had been corrupted by Shima.

"I see," said Arai thoughtfully.

In Tokyo they were still guessing about the Shima files. At the Sloan they already knew.

"John," said Walter Bowman, from New York, "the word is that they've found enough for a civil suit on industrial espionage. Nobody's talking criminal action — at least not yet. Do you think we should start finding another bride for RR&H?"

By now Thatcher had taken Ridgeway's measure. "Len is worried about legal restrictions on Shima's activities. A civil suit won't bother him, particularly one that won't get to court for years."

"The problem may not be what happens to Shima in the U.S."

"You expect repercussions in Japan?"

Bowman went on to relay the predictions of his experts.

"The government there has accepted the fact that this exposé isn't going to die down. And they'd rather have Shima being crucified than their own cabinet ministers."

"How would that sit with the rest of the industrial community?"

"I suppose they'd agree to anything that would keep the government in power. It would be a real plus if they could load most of the scandal on one culprit."

Thatcher's errant imagination immediately produced the one twist that could blast this strategy to smithereens.

"All they need now is for Matsuda to tell the world that the bribe came from Yonezawa."

"The opposition would love it. It would destroy the one-rotten-egg theory and support their claim that corruption is rampant."

After witnessing the day-to-day performance of Lackawanna in Tokyo, Thatcher had never been able to believe that its personnel had the know-how to swim sharklike through the currents of Japanese bureaucracy.

"Well, it stands to reason that it must have been either Shima or Yonezawa. So the government has a fifty-fifty chance of being right."

"Shima had the most to lose," Bowman pointed out. "Wouldn't that up the odds to sixty-forty?"

"Except for one thing. Gene Fleming says that Arai is the real wild card in that bunch."

Chapter 24

The information that Pamela Webb had provided to the fax station was, as usual, absolutely correct. Calls to Mr. Alderman's room during the day were fruitless, but he appeared in person at five o'clock, his raincoat still dripping and his hands filled with the mail and messages he had just picked up.

"Has my stuff come in?"

"Yes; I'll have the girl get it." The manager lifted an appraising eyebrow. "Incidentally, that report Mr. Kruger has been waiting for also arrived."

Bennet Alderman was more obliging than Pamela had been.

"Then I'll take that along too," he said casually.

"We'll have them for you immediately," promised the manager, knowing full well that a major search would be necessary.

"No hurry."

Alderman had disposed himself at the counter and was dealing with his mail as if he had all the time in the world.

"Well, now, look at this," he muttered.

"They're not riding so high now."

The clipping announced that Shima Computers had filed a motion to delay sentencing. There was also a photograph of a grim-faced lawyer toting a laden briefcase up the steps of the federal courthouse in San Francisco.

"I'll bet they sock it to them," Alderman said under his breath as he continued the process of scanning, crumpling, and discarding.

All his comments were in the same optimistic vein — and equally meaningless to the manager — but they lasted until two packets and two bills were produced.

"If you'll just sign here."

But Alderman had one last message to read, and this one capped his elation.

"Everything's going my way," he announced. "Even the great Matsuda is coming down from his high horse."

"Splendid," said the manager cordially.

Then, in all innocence, he placed Johnson's damning report into Bennet Alderman's outstretched hand.

As John Thatcher watched Matsuda parade through the lobby on his daily visit to the fax station, it was apparent that the bureaucrat had changed his manner toward his watchdogs. Matsuda was no longer ignoring their presence. These days he was pretending they were menials, crisply directing them to open doors or to retrieve his coat. It was probably, Thatcher decided, the only way a proud man could live with the situation.

This opinion received unexpected endorsement.

"I am afraid that Deputy Secretary Matsuda is irritated by the surveillance of my men," said Inspector Hayakawa, materializing from behind a column. "It is regrettable that a man of his experience does not appreciate the necessity for my action."

"Yes, indeed," Thatcher said briefly.

He and Hayakawa had been inhabiting the same hotel for three days without a single encounter. The policeman would not have engineered this meeting unless he wanted something.

Hayakawa came to the point with commendable dispatch. "I understand there was an unfortunate display of temper by Mr. Bennet Alderman yesterday evening."

"And I was a witness," Thatcher agreed. "But I have every confidence that you know as much about what happened as I do."

Hayakawa did not deny the assumption. Instead he went on to demonstrate its accuracy.

"They tell me he has suffered some setback in his career that occasioned a spate of anger toward most of his associates."

Thatcher fully expected them to move briskly on to the fracas between Alderman and Hodiak. If the Japanese needed any reinforcement for their conviction that Americans resort to violence at the drop of a hat, that should have done it.

"I am sure they also reported Alderman's condition."

It was a small point, but any distinction between last night and Tokyo was worth making. Say what you would about the tedium of the MR hearings, everyone had been irreproachably sober.

"Oh, yes." Hayakawa shook his head disapprovingly. "You would not believe the amount of work caused to our police force by those who become hostile with drink. We are rarely troubled by those who simply mellow."

He then abandoned his professional reverie and returned to the attack. "I am not very interested in the internal dissensions at Lackawanna. But is it true that Mr. Alderman also singled out Mr. Matsuda for his personal invective?"

"In a sense. He said it was time someone choked the truth out of Matsuda."

"I was afraid of that." Hayakawa sighed. After a moment's reflection, he reached a decision. "I wonder if you could spare the time to join me in a cup of coffee, Mr. Thatcher?"

Intrigued by the unexpected cast of their conversation, Thatcher followed the inspector to a table. After their order had been served, Hayakawa leaned forward earnestly.

"Mr. Matsuda is an intelligent man with a vast amount of experience in certain areas. In other ways, however, he is an innocent. He assumes, for instance, that I have assigned two men — from a tightly budgeted staff, I might add — in order to monitor his communications with those involved in the MR hearings. Offhand, I can think of many criminals with limited mental ability who would not make this mistake."

"You mean you're not worried who he talks to? Or whether he takes a plane for Brazil?"

"Mr. Matsuda is not confined. He can enter a public phone booth at will. And he would not be in London if there were any possibility of flight. The man must think I am an idiot," Hayakawa burst out. "I, too, know that the government situation is reaching a crisis and the time for silence is nearing an end. But Secretary Matsuda is so busy weighing the factors he understands that he forgets entirely that murder has certain consequences."

Thatcher was beginning to see why they were sipping coffee together.

"And your two men?"

"They are bodyguards, of course. If Mr. Matsuda did not kill Ushiba himself, then someone else did. And while the deputy secretary is so busy calculating his moves, he has never even noticed the fact that he represents a threat to the murderer. In this situation I am very alarmed at the prospect of Mr. Alderman trying to exert pressure on Mr. Matsuda. Once word of that spreads, the possibilities could be disastrous."

Thatcher nodded. "I agree, but I fail to see how I can help."

"You have a greater familiarity than I with the value of these proposals made in a drunken fit of spleen. Is it your considered opinion that Alderman will try to implement his suggestion?"

Inspector Hayakawa was so serious that Thatcher reflected for some time before he framed a reply.

"Let me first tell you about Alderman's ramblings yesterday. He was not forthcoming about the nature of his problem, but it was clear he had in some way lost ground with Kruger. He blamed Pamela Webb for this occurrence, and she was the principal target of his venom. It was almost as an afterthought that he considered forcing Mr. Matsuda to disclose what he knows."

"So you think he might not be serious about Mr. Matsuda?"

"For what it is worth, I think Alderman's instinct will be to play politics in the arena he knows, namely Lackawanna." Native caution forced Thatcher to add a rider. "Of course, just bumping into Matsuda could set him off."

Hayakawa did not sound encouraged as he replied: "I do wish that Mr. Alderman had not raised the matter in a public place. If I heard about it, others did too."

"You think there is real danger?"

The inspector nodded gravely.

"Enough so that Mr. Matsuda will be accompanied every moment of the day until he is safely in his bed."

If not in bed, Matsuda was irreproachably occupied in his room. He allowed his usual dinner hour to come and go as he drank in every word of current thinking in Japan.

"Preposterous!" was his first reaction to the growing belief that all elements of the bureaucracy were tainted.

Having vented his ire, he was able to turn his second reading into a dispassionate analysis of the positions being taken by official and semiofficial spokesmen.

At this point he broke off to make his delayed appearance at the dining table. Without haste, he worked his way through the courses, exhibiting no sign of impatience as he produced stately conversation for the benefit of his guardians.

It was ten o'clock before he returned for his last, and most important, reading.

"I was right," he finally declared, congratulating himself on his acumen. "The time has come for them to make approaches."

The balance had shifted so that someone out there would be grateful for the right words from him.

While the architects of Tudor House had badly miscalculated the space requirements of the fax station, they had more than compensated with the grandeur of the penthouse floor. Here, lavish provision had been made for a state-of-the-art health club, stretching expansively in all directions.

An unqualified triumph by every measure, the facility was the envy of every other deluxe hotel in London. From seven in the morning until eleven at night the elevator banks were busy delivering guests intent on utilizing every known aid to physical fitness.

But with the departure of the cleaning crew at midnight, the health club became a vast, shadowy wasteland. Widely spaced night lights cast feeble pools of illumination on the floor, as walls and ceilings disappeared into cavernous heights.

Time, however, had lost all meaning for Mr. Kyle Mendelsohn. Mr. Mendelsohn had crossed the Atlantic for a reunion of his World War II army unit. When he was poured out of his taxi at two o'clock in the morning, he had long since cast aside his respectable Arizona identity. Still crooning imperfectly remembered snatches of "Lili Marlene," he was received by the night staff with practiced efficiency. They steered his wavering steps across the lobby and into the elevator, where the night porter firmly punched the correct button.

"Good night, sir," he said politely.

His charge, overcome by sorrow for lost youth, half sobbed in reply:

"Poor Lili!"

The staff, unfortunately, was not familiar with domestic habits in Phoenix, where Mr. Mendelsohn regarded his own swimming pool as a precaution against morning-after woes. Subliminally aware of the need for preventive action, he lingered in his own room only long enough to collect his gear, then continued journeying to the penthouse floor.

Once arrived, he paid no attention to the tomblike silence or the all-pervading obscurity. Instead he supported himself against the wall to study the bewildering array of directions. Having finally deciphered the word POOL, he carefully aligned his forearm along the length of the arrow.

"That way," he muttered triumphantly.

He caromed off one wall and then the other before successfully negotiating the first turn. By now vague doubts were beginning to make themselves felt, and he was relieved to see a blurred figure at a distant corner. Encouraged by this sign of human occupancy, he hastened his unsteady pace.

Stumbling forward too quickly, he never noticed the waste receptacle until he collided with it.

"Hey!" he cried in protest.

And immediately the narrow hall reverberated to the echoes of a gunshot and an agonized scream.

Chapter 25

"I tell you, I'd just gotten out of the elevator when this maniac tackled me," Bennet Alderman said for the third time. "Why the hell would I want to shoot Matsuda?"

Kyle Mendelsohn did not argue with the description. Now on his third cup of coffee, he was appalled at his recent act of folly. The sound of enemy fire had awakened every instinct dormant since VE-day. When he had rounded the corner, to see one twitching figure lying inside the open door to the swimming pool and another halfway to the adjoining elevator, he had not prudently retreated. Instead former Technical Sergeant Kyle Mendelsohn had charged into combat.

The first arrivals on the scene, drawn by the sounds of a melee, had found Mendelsohn and Alderman frantically wrestling on the floor, while Mr. Tomaheko Matsuda pumped his life's blood into the tiled gutter surrounding the pool.

"I could have gotten myself killed," Kyle moaned.

The ambulance had long since removed Mr.

Matsuda, still alive, to the hospital. That had been the only departure. Since then it had been nothing but arrivals. Two members of the Japanese Embassy were maintaining a watching brief for their fallen countryman. By their side, offering assistance and support, was a representative of the British Foreign Office. Circling the entire group with clucking solicitude was the general manager of the hotel. The police had come in waves of increasing importance, which culminated in the person of Superintendent McLeod. It was he who was questioning Alderman.

"But you were meeting with Mr. Matsuda at the pool?"

"I've gone over this again and again," Alderman grated. "I got a note from Matsuda this afternoon asking me to meet him there at two A.M."

"And you did not regard that as astonishing?"

Alderman was openly snarling.

"Why the hell should I? Everybody in the hotel knew that he had the cops on him all day. I figured the only time he could shake them was in the middle of the night."

"I wasn't referring to the time," McLeod said patiently. "Weren't you surprised he wanted a meeting at all?"

"Of course not. The heat was on Matsuda.

It's common knowledge he was on the take and he'd missed out on his big score. So he wanted to see how much Lackawanna would ante up for his testimony."

The superintendent considered this and saw a flaw.

"Then why you, instead of Mr. Kruger? He's the one who'd have to decide, isn't he?"

"They call it deniability, Superintendent," Alderman said with world-weary superiority. "By using me as a go-between, Matsuda could back out if we didn't come up with a deal. Then he could peddle his papers someplace else."

The Japanese had stiffened as Alderman began his exposition. Now their outrage could no longer be contained.

It was intolerable, the embassy spokesman declaimed, that such slander remain unrefuted. They must protest not only these baseless allegations but also the laxity of the host country in permitting this act of violence.

Alderman snorted contemptuously. "What gives you the right to complain? You didn't do such a hot job of protecting our people in Tokyo."

There was a shocked silence at this first overt reference to the demise of Mr. Ushiba, which Superintendent McLeod noted thoughtfully. Upon being summoned to duty, he had received a hasty briefing on the Midland Research scandal and a very thorough briefing on the best interests of his own government. He waited a moment to see if anyone would take up the implied challenge, then continued his interrogation.

"Then you were simply on your way to this meeting, Mr. Alderman?"

"That's right. I'd just taken a couple of steps from the elevator when the door to the pool opened and I could see this vague silhouette. Then all hell broke loose — a shot, Matsuda screaming and going down. So I was ducking back into the elevator when Mr. Gung Ho here came leaping out of nowhere."

Everybody looked respectfully at Kyle Mendelsohn, who gave a visible shudder.

"And you still claim Mr. Matsuda instigated the meeting?"

"For Chrissake! I opened his note at the fax station and mentioned it to the guy there. Ask him if you want, but I'm through going over this."

McLeod wanted less officialdom, not more, and Alderman's tone suggested that his next utterance would be a demand for the U.S. Embassy.

"It is getting late," the superintendent conceded. "I'll take statements from the others tomorrow, but right now I think the best thing you gentlemen can do is go back to bed."

McLeod himself was planning to work through the night, even though the two men he most wished to question were presently beyond his reach. According to the doctors, Mr. Matsuda would first undergo surgery and then be incommunicado for a period of up to forty-eight hours. The other promising source of information was Inspector Hayakawa, who had been modestly lurking behind the embassy delegation. But approaching him would be fruitless until he had been instructed as to the best interests of *his* government. Presumably that process had commenced the moment the Japanese were alone.

In the meantime, McLeod, having been yanked from his own bed, proceeded to deal out the same treatment to key members of the Tudor House staff.

"Why was the swimming pool unlocked?" he asked the director of the health club.

"Because the key was missing when they wanted to close up at midnight."

There was not an ounce of censure in the superintendent's voice: "So you just left it open?"

"That's right. It wasn't important enough to wake up the manager for the master. After all, what is there to steal? The pool?"

"Tell me about this key. Where was it missing from?"

The director explained that the life guard, after opening up in the morning, placed the key in the top drawer of the sign-in desk.

"So everybody who uses the pool first thing would be aware of this?"

"And a lot of others. The ones coming out of the elevator by the pool, the ones passing it on their way to the weight rooms or the exercise classes. You have to remember that's our busiest hour of the day."

"Then the next thing I'd like you to do is check on the use made of your club by these people." McLeod produced a list of those who had attended the MR hearings in Tokyo. "Is that going to take a long time?"

"Not with our computer," the director said proudly.

As McLeod was led toward this paragon, he had a final question about the physical layout of the facility. "If someone with only the pool key ambushed Matsuda, could he have gotten out to some other corridor?"

"Oh, yes. All the dressing rooms open to the corridors from the inside. You don't want some fool woman being locked in. From the swimming pool you could get to two other corridors."

The director had already settled himself at

the keyboard and was conning the list. The Lackawanna delegation had pride of place.

"Carl Kruger." He tapped out the name and instantly the screen became busy. "He swims every day at opening time. Oh, and while she's not on your list, I see Mrs. Carl Kruger attends the seven o'clock low-impact aerobics class."

McLeod had not realized they had a Mrs. Kruger in their midst.

"Go on," he urged.

"Bennet Alderman uses the weight room and Pamela Webb the jogging track. Both of them are early birds too. We have no listing for Donald Hodiak, and John Thatcher has only been swimming once, at five-thirty in the afternoon."

"Now let's have the Japanese."

Without bothering to punch keys, the director said chattily: "Well, of course Mr. Arai and his staff are a special case. They're in and out all the time."

"Why?" McLeod asked economically.

"Mr. Arai has the penthouse suite. It's the largest accommodation in the hotel. There are about eight of them in there."

Geography had not been included in McLeod's briefing. "I thought your club took this whole floor."

"With the exception of that suite. Apparently they don't work to any established schedule, so they come in here whenever they have free time."

"God!" They all sounded impossibly athletic to Superintendent McLeod, who could rarely steal enough time for a long walk. "And Matsuda himself? Does he relax by running a four-minute mile?"

But Matsuda, in the eyes of the director, was even worse than Don Hodiak.

"He's only been here to use a steam box three times, and he's had a massage twice." These symptoms were all too familiar to the director, who ended darkly: "Stress."

"And quite a lot of it, from what I hear," McLeod murmured before adding: "You needn't bother with Noriko Iwamoto. The desk says he's not staying here."

The director's fingers, however, had already alerted the computer's memory.

"Maybe not now. But he was swimming here at seven A.M. last February sixteenth."

"Thank you," McLeod said thoughtfully.

Unlike everybody else who had been levered out of his suburban bed, the manager of the fax station appeared to enjoy the change. He received McLeod in his own domain — now occupied by one drowsy attendant — and invited the policeman to share his appreciation.

"I've never seen it like this before. It's really

quite pleasant," he marveled.

McLeod had learned to handle discursive witnesses years before.

"You do a lot of business?"

"It's a madhouse in the daytime."

"Then I hope you've got a good memory. I want to know about Mr. Bennet Alderman's visit here."

The manager frowned. The previous day had featured a transmission sent to the wrong bank in Hong Kong. At the height of the subsequent hysteria, the client had been threatening a lawsuit.

"Alderman?"

"He's the publicity director for Lackawanna," McLeod prodded.

"Lackawanna," the manager repeated on a more hopeful note. "Yes, they send and receive all the time."

McLeod knew some kind of cue was needed. "I thought you might have a log."

"Of course." A substantial ledger was produced and consulted. "The Alderman material arrived at eleven-fourteen in the morning."

"I really wanted to know when he was here."

"Wait!" the manager cried. "It's beginning to come back. There were two batches of material for Lackawanna, and they arrived in the wrong order. Of course that always happens."

The manager placed the tips of his fingers on either temple as if by steadying his head, he could bring to rest the whirling fragments in his mind.

"Yes, it was Miss Webb who was here when this arrived," he said, indicating the morning entry. "And when I showed it to her, she said it was Alderman's and he wouldn't be back for hours."

McLeod hoped it was all going to be this simple. "Well, if he was here when her transmission came in, you just have to look that one up."

But the manager was shaking his head.

"No, I remember now. Everything for Lackawanna was here by the time Alderman stopped by. Let's see, the second arrival was at one-fifteen. And it must have been here for some time, because I chatted with him while the girl was digging through the piles in the back. He was willing to take both lots."

McLeod congratulated himself on having arrived at the target area.

"Tell me about this chat," he invited.

"It wasn't anything in particular. Alderman had just returned to the hotel, and he'd picked up his mail. He was riffling through it, throwing some of it away and making casual comments. I was keeping him happy while the clerk searched the shelves."

Now, if ever, was the time for caution.

"Do you remember what he said about his mail?"

"Not in any detail. He was really talking to himself. But he did seem very cheerful about it, and oh, yes, at the end he made a remark about one of the Japanese. I was worried because I was afraid Mr. Matsuda might have overheard."

McLeod stared. "You mean he was here too?"

"No; he came in just after Mr. Alderman left. But with all that greenery, you can't tell when someone's within earshot."

"So Alderman was insulting?"

"Oh, no; it was one of those jocular remarks that Americans make. But you know the Japanese; they wouldn't understand. Sometimes I'm not sure that I do. But I have an idea."

Once again the manager immersed himself in the log, turning pages busily as he explained.

"Mr. Matsuda knew exactly when his transmission was due, and he arrived on the dot. Here it is! Five-oh-three. So Mr. Alderman was here a minute or two earlier."

For the manager, this was total vindication of his system. For the superintendent, it was only partial triumph. Try as he would, he could evoke no further recollections. Bennet

Alderman had ripped open an envelope, read a message, made one of those American remarks about Mr. Matsuda, and then discarded the note.

One last effort was in order.

"Is there any chance it's still in your wastebasket?"

"Superintendent!" The manager waved toward shelves already overflowing with the night's receipts. "All debris is removed on an hourly basis. Otherwise we'd never keep our heads above water."

By the next morning the hotel was buzzing with tales of nighttime dramatics at the swimming pool. To a man, all the guests on Superintendent McLeod's list claimed to have been asleep in bed at two A.M., and equally, all failed to produce any confirmation. Even the Krugers would only say that Audrey had retired at eleven, while her husband remained huddled with his staff until after midnight. The only surprise emerged when McLeod finally tracked John Thatcher to the dining room, where he was breakfasting with a companion.

"This is Eugene Fleming, Superintendent. He's in charge of the Sloan's Tokyo branch."

For a moment McLeod doubted the accuracy of his list. "You weren't present at the

Midland Research hearings, Mr. Fleming?"

"Not guilty." Gene grinned while lavishly spreading marmalade.

Thatcher hastened to explain.

"The Sloan is not a party to the MR negotiations. My own involvement rests on the formal need for the presence of a bank officer." He did not feel it necessary to enter into the intricacies of creditors' agreements.

"I see. Well, Mr. Thatcher, you'll have heard of the attack on Mr. Matsuda last night. We're asking people if they saw him yesterday evening or if they noticed anything unusual in the hotel last night."

Pouring himself another cup of coffee, Thatcher shook his head. "I'm afraid not. In the evening I was out to dinner at the home of our London branch manager. I returned at eleven and went straight to bed without seeing anyone."

Still trying to place Gene Fleming in the scheme of things, McLeod turned to him. "And you were with your colleagues?"

"Oh, no, I was busy someplace else. I didn't get back until late."

"But aren't you the Japanese expert for your bank?" McLeod persisted.

"Yes, but I'm also on the board of the International Federation of Motorcycle Associations. Yesterday afternoon I spent some time watching the trials of Shima's new line of motorcycles. Rick and I arrived at Euston around eleven."

The mention of the missing element from the MR hearings was enough to convince McLeod that his instincts had been sound.

"Rick?"

"Noriko Iwamoto," said Fleming with an impressive roll. "We came back here for a nightcap, and it must have been about twelve-thirty when we broke up. Then I went to bed, and Rick left for the Shima apartment."

As the cheerful, unconcerned voice dropped another suspect into the hopper, McLeod took a deep breath.

"And would you know where this apartment is?"

Fleming nodded briskly. "Sure. It's on Half Moon Street, just a two-minute walk from here."

"I see," McLeod sighed.

Inspector Hayakawa was obliging enough to state his official guidelines at the outset.

"After extensive conference," he said with gentle irony, "it has been decided that continued homicidal assaults on our personnel cannot be tolerated. I have been instructed to render all possible assistance."

"Thank God," said McLeod frankly. "I

318

don't see how we can get anywhere without your cooperation."

Hayakawa was not encouraging.

"You will be disappointed. We have not succeeded in eliminating anyone. There are, of course, outstanding probabilities. It is received truth in Tokyo that Mr. Matsuda took a bribe and then killed his underling, Mr. Ushiba, to protect himself."

McLeod had nothing but contempt for the received truth of political and journalistic circles. "I don't care about all that. I want to know what you think," he said bluntly.

"I don't believe it's that simple at all. My men did produce substantial dossiers on Matsuda and Ushiba. Matsuda would never have brought that letter into the office, let alone left it carelessly lying about. Furthermore his record shows he would have been perfectly capable of dealing with Ushiba. And there is complete agreement that Ushiba was stupid, lazy, and unenterprising. Even his wife, in defending him, confirms this picture." As he spoke, Hayakawa could see again that small, wiry woman with the disillusioned eyes. "She says he never would have had the initiative to do anything with that letter. I think someone obtained it with a good deal of effort and decided to use Ushiba as a tool. He was impressionable enough to be persuaded that it was his duty."

"So Ushiba was a cat's-paw?"

For once, the inspector's command of the English vernacular failed.

"Cat's-paw?"

"To take the chestnuts out of the fire."

Hayakawa carefully considered this hoary figure of speech, then nodded. "Exactly. It was a dangerous maneuver, at least politically, and Ushiba would be too dense to realize how exposed he was. Indeed, I even contemplated the possibility that the letter was forged."

"That wasn't mentioned in my briefing."

"It had to be considered. The Swiss, however, can be cooperative when no names are involved. They tell me that physically the letter is above reproach. The paper is that used over there, the typeface is appropriate for that kind of office, the language conforms to their trade usage. It would have required knowledgeability to produce that result, but not, of course, beyond the resources of the principals. They all have international offices dealing with Switzerland."

McLeod examined his colleague.

"But there's something more, isn't there?" he asked acutely.

"Curiously enough, it's the lack of incriminating content. The only reference to Midland Research is the scrawled initials. Surely, if anybody had been fabricating evidence on this level, they would have made the contents more damning. I know I would have."

"So we have a genuine document stolen from Matsuda and exactly the right person in the ministry pressed into service. It doesn't sound much like the Americans."

"Not alone, certainly not," Hayakawa agreed readily. "They could have conspired with Yonezawa to bribe Matsuda, and Shima produced a counterplot. Or else Yonezawa discovered a bribe by Shima and took action. I find it very easy to believe that they all have something to hide."

McLeod thought it was time to move from theory to fact. "The one who was on the scene last night was Bennet Alderman."

"Yes, and he's in some kind of difficulty at Lackawanna. It is possible that he acted independently in Tokyo, that Mr. Kruger has just grown suspicious, and it became essential to silence Matsuda."

With three corporations involved, there were already enough combinations, as far as McLeod was concerned. If individual employees were striking out on their own, the situation became even more complex.

"Do you think he would have?" McLeod asked doubtfully.

"It happens. After all, Shima is now involved in that export violation because of something the head of computers did without knowledge by the parent company."

McLeod nodded gloomily. "Speaking of Shima, I have a piece of news for you."

He related Gene Fleming's story, then continued: "We've been unable to find anybody in the hotel who saw Iwamoto leave. There were some guests taking the same elevator as Fleming who heard the two of them say good night."

"Iwamoto could have remained here someplace unobtrusive until two and then attempted to kill Mr. Matsuda. But that does not address the basic problem."

"I know, I know," grunted McLeod. "If Alderman didn't shoot Matsuda, then how did a third party become aware of their meeting? It's much simpler to believe that Matsuda asked for the meeting to make some kind of deal, and Alderman decided to rid himself of a threat."

The Japanese inspector had been looking more and more dissatisfied.

"Not for me, it isn't," he said decisively.

"You don't think Matsuda would have set a price on his silence?"

"That's not what I meant. Matsuda is subject to the temptations and alarms of all human beings. He might take a bribe, he might even commit murder. But under no circumstances would he appear at his office in Bermuda shorts. He would also not arrange clandestine meetings at deserted swimming pools. Even if a nighttime rendezvous was necessary, what was wrong with Alderman's room?"

McLeod tried to transpose Matsuda into a comparable British civil servant.

"In a way, you're right. But you know the basic flaw as well as I do," he said at last. "No matter what the compulsion, Matsuda *was* at that swimming pool."

Chapter 26

For forty-eight hours the world awaited Mr. Matsuda's story. During this period his wife and son emplaned for London, the Prime Minister expressed the deep regret of the British people, and the Japanese ambassador announced that his government was following developments.

The only meaningful public statement emanated from St. Ethelred's Hospital. In spite of medical technicalities, the message was clear. Mr. Matsuda was in no immediate danger.

Inside Tudor House, an army of Superintendent McLeod's minions moved purposefully through the vast complex, acquiring snippets of information here and there. The gun was discovered at the bottom of the swimming pool.

"No fingerprints, and it was reported stolen from a collector's home six years ago," a subordinate reported.

"What about witnesses?"

They were few and far between. A porter, after replacing a light bulb, had used the elevator bank servicing the Lackawanna rooms at one-fifty. Of the three cars available, two had been down in the lobby and the third had been at rest on the penthouse floor. At one forty-five, two guests had walked past Don Hodiak's door without seeing signs of life.

"Keep at it," McLeod directed.

Outside Tudor House, a pack of reporters circled like wolves. In Tokyo, where the press had come on the scene after the participants had scattered, the emphasis had been on the ministry scandal. Here, with a public shootout and the entire cast onstage, the focus was on personalities. There were photographs of Mr. Arai on his morning promenade, of Kruger and Pamela Webb fighting their way to a taxi, of Kyle Mendelsohn, now sober as a judge. The only person coming and going with any freedom was Haru Fleming, who returned from her sorties with bright-eyed accounts of what was going on.

"They were shouting to Mr. Kruger, asking if he expected Mr. Alderman to be arrested. He said he had no comment."

Nobody was asking Bennet Alderman, because he was spending full time assisting the police with their inquiries.

Among those feeling the strain was Inspector Hayakawa. The bullet that smashed into

Mr. Matsuda had destroyed the Japanese government's opportunity to handle a ticklish situation with discretion. Bowing to the higher realism, Tokyo had issued its edict. Hayakawa, by cooperating with the British, was to remain close to the investigation and obtain early news of progress. It went without saying that his frankness was to be restricted. The inspector's case notes on Messrs Arai and Iwamoto were not for foreign eyes — at least not yet.

"The circumstances are unavoidably embarrassing," a testy embassy official explained. "But an unexpected statement by Mr. Matsuda could render them far more difficult. In many ways it would have been simpler . . ."

His voice died away as Hayakawa remained impassive. It was not his place to acknowledge that he understood this sentiment, let alone to share it. The official position was gratitude that Deputy Secretary Matsuda's life had been spared.

Clearing his throat, First Secretary Sessue continued. "In order to avoid this predicament, I gave his son a message to take to the hospital."

"And was Mr. Matsuda receptive?" Hayakawa asked, now able to evince legitimate interest. The answer might well establish open season on Noriko Iwamoto.

But Sessue's program had been thwarted by human frailty.

"It is impossible to tell. According to the son, Secretary Matsuda was too weak to do more than send his thanks to the ambassador for wishing him a speedy recovery."

Both Hayakawa and his embassy believed that correct preparation could prevent unpleasant surprises. Unfortunately the tempo of events was no longer in their hands.

"The doctors say that Mr. Matsuda is now fit to be questioned," a clerk from Scotland Yard informed Sessue on the phone.

"Excellent news," said the first secretary, mentally cursing the medical fraternity for unseemly haste. Another round of communication via the younger Matsuda might have accomplished much.

". . . know that you and Inspector Hayakawa wish to attend," the youthful voice went on. "Superintendent McLeod expects to be at St. Ethelred's at two o'clock this afternoon and will welcome your presence."

"Please thank the superintendent for me," said Sessue, foreseeing a difficult passage ahead.

In this he was not alone.

Superintendent McLeod, normally the most phlegmatic of men, was beginning to regard the Matsuda case as punishment for whatever sins he had committed. Twenty-five years on the force had inured McLeod to crime in odd places, to stories so thin they might even be true, to suspects claiming to have slept through critical moments. Nine times out of ten, he knew, methodical plodding could clarify matters.

But methodical plodding held no attraction for the forces that had been unleashed. The press assailed him with pleas for startling revelations. The experts concerned with Anglo-Japanese relations and U.S. investment in the U.K. peppered him with warnings to avoid giving offense to anybody. His superiors urged him to provide material that would ready the home secretary for hostile questions in the Commons.

Before setting forth for St. Ethelred's, the superintendent was subjected to yet another round of advice from the Foreign Office.

". . . and God knows we don't want any official protest lodged, either."

"No, sir," said McLeod, keeping his opinions to himself.

"So you must exercise extreme care in dealing with Mr. Matsuda. There must not be the slightest suggestion of harassment or of overtaxing his strength. Simply ask neutral questions and accept his answers at face value. Remember, no matter how Mr. Matsuda is viewed in Japan, here he is a victim, pure and simple."

Senior police officers are hardened to situations in which they are instructed to moderate efficient investigative procedures. At the same time they are asked to produce speedy results. McLeod frequently wondered how many areas of government were conducted with the same lack of elementary reason.

"That may make our interrogation of Mr. Matsuda less productive," he pointed out.

"I know, I know," said the anxious official. "Really, in many ways, it would have been simpler if . . ."

Firmly clamping down on this thought, he indicated appropriate guidelines. "You can take your cue from the Japanese representatives present."

McLeod had much to learn about diplomacy.

"I suppose things could be worse," he said sourly. "We could have the Yanks butting in as well as the Nips."

The Foreign Office shuddered.

The only person looking forward to two o'clock was the man already installed at St. Ethelred's. Tomaheko Matsuda was still lying motionless upon his hospital bed. His words to his wife and son continued to be little more than criticism of their needless histrionics. If anything, his withdrawal into self was increasing with the return of physical strength.

However, contrary to appearances, Matsuda was now ready to shed the habits of a lifetime and replace endurance with candor. The attempt on his life had been a severe shock. Matsuda was bitterly energized by the conviction that he had been subjected to one indignity too many.

"You ask why I should be at a health club in the middle of the night," he told McLeod. "I am eager to tell you."

Only their rigorous training kept Inspector Hayakawa and First Secretary Sessue from exchanging dismayed glances. The very timbre of Matsuda's voice suggested emotional recklessness.

"Glad to hear it," said McLeod laconically.

Although supine, Matsuda seemed to draw himself up. "In the course of my duties here, it is vital for me to maintain close contact with my office at MITI, often by fax. So I had occasion to stop by the station in the hotel — to gather important material that I was expecting."

McLeod, Hayakawa, and Sessue were about as dissimilar as three men could be. Nevertheless they all registered the same cautionary note. With his phalanx of flunkies, why should Matsuda have been running his own errands?

Incongruous or not, his story tumbled out.

". . . While I stood waiting, what should I happen to discover but a note carelessly left on the desk. Quite casually I glanced at it — and to my astonishment I found a message, purporting to come from me. A rendezvous, if you can believe it, to meet Bennet Alderman. Late, late at night!"

The mere memory enraged Matsuda so much that he missed audience impatience.

"I determined to learn who was misusing my name and for what purpose," he continued with hauteur. "The very nature of the meeting — after midnight and in such unsuitable surroundings — suggested furtive and possibly criminal dealings. I considered it my duty to expose the impostor."

His defiance invited challenge, but none was forthcoming. McLeod, who knew all about the visits of the younger Matsuda, realized that this testimony might be hand-tailored to accord with Bennet Alderman's story. Orders, however, are orders. He was supposed to accept any answers, no matter how farfetched.

"Go on," he invited.

But Matsuda's recital had effectively ended. He remembered emerging into a deserted corridor and opening the door to the pool. After that, all was confusion. There had been a loud noise, intolerable pain, then blankness.

Secretary Sessue had armed himself with medical support. "The doctors say this is quite a common response. Trauma, I believe they call it."

"Yes," said McLeod uncommittally, noting that Matsuda's attention had wandered.

". . . as I am sure Inspector Hayakawa's experience will confirm," Sessue prattled on.

McLeod made no pretense of caring about Hayakawa's experience.

"Mr. Matsuda," he said, "this note you — er — happened to come across. We didn't find any sign of it."

Matsuda was listening after all. "Naturally I destroyed it at once. As the message was totally invalid, I deemed it necessary to ensure that it did not fall into other hands."

"I see. You did not feel it desirable to inform Mr. Alderman of this invalidity?"

In spite of being flat on his back, wearing inappropriate attire, Matsuda sounded every inch the civil servant.

"I carefully considered the available alternatives. In my view it was imperative that the meeting take place in order that the identity of the impostor should be discovered. I had no assurance that I could rely on the cooperation of Mr. Alderman."

McLeod, knowing that he was now on thin ice, proceeded cautiously. "Very well. But what about notifying the authorities? It isn't as if you had to report to us. You had Inspector Hayakawa here, at your beck and call."

Constraint descended like a fog. Then, in a dead heat, the Japanese all spoke:

"I must protest —" Sessue began hotly.

". . . limited jurisdiction," Hayakawa declared.

"The situation has been made very complicated for me by earlier events," said Matsuda, with a wary look at Sessue.

McLeod blinked. "No offense intended," he said, "but tell me, what do you mean about very complicated, Mr. Matsuda?"

To the great relief of Inspector Hayakawa and Sessue, St. Ethelred's intervened.

"I'm afraid that's all the time we can allow now. Mr. Matsuda needs his rest."

"Fine, fine," said McLeod genially. "We'll just all have to come back tomorrow, then."

". . . So despite everything, it's beginning to look as if Bennet may be telling the truth," said Carl Kruger a day later.

"Before I believed Bennet I'd need a lot of confirmation," said Audrey.

Pamela, in the Kruger suite with them, looked up from the newspapers she was reading. "Apparently Matsuda's provided it, Audrey. I admit the whole story's weird, but it seems to be holding together. At least the press is beginning to back off Bennet. Unfortunately they're still fascinated by the shooting."

While Pamela, Don Hodiak, and Carl struggled to go on about their business, Audrey had remained at the hotel.

"And I'm getting cabin fever," she complained.

"Going to Grosvenor Square with me wouldn't have given you much joy," Carl told her. "The reporters who aren't circling the fort here are camped out in front of the embassy."

Nevertheless the embassy was proving to be a more reliable source of official information than the newspapers. Kruger was getting fully briefed.

". . . and I'll bet Arai is too," he said reflectively. "And probably Iwamoto as well. God, the Japanese must be going crazy trying to figure out what the hell is happening."

Pamela remained more positive. "Let's hope that Mr. Arai already knows. At least he understands the politics involved and how MITI is likely to react."

But hope was not enough for Kruger. "We're doing more than that," he announced. "I want you to go right up to Birmingham."

"Why on earth?" she demanded.

"Look, we were on a pretty even keel,

counting down to Ali's presentation," he said. "Then Matsuda gets shot, and Bennet's detained. And we're back in the mud. Well, by God, I'm not going to let them screw Lackawanna again."

"I read what you told the *Financial Times*," Pamela said dryly. "But, Carl —"

He did not let her finish. "Naturally we've postponed Ali's big show until the smoke clears," he said. "It wouldn't look right to forge on as if nothing had happened. Besides, the Japanese need time to get their act together. But meanwhile I'm not going to let us sit here twiddling our thumbs. So here's the scenario. I'll stay here in London to show sympathy and incidentally stand by Bennet. That shouldn't be more than a couple of days."

"When you'll need me," Pamela argued. "You just said this is where everything is happening."

"No, I need you in Birmingham, keeping Ali up to speed," he responded. "MR has to be just as sharp as if we were right on schedule. Somebody has to go, and that somebody is you."

"What about Don?" she replied, casting around for another objection.

"Don't be silly," Kruger said baldly. "You know how Don feels about the whole project.

You get up there tomorrow morning, and I don't want to hear any more about it."

His tone made her flush angrily. "All right, all right," she said with resentment. "I'll check back with you before I leave."

She was storming out when Audrey called after her: "Be sure you do that, Pamela."

Audrey's brightness remained when she was left alone with her husband.

"It isn't as if she cares what happens to Bennet," she said. "Why do you suppose it makes her so mad to have to go to Birmingham?"

"Who knows?" he replied abruptly.

Being a wise woman, Audrey did not ask another question that occurred to her.

Why was Carl hell-bent on getting Pamela out of town?

Chapter 27

Mr. Matsuda was still lying on his hospital bed when Shima's day of judgment arrived in Washington. There, the original cries for vengeance had been replaced by a growing desire to maintain a low profile in the Midland Research scandal. In consequence the announcement was anticlimactic.

John Thatcher scanned the fine print before laying it aside.

"It's confined entirely to Shima Computers. There's not a word about the parent company. I expect Len Ridgeway to start calling any minute."

"This doesn't mean a thing," said Gene Fleming, who was fresh from an hour on the phone with his office.

Thatcher had suspected as much. "Now we wait for the other shoe to fall?"

"Right. And what they decide to do in Tokyo won't be tied to the violation or even the MR situation. The government is trying to stay in power by painting Shima as black as possible, then clobbering them."

"All right, that's what the government wants

to do. Will they succeed?"

"It won't be easy now they've got this attack on Matsuda. Mysterious notes, assignations in the middle of the night, shooting!" Every fiber of Gene Fleming's sturdy common sense recoiled. "It's hard to believe even when you're sitting in the same building. This must make great reading in Tokyo."

Thatcher thought this was too parochial. "Not just in Tokyo," he said.

"It's more than this frolic upstairs," said Fleming, with a contemptuous jerk of his thumb toward the ceiling of the Tudor House bar. "I'm talking about killing Ushiba. That's what doesn't make sense to the Japanese. Everybody involved had access to a hell of a lot of money. The normal procedure would have been to buy his silence. Then, as Matsuda's role clarified, the government remembered that he didn't have the key to a corporate bank account."

"Come now, that's not entirely true," Thatcher objected. "He had a million-dollar bribe he could offer to split."

"There's still lingering bewilderment. Because no matter how you slice it, the stakes just weren't high enough then for murder."

Thatcher could think of one other factor. "That is tenable only if the suspects identified entirely with their companies."

"So? Arai *is* Yonezawa. And the same could be said about Kruger and Lackawanna."

"But not about everybody. Which brings us to Bennet Alderman and the latest developments about him."

Thatcher went on to explain Carl Kruger's growing suspicions.

". . . and Alderman's dirty tricks are outside normal corporate practice. He compiled a dossier on Hodiak's personal life that infuriated Kruger. I don't know what was in it, but it seems to have included dirt on Mrs. Hodiak. Then he's been trying to get Pamela Webb dismissed for a long time. But Kruger has just learned that Alderman went behind his back in an attempt to enlist Mrs. Kruger in this campaign."

"He must be everybody's little friend," Gene remarked.

"There's more. The political polls that alerted Kruger were discovered by Pamela Webb, which has inspired a full-scale vendetta against her. Even worse, there was another row with Kruger this morning. As Alderman stormed out, Hodiak overheard him saying Kruger couldn't fire him because he had plenty on Kruger."

Gene Fleming's imagination was fired. "My God, that could be anything from a convivial weekend to seeing Kruger shoot Matsuda."

At the moment, Thatcher was more interested in Bennet Alderman than in the sins of his employer.

"Alderman has devoted years of his life to making Kruger his entry ticket to the White House. If anybody tries to take that ticket away from him, he's ready to attack without compunction. Now, what would his reaction be if an insignificant Japanese clerk suddenly became an obstacle?"

Fleming nodded. "I see your point. In his case, the stakes might be so high he'd flake out. And if Alderman lost his head, he could have Ushiba's corpse on his hands before he knew it. Was that physically possible?"

"As Alderman and Ali Khan did not know the afternoon session had been rescheduled, they arrived early. While Khan was working with the staff to prepare for his lecture, Alderman was out of everybody's sight."

Gene Fleming was trying to put himself in Alderman's shoes, but the exercise was too much for him.

"If I had gotten away with killing Ushiba," he said doubtfully, "I sure as hell wouldn't risk that attack on Matsuda. Not when it puts me front and center as a suspect."

Thatcher promptly demolished this reasoning.

"Only because things went wrong. If Alderman had slipped back to his room and a dead Matsuda had been discovered at seven o'clock in the morning, the field would have been wide open."

But Fleming had now become a devil's advocate.

"Not after Alderman had just threatened to choke the truth out of Matsuda."

"In a public place with witnesses," Thatcher said dryly. "That, if anything, placed him with those who wanted Matsuda to speak — as opposed to someone determined to silence him permanently."

His back to the wall, Fleming was prepared to concede some merit to Thatcher's argument. "And the Japanese would love it," he pointed out. "Because it gives them an American not only reacting with violence but doing so for selfish reasons. It would confirm their gut instincts."

"And what about your instincts?" Thatcher asked, genuinely curious.

"Maybe they've brainwashed me, but I feel the same way. In fact, there's only one Japanese I could begin to see as the killer."

"Iwamoto?"

"Hell, no! I'm talking about Mr. Arai. He didn't get where he is by being submissive to group loyalties. Oh, he's lived down his past, and he's bright enough to affect a super-

Japanese personal life. On state occasions you see pictures of him in a kimono, surrounded by his descendants. The older he gets, the better it looks."

Thatcher was not convinced. "Are you serious?"

"I admit that I have a tendency to see Arai's fine hand behind too much," Fleming replied. "Bennet Alderman makes a more plausible murderer. He had a lot to lose, he's half crazy on the subject, and he was right at the scene of the crime. What's more, now that he's declared war on Kruger, Hodiak, and Pamela Webb, it won't be just the Japanese who favor that solution."

But Gene Fleming had forgotten that Japanese xenophobia had been superseded by Japanese self-interest. In Tokyo a report was being made to select members of the Diet.

"Mr. Matsuda claims he was shot by an unknown assailant. He strongly suspects the Americans."

"That is no longer satisfactory," Minister Sato said severely. "It may even be counterproductive. We are now dealing with an internal problem."

The opposition papers were suffering an embarrassment of riches. Half the front pages covered the Matsuda shooting, while the other half were devoted to the judgment against Shima.

"The United States government," said one legislator sourly, "has clearly left the ultimate decision to us. And in view of their strong feelings about export violations, this can only mean they do not wish to figure in these headlines."

A more optimistic note was sounded across the table.

"The opposition, however, may have made a serious mistake. They are giving so much publicity to Shima that a strong step against the company by us could have a very positive effect."

Sato turned accusingly to the bearer of bad tidings. "Has this not been made clear to Mr. Matsuda?" he demanded.

"It is difficult to persuade a man whose doctors permit only fragmentary visits," the emissary apologized. "In addition, I am told that Secretary Matsuda appears deeply suspicious of the overtures made to him."

"*He's* suspicious!" The minister was affronted. "It is Secretary Matsuda who has been taking bribes, not us."

Unfortunately this reminded everyone that the Recruit scandal was the ultimate source of current pressures.

"Yes, yes," they chorused hastily. "But it

is only natural that Mr. Matsuda should seek some assurance as to the future if he admits his past errors."

Like so many politicians, Sato required unimpeachable ethical standards from the senior civil service.

"There can be no question of a public future," he announced grandly.

The emissary had been biding his time until this moment. "Naturally not," he agreed gravely. "However, it did occur to me that under these unique circumstances, an arrangement with the private sector might meet the needs of all parties."

Everyone instantly began to calculate which executive office Yonezawa might be willing to contribute to the commonweal. As no answer could be forthcoming in the absence of Mr. Arai, there was a general disinclination to pursue the topic.

"That is a possibility," said Sato dismissively. "To a certain extent we face the same problem with Shima. The action we take against the company cannot be permanently crippling. When, then, can we plan for them to return to business as usual?"

That was exactly what Len Ridgeway wanted to know.

"Well?" demanded the familiar voice from

Anchorage. "The penalty was just against the subsidiary."

Thatcher explained about the second shoe. "Gene Fleming says it's impossible to predict what action the Japanese government will take. If the Prime Minister were to criticize the Shima Trading Company in one of his upcoming public addresses, then Iwamoto would be expected to resign with a handful of his officers."

Ridgeway had no intention of starting again with a new, and probably nervous, group of Shima executives.

"And when is all this supposed to happen?"

Thatcher's reply was cold comfort.

"There's no telling. I know you like the deal, Len," he continued, "but I wouldn't wait more than ten days. These things can drag on for quite a while."

They already had, as far as Pamela Webb was concerned.

"Hello," said Ali Khan, when she reached Birmingham. "The car's just outside."

Oh, Lord, who needs another long face? she said to herself. But clearly a pep talk was needed. She began cautiously. "This is turning into a real endurance test."

Khan was not as docile as he had once been. "It's turning into a nightmare," he replied sharply. "If I'd known what I was letting my-self in for, I would never have gotten mixed up with Lackawanna. Murder and attempted murder are more than I bargained for."

His self-pity stung her. "Try thinking about others for a change!"

She regretted the outburst instantly. Khan withdrew into offended silence until they reached his car.

"Look, I'm sorry I bit your head off," Pamela said at the first red light. "But you've got to understand that it's really been a pressure cooker in London."

He kept his eyes fixed on the road. "Tell me exactly what happened," he said, reversing their usual roles.

Pamela had always known this might happen. When she first met him, Ali was a raw young genius with everything to learn. Now he was a key figure in a high-stakes business.

"I've got to know what's going on," he told her. "Otherwise there's no way I can make plans for the future."

"It isn't as negative as you may think," she said.

"Let me be the judge of that."

As dispassionately as she could, she described the events leading up to the attempt on Matsuda's life.

"Christ!" he said when she finished.

"Ali, Matsuda wasn't actually killed. They're saying he'll probably recover soon enough to come up for the demonstration."

"Ah, yes, the demonstration," he said bleakly. "That's still going on, is it? And is Bennet Alderman going to be free to attend too?"

In her dealings with Khan, Pamela had come to understand some, but not all, of his thought processes.

"Yes, Bennet will probably be here," she said flatly.

"Once more into the breach," he muttered.

"All we're going to do is concentrate on getting the sale to Yonezawa finalized," she said patiently. "When that's done, we can lean back and brood about everything that's happened. But doing it now is just a distraction. And God knows, we've had enough distractions already."

"If you say so," he said, creating another pool of silence.

When Khan pulled into MR's parking lot, he switched off the ignition but remained sitting. Through the windshield, he studied his creation as if he had never seen it before. MR occupied a small, undistinguished compound.

"Doesn't look like much, does it?" he said reflectively.

"It's what's inside that counts," she said

with matching detachment. "Carl realized that, and so will the Japanese."

"Maybe," he said dubiously. Then, in an abrupt mood change, he shook himself and clambered out of the car.

"Was it your idea to come up early, or did Kruger send you?" he demanded when he joined her.

Khan was both proud and touchy. Without Pamela as intermediary, his relationship with Kruger would have been strained. Her skills did not desert her now.

"Nobody's trying to boss you around," she said, concealing weariness. "The only reason I'm here is to make sure that all the right preparations are in place. This is our last chance, and time is running out."

"I think time has already run out."

"Don't talk like that," she said. "Just be realistic. If we can pull this off, we'll be home free. Once the sale is well and truly made, the Japanese will close the book on what happened in Tokyo."

"Murder and bribes?" he countered stubbornly.

"They've covered up worse and lived happily ever after," she insisted. "And once Carl gets what he wants, things at Lackawanna will simmer down too. You called it a nightmare. Well, nightmares end."

"For Hodiak and Alderman too?" he asked softly.

"I don't know what's going to happen to them," Pamela said unhappily.

Alderman's fate was being decided at that very moment.

"This is the kiss of death as far as I'm concerned," a bald congressman declared in Senator Will Trowbridge's office. "For all we know, they've arrested Alderman by now."

The lawyer from Alexandria had checked with London before setting forth.

"Not yet. They don't have enough of a case."

"Who cares?" demanded the Texan in the corner. "The point is, he got caught at whatever he was doing."

In this group, there was no more unforgivable sin.

"He got caught at more than that," Sam reported. "Apparently Kruger's wise to Benny's moonlighting."

The others looked at Sam with interest.

"Did Alderman tell you this?" Trowbridge asked.

"No."

The single syllable was damning. Their inside man was no longer a reliable conduit of information.

"Then how did you hear about it? We don't have anyone else planted."

"No, but Kruger's ordered a search of Alderman's files, and the news is going through Lackawanna like wildfire. One thing that Bennet never learned is that it doesn't pay to make enemies when you don't have to."

Baldie was growing impatient with trivia. "Then the decision about Alderman has been made for us. His usefulness is over. I'm surprised he hasn't been thrown out on his ear."

"That wouldn't look so hot right now," the Texan reasoned. "I suppose Kruger'll hold off until they're all back from England. Then he'll dump Alderman good and hard."

Sam, also eager to attack the important part of the agenda, shrugged.

"Look, Alderman's not important, and he never has been. The question is, do we forget about Kruger?"

Senator Trowbridge's only personal knowledge of Carl Kruger stemmed from the forty-eight-hour descent on Washington.

"He may look good on paper, but I wasn't all that impressed when I met him. Besides, wherever he goes, bodies start hitting the floor."

"You don't want to be fooled by the clean-cut act," Sam cautioned. "The guy knows how to counterpunch. I admit I thought he was down for good before, and look how he handled Shima. He might pull it off again."

Very few things still had the ability to outrage Trowbridge, but being asked to hurl himself into a meat chopper was one of them.

"You've got to be kidding. Going anywhere near Kruger is too risky."

The Texan agreed. Sad, but resigned, he said: "It's a shame. We won't find anybody else with that recognition value."

Unlike everybody else in the room, Sam was not protecting a political fiefdom. His role in these councils was that of impartial analyst, espousing no cause but giving due weight to every factor. He routinely took every side of an argument.

"That recognition simply means everybody knows about Kruger," he pointed out. "And what they know these days isn't going to do us a hell of a lot of good."

"Not to mention that he's got that blonde with him wherever he goes," Trowbridge grumbled, becoming more negative by the moment.

The Texan prided himself on keeping up with the times. "Nobody cares about that anymore if it's handled right. Kruger could square things by marrying her. No, what bothers me is Alderman."

"But we've settled that. We're cutting him

off," Trowbridge insisted.

"Yeah, but he can still spell trouble. We don't have any idea what he was up to. Of course I don't know him," the Texan said, reminding the others that they were responsible for bringing Alderman into the fold, "but you all say he's got big ambitions. He could have been cutting a deal of his own with the Japs. Maybe he wanted to get his hands on some of those big bucks in Tokyo."

Trowbridge stiffened. "Come on! I figure he got overeager. Benny was hot to bring Kruger back a hero. So he stepped out of line trying to make it a sure thing. God knows what he got involved in, but he wouldn't set up for himself."

"Why not? That's what he was doing with Kruger." The soft drawl continued with unimpeachable logic. "For Chrissake, Will, we didn't tell him to start running around, meeting Japs at midnight — with or without a gun."

Like so many other Olympians looking down at the activities of mortals, Senator Trowbridge had never thought to see himself on that lowly plane. The possibility that Bennet Alderman had been no more loyal to him than to Carl Kruger was hard to swallow.

"I don't see it," he said stubbornly. "Benny was real shook up when Paul's crowd started that smear campaign. He lost his head completely."

Noting this reaction, Sam smiled thinly.

"Nonetheless it's a valid point, Will. Kruger could be hit by some of Alderman's dirt at any time. It would be silly to take a chance like that."

"Then thank God we did it my way. I was never crazy about a dark horse in the first place. But if we'd approached Kruger directly, pulling out would cost us. Now nobody outside this room has to know. . . ."

As Trowbridge continued shoring up his self-esteem, the Texan picked up a pad and drew a thick black line through the name of Carl Kruger.

Chapter 28

The postponement of the MR hearings had left most of its cast in a state of suspended animation, but John Thatcher was pleased to find his own extra time in London being exploited for worthwhile ends. Toby Lemieux was not only systematically canvassing possible Japanese acquisitions; he had injected the Thatcher presence into several all-British negotiations.

Gene Fleming responded to this challenge with a last-minute coup of his own. Like a magician producing a rabbit out of the hat, he dangled the French representative to the IFMA.

"But why?" Thatcher asked, upon being informed of the appointment.

Motorcycles, he was told, were only one facet of Raoul Thibault's activities.

"These days he's the biggest wholesaler of china in France."

"So naturally he knows every manufacturer in the country?"

Fleming was smug. "Including a small family firm that's run out of descendants."

The subsequent hour was a lesson to Thatcher. He had always assumed that Gene Fleming was an eccentric in the world of motorcycling, a sober man of affairs surrounded by leather-jacketed fanatics. But Monsieur Raoul Thibault disabused him of that notion. A stocky man with glistening dark eyes, Thibault discoursed learnedly about the distinction between earthenware and porcelain, about varying admixtures of ash and clay, about rival traditions in Limoges and Staffordshire, Dresden and Nanking.

While he necessarily appreciated the commercial value of dinnerware, Thibault reserved his real approval for ornamental pieces. Antoine Poirier et Fils, he said, had been producing vases and urns and figurines for a hundred and fifty years.

"But Léon's health is forcing him to consider retirement," he added sadly.

Nor did Thibault's helpfulness end there. He could name the Poirier bankers, estimate the firm's annual gross, and make a shrewd guess about net profits.

"Very timely," Thatcher observed as they were returning to Tudor House. "Toby will be able to get to work on this right away."

"And if we should ever be thinking in terms of European insurance companies," Fleming said blandly, "we could do worse than consult the IFMA rep from West Germany."

It was a humbling reminder that virtually any extracurricular activity could prove useful to a working banker. But then simply existing and moving about ensured contacts of some nature. As they crossed the entrance arcade, lined with boutiques and other gilded offerings, they met Audrey Kruger, emerging from the beauty salon.

"Oh, you're still here," she said. "I thought you'd gone to Birmingham with the rest of them."

"We're not leaving until this afternoon," Thatcher replied.

"What a shame! They could use some dilution."

In fact, the Sloan contingent had cunningly ascertained Lackawanna's travel plans before making its own. Now Thatcher was doubly grateful for his foresight.

"What with the police leaving us alone and the press finally beginning to thin out," she continued, "I thought I could get Carl calmed down before he left. But there's just so much I can do when these fax people let everybody read everybody else's mail."

Fair-mindedly Thatcher tried to defend the fax station. "If Alderman is going to crumple his messages and leave them on the counter, it really isn't their fault."

"I'm not talking about the note that either came from Mr. Matsuda or didn't, and who cares anyway?" she replied with uncharacteristic fretfulness. "I'm talking about —"

In the midst of her irritation she stopped short, clearly debating whether Thatcher and Fleming were appropriate confidants. Audrey Kruger might babble nonstop, but Thatcher could not recall indiscretions about Lackawanna.

Her second thoughts had reminded her of the worldwide publicity surrounding Tudor House.

"I suppose everybody knows by now that Carl was mad at Bennet."

"I was privileged to witness Alderman's reaction," Thatcher said dryly. "That was when he and Hodiak went to the mat. And your husband has since told me that he's beginning to fear Alderman might have had a hand in bribing MITI."

In the face of this comprehensive knowledge, Audrey had no qualms about continuing.

"That's why Carl had some kind of report on Bennet's work sent over. But the fax people let Bennet get his hands on it first. And Carl didn't need the extra annoyance."

Thatcher could mount only qualified sympathy. Life should have taught Audrey her limitations. She could send her husband forth in fighting trim; she could not insulate him from the buffetings of fate.

"Well, your husband will have turned his mind to selling MR by the time we all gather tomorrow."

"At least Carl is in good physical shape. He's even been going swimming, though I don't know how he can bear to use that pool," she said with an involuntary shudder. "Just look at *him!*"

Mr. Tomaheko Matsuda had been unloaded from a limousine and supported through the front doors. His progress across the lobby was halting, his face pallid, his left arm obscured by a bulky and complex sling. Although he looked like a candidate for a rehabilitation center, he was swift to announce his intentions.

"Ah, Mr. Thatcher, Mr. Fleming. I thought everybody had already departed for our session. I am looking forward to it with great interest. And Mrs. Kruger too. You are not accompanying your husband?"

"I'd just be in the way," she replied automatically. "But you mustn't stand around like this; you're not well. And — pardon me — should you be going to Birmingham at all?"

Matsuda, clearly fresh from some victory

over Japanese bureaucracy, was kindly. "My doctors have assured me that I am ready to resume my duties," he explained.

Part of his tolerance was probably due to Mrs. Kruger's womanly behavior. Thatcher suspected that it was easier on a conservative Japanese than Pamela Webb's efficient grasp of corporate finance.

"Actually that wasn't what I meant," she rejoined. "Aren't you afraid someone will try to shoot you again?"

Even this bluntness failed to puncture Matsuda's self-satisfaction.

"My wife, too, suffers from these alarms," he explained grandly to Thatcher. "That is because she does not understand the situation. It was incautious of me to intrude upon a clandestine meeting. But as I no longer constitute a threat, there is no reason to anticipate further violence."

That might be Matsuda's interpretation; it was certainly not that of his watchdogs. They were standing on either side of their charge, vigilantly scanning the lobby.

"I need not say how happy we all are to see you recovered," Thatcher said. "And we certainly hope you are correct about the future."

"There is no alternative explanation," Matsuda declared. "I blame myself for not realizing that the forces unleashed in Tokyo could represent a danger to the most innocent by-stander."

If there were misgivings about his physical safety, there was roaring doubt about his innocence. That, of course, was a subject upon which even Audrey Kruger was not going to venture.

Without a flicker, Thatcher retreated into generalities. "We can only be grateful there have been no tragic consequences."

Even stray Americans were receiving the Matsuda accolade. "I have forwarded my expression of appreciation to the hotel guest who acted so promptly in my behalf. Without him I fear the results might have been quite different."

By now it was only too apparent that tomorrow they were all going to have a bellyful of Matsuda as gracious higher being.

"And will we have the pleasure of traveling by the same train with you?" Thatcher asked, prepared to take evasive action.

But there was no need for concern.

"I am afraid not. My surgeon has advised me that it will be less of a strain to go by limousine. Indeed, you will have to excuse me now," he said, consulting his watch. "I still have to ensure that my papers are packed properly."

* * *

"He sure doesn't act frightened," Fleming admitted as they made their way to their rooms.

Thatcher fell back on the opinion of an expert. "Inspector Hayakawa says Matsuda doesn't factor violence into his analysis of the situation."

"That's what Hayakawa said before the shooting," Fleming pointed out. "Anybody who's been hospitalized by a gunshot wound has had the possibility brought to his attention."

"I would certainly think so."

"All things considered, Matsuda is carrying this off better than I expected. Of course everybody in Japan is learning new tricks."

As they emerged from the elevator, Thatcher demanded an explanation.

"Before Recruit, there were certain givens," said Fleming. "Now it's a new ball game. If the Japanese hadn't been in the middle of that scandal, our troubles would have been handled far more discreetly."

"You're not forgetting they had a bloody corpse in an MITI office? They couldn't just ignore it."

Fleming cocked his head. "No, but they wouldn't have let it shape government policy."

When they arrived at Thatcher's door, he was trying to imagine the murder of Mr.

Ushiba and the attack on Mr. Matsuda in a less frenzied context.

But Fleming was already moving on. "The two-forty seems to be safe. We still taking it?"

"Yes, of course," said Thatcher, fumbling for his key. "I'll meet you downstairs in twenty minutes."

As Thatcher proceeded with his packing, he reverted to Matsuda's serene dismissal of physical peril. What could make him so confident? Surely, after the happenings in Tokyo and London, any man privy to the identity of the briber had cause for alarm.

Methodically stowing shirts and underwear, Thatcher continued to speculate. But try as he would, he could produce only one explanation.

"It doesn't make sense," he muttered to himself. "Or rather, if it does make sense, then nothing else does."

But the clock was ticking, and he sternly put the entire problem from his mind. With his two-suiter deposited by the door, he attacked his attaché case. He was just lowering its lid when he discovered, to his annoyance, that there had been a fresh delivery while he was out.

Miss Corsa had embraced the fax era with such gusto that a nonstop stream of documentation followed in her employer's wake. The net result of this modern technology was that he had to find space in an already bulging case. Somewhere else in Tudor House, he reflected, Mr. Matsuda was similarly encumbering himself with useless and time-consuming paperwork.

In a spirit of rebellion, Thatcher began to reverse his movements. But even as he did so, his subconscious speculations began to bear fruit.

"Good God!" he exclaimed, jerking upright in the act of consigning a memo to the wastebasket. "But that would make everything simple."

Too simple, perhaps?

Thatcher shook his head. He had listened to Haru Fleming analyzing the concept of *uchi* and her husband emphasizing the importance of Recruit. And, naturally, these two crafty Japanologists were absolutely right. But they had not gone far enough.

Thatcher could think of another solution. Since it would upset a major applecart, the prudent man would neither voice fanciful theories nor dismiss them. Instead he would acquire supporting evidence. Happily, in the sea of Midland Research paper there was one unexamined document that had no doubt been printed in bulk, filed in triplicate, and made available on demand.

To think of it was to reach for the phone.

Five seconds later, Mr. Matsuda, courteous as ever, was sounding baffled.

"Mr. Ushiba's report? Yes, of course it was introduced into the record. And I would be happy to provide Mr. Fleming with a copy, if you feel it would be of help. But I should warn you that . . ."

As Thatcher listened to the familiar refrain about poor Ushiba's lack of the smarts, he realized there was a long road ahead. The report might provide an indication. By cudgeling his brains, he might slowly amass further corroboration.

But the participants in this drama were not interchangeable robots. They were living people with very human concerns. Don Hodiak had to deal with a problem wife, Mr. Arai had to rewrite his buccaneer past, Pamela Webb had to live with gossip. And men and women do predictable things. When moving to exposed positions, they try to shield themselves. Could protection, in this case, have taken a time-honored form?

Every now and then a poker player is actually dealt a royal flush. Overcome by the possibility that he might strike it lucky, Thatcher could barely produce farewell remarks for Matsuda before dialing again.

"Toby?" he said. "A wild idea has crossed my mind, and I'd like your people to check it out."

Chapter 29

"But we don't need a dress rehearsal, Carl; we've already had one," Ali Khan insisted within hours of the arrival of the Lackawanna team. "The actual demonstration will be exactly what we did for Kwai Dong. Of course Pamela says she has to have some alterations, but those just affect the presentation."

Pamela sounded long-suffering. "There have to be changes because you were busy setting up municipal appointments when Dong was here. You ought to welcome them, Ali; they put you front and center."

"I don't object. I'm simply explaining that I can't be everywhere at once. You want me for the changes, Carl wants me to run a rehearsal, and on top of everything else, that producer wants me."

"Just a minute!" Kruger held up a hand as he scented an opportunity to solve one of his minor problems. "What producer?"

"It's big news here when the Japanese and the head of Lackawanna come to town," Ali explained. "The TV people are coming out to MR this evening to prepare for their coverage tomorrow, and the papers are asking for some kind of handout. God knows who I'll get to do that."

Bennet Alderman, sitting slightly apart from his colleagues, raised his head automatically at the mention of television, but Carl Kruger gave him no chance to speak.

"There's no reason for you to bother about publicity, Ali. Not when we have a PR expert here."

Ali, who had witnessed the press circus in Tokyo, made things absolutely clear. "This isn't worldwide coverage by CBS, Carl. This is just a local feature. I don't know why they have to come out today, but I suppose they know what they're doing. Anyway, I don't have time to hold their hands."

"Of course. You go right ahead and work out those details with Pamela. Bennet will go over to MR this evening to take care of the TV people."

"Absolutely," said Alderman, rising and moving to the door. "And while I'm there, I'll see about that press release too."

No one was more gratified by his departure than Don Hodiak. "Well, at least you've gotten him out of our hair for tonight," he said in tones of congratulation.

Pamela drew her own inference.

"You must have had a merry train trip together," she suggested.

Carl Kruger grimaced.

"It was easy in London," he said. "Bennet was always with the police or the lawyers. God knows what we're going to do with him now that we've got him full time."

"There's always Lackawanna U.K.," Pamela reminded him. "Maybe you should decide they need an expert PR man too."

Then she briskly returned to her chief preoccupation. "Come on, Ali," she invited. "Let's find someplace private and get to work. It may take quite a while."

"That's not a bad idea," Kruger mused after they had both gone. "I mean about saddling U.K. with Bennet."

"Have the police decided he didn't shoot Matsuda?"

Kruger shrugged. "Hell, Don, they don't seem to know what's going on."

"This should be some meeting. The Japs are stuck with Matsuda, and we've got little Bennet."

For days now Kruger had been deprived of his usual confidants. Pamela Webb had been up north, and Alderman was no longer one of the faithful. Insensibly Kruger had begun turning to Don Hodiak.

"Even if Bennet is telling the truth about the shooting," Kruger continued, "I don't like the other things he's up to. Did you know he got hold of Johnson's report before I did?"

Without any ulterior motive, Hodiak grumbled: "Privacy is getting harder and harder to find."

"You can say that again." Kruger's eyebrows drew together in a forbidding line. "You heard Bennet say he had something on me, didn't you? I thought I saw you in the hall."

Hodiak was uncomfortable. "That's all I heard," he said gruffly.

"Bennet's got a one-track mind," said Kruger with a twisted smile. "Look, I'm not a chaser, Don, but I'm no saint, either. He knows about a couple of weekends when I forgot myself. No big deal."

Nodding, Hodiak said deliberately: "He never gives up. Right now Bennet's trying to dig up dirt on Pamela. He thinks that if she's got something going on the side, that'll be the end of her."

"For Chrissake, I don't give a damn what she does on her own time," Kruger blurted. "But that doesn't mean I want to read the details any more than I want to know about your troubles."

Hodiak was content to let the matter drop. "Well, by this time tomorrow, the pressure will be off. Then we can get back to business as usual. You eating in the hotel?"

"No," said Kruger without elaboration. "I have something on."

Two hours later, he was smiling lazily as he accepted a drink in a house set well beyond the urban sprawl of Birmingham. Mr. Arai, after Tudor House had placed him cheek by jowl with an assassin, had decided to distance himself. He was perched on the extreme edge of an overstuffed chair covered with a faded floral chintz. Echoing this theme on the far wall, a magnificent bouquet was reflected in a gilt mirror. Its profusion of color, variety, and form was a tribute to the English cutting garden and an offense to every Japanese aesthetic standard. Furthermore, it was all too apparent that the Yonezawa commissariat had been left behind. On Kruger's arrival, a maid coming through the service door had been accompanied by a tantalizing aroma of roast beef. And Mr. Arai, like everyone present, was drinking Scotch. There had been no suggestion that anything else was available.

Kruger leaned back at his ease and listened to his host. Mr. Arai spoke at some length before permitting the translator to take over, but the only material fact emerged at the end of his discourse.

"Mr. Matsuda's caution, normally an admirable characteristic, is now entirely misplaced. He is considering our proposal."

"Maybe he's reluctant to make a vital decision while he's still weak," Kruger suggested.

Arai sipped his drink with catlike fastidiousness while he weighed this possibility.

"No," he decided. "The man has been released by the hospital. There can be no medical grounds for his hesitation."

Kruger was not so sure. Earlier that afternoon he had witnessed Matsuda's arrival at the hotel. The watchdogs seemed to have begun playing the role of male nurses. For that matter, Arai himself was showing signs of the extended strain.

Little by little, an atmosphere of geriatric frailty was engulfing the MR hearings. It was not the ideal background for a thrilling demonstration of groundbreaking technology. In a brief spurt of nostalgia, Kruger remembered Pamela Webb and Ali jogging into the Tokyo Hilton. Tomorrow's critical gathering could certainly use an injection of youthful vitality.

Youthful high spirits had no place on Pamela Webb's agenda as she painstakingly reviewed detail after detail.

"And you're sure everything is set?" she asked in one final omnibus caution.

"Absolutely," said Ali with growing confidence. "Everything at MR has been taken care of."

She frowned. "Remember, we won't get a second chance this time."

"And we won't need one. As a matter of fact, it's an advantage to be doing it in Birmingham. I wish you'd stop worrying."

"What a hope!" The frown was replaced by a rueful grimace. "I won't stop worrying until we've pulled it off."

Ten miles away, there was another worrier.

"This could make a big difference," Rick Iwamoto said unnecessarily.

His chief mechanic was making no promises. "Race results cannot be guaranteed. From what I have seen, we have a very good chance."

"A big victory could have an impact in Tokyo," Iwamoto said, talking more to himself than to his companion. "Shima needs some favorable publicity. If we have a first-place finish, I will accept the trophy personally."

The mechanic thought that would be appropriate even in the absence of larger issues, but he contented himself with saying:

"Certainly, Mr. Iwamoto. In the meantime, we've finished tuning up the SR-10, and I thought you might wish to look at it."

Iwamoto, striding toward the sheds, paused. "Not right now. But later on, after I've talked with Kanakura, I might take it out for a spin."

Carl Kruger was not the only one with dinner plans that did not include his subordinates.

"I'll be dining out," Thatcher announced.

"Fine," said Gene Fleming absently, his eyes glued to the traffic light on Hagley Road.

A leisurely stroll after their train trip had seemed like a good idea, but they had not bargained for the obstacles to pedestrian movement. Nearby was a complex highway interchange, but that failed to explain the clotted traffic streaming before them.

"I don't think I've ever seen such a density of motorcycles," Thatcher observed as a group of at least thirty helmeted riders gunned past. "Is Birmingham the home of British cycling?"

"For the next three days it is. The All Midland Rally starts tomorrow. It's got everything — even an event to showcase the new racing models," explained Fleming, waxing rhapsodic. "There are motorcycle clubs coming to attend from all over the country. You don't know what you're missing."

"And I intend to go on missing it," Thatcher said firmly. "But at least I don't have to feel that I'm abandoning you for the evening."

"Far from it." Fleming grinned. "I'll go out

to the track and see how things are shaping."

When they returned to their hotel, both men changed clothes. Thatcher, after a long summer day, decided on a shower and a clean shirt. He emerged to find that Gene Fleming had discarded his banker's suit in favor of a windbreaker and fatigues. Apparently notables of the motorcycle world were just plain folk when not carrying out official duties.

As for himself, Thatcher knew he was on duty, even if the schedule called for an informal dinner in a small Pakistani restaurant.

"This place is owned by Mr. Khan's father," Inspector Hayakawa said, rising from a corner booth to greet his guest.

Thatcher examined his surroundings with new interest. The tables in the center of the room were occupied by large parties. The high-backed booths along the walls contained couples and foursomes. The crowd included a broad range of local residents.

"It seems to be popular."

"They say the food is good and inexpensive. But the Khans own a fancier restaurant out in the suburbs."

This display of omniscience was clearly deliberate.

"Have you been getting background on everybody?"

"Insofar as possible. For instance, did you

know that your Mr. Fleming acquired a house in Hawaii last year that is valued at" — Hayakawa consulted a small notebook, then continued ominously — "at close to one million dollars?"

Thatcher might play the admiring layman in a discussion of the Khans, but not in one about Sloan personnel.

"The date is misleading, Inspector," he said calmly. "True, Fleming built the house last year, but he acquired the land — Maui oceanfront — almost twenty years ago. Naturally it has been an outstanding investment."

Unmoved by this tale of financial wizardry, Hayakawa jotted a note and murmured: "That explains it. The timing was wrong anyway."

Thatcher yielded to curiosity.

"And what do you have on me?"

"Widower, three children with their own families, expenditures within your income," Hayakawa recited. "From a police point of view, you are unpromising material."

"I'm glad to hear it," said Thatcher sedately. "But according to your thinking the other day, all this information is irrelevant. A cover-up of corporate misconduct would not necessarily be reflected in sudden affluence."

Hayakawa waited until a burst of noise from a large group celebrating some team victory abated. "That is why I wished to consult you. My thinking has changed. This afternoon I was received by Mr. Arai, who is puzzled by the latest turn of events. A very lucrative position at Yonezawa has been offered to Mr. Matsuda that would permit his tactful resignation from the ministry."

"And he has refused?"

"He has said that he requires time to consider the offer thoroughly."

Thatcher was relieved to hear that Mr. Arai was capable of perplexity. He did not, however, expect Hayakawa to share his appreciation.

"Inspector, Mr. Matsuda must recognize the danger of violence now."

Hayakawa recanted some of his earlier beliefs.

"Of course he does. But he still assumes that he intruded on a secret meeting and his presence constituted a danger. I do not agree."

Thatcher realized that he and the inspector, although starting from different points, were slowly converging on the same conclusion.

"You did say that the door to the swimming pool was closed?" he prodded.

"Exactly. When Mr. Matsuda opened that door, he was silhouetted by the night light in the corridor, and he was shot within one pace. There was no time for the murderer to notice distinctions in outline or movement. He shot the moment he had a target."

Thatcher was more than ready to complete the thought. "Which means that Bennet Alderman was the intended victim."

"And this is what I find bewildering. Why should anyone wish to kill Alderman? Yonezawa could brush aside anything he said. And while he has enemies at Lackawanna, his days there are numbered. He is too insignificant to be a threat to the interests involved."

"Just like Mr. Ushiba," Thatcher murmured.

Hayakawa was startled.

"Yes," he agreed warily. "Just like Mr. Ushiba. You are not suggesting that *he* was murdered by mistake? He was attacked in his own well-lighted office."

"No, I am suggesting we have misconstrued the forces involved."

The inspector was not lightly relinquishing his only sheet anchor.

"But the basic situation — MR's sale to Yonezawa — is what defines those forces."

"Not entirely. I suspect we have overlooked what might have been obvious in the United States."

Hayakawa was so incredulous that Thatcher waited for the remains of their curry to be removed before expounding his theory. When he finished, the expression on the inspector's face was not encouraging.

"Extraordinary," Hayakawa said severely, more as an indictment of the behavior outlined than of the reasoning followed. "And, I must point out, nothing but sheer speculation."

Thatcher was beginning to think that the inspector would rather have an unsolved murder than a world containing unruly human beings.

"True, but proof is available. And very quick proof, if I am right about one point that the Sloan's London branch is checking. Thank God we're in England."

Still ruffled, Hayakawa retreated into chauvinism.

"It would be equally simple in Japan."

As a concession to international harmony, Thatcher not only yielded the point; he did it generously.

"Only in my own disorderly country would we face an insurmountable problem," he admitted.

After days with hostile authorities, followed by a journey with outright adversaries, Bennet Alderman was delighted to spend a few hours in an atmosphere of normalcy, doing the work he did best. Even the inevitable pinpricks were a source of satisfaction, proving as they did the necessity for his expert touch.

This need became apparent as soon as he pulled into the Midland Research yard. The small strip of executive parking immediately outside the offices had been entirely pre-empted by the television crew. As he strolled back from the employees' lot at the opposite end of the compound, Alderman reminded himself to see that this error was not repeated in the morning, when that space must be reserved for more distinguished guests.

Inside, he found more to criticize. The TV personnel were wandering at will, issuing their commands in a lordly manner while MR clerks scurried to obey. Mentally rolling up his sleeves, Alderman took charge.

"You realize that we can't have the proceedings tomorrow disrupted. You'll be able to take footage of the robotics demonstration but not of the meeting. As for your background clips, they should be filmed tonight."

The producer, condemned to a life of local features, rarely got his hands on an international celebrity, and he wanted as much mileage as possible.

"We're hoping to start with an introductory statement by Mr. Kruger himself, explaining the applications of MR's technology. I've prepared some remarks —"

"Let me see," said Alderman, stretching out

one hand for the script and reaching for his editorial pen with the other.

It was a busy and productive evening. The crew was harried into doing all its outside work and as many interior shots as possible. Beautiful phrases were formed to issue from the mouths of Carl Kruger and Ali Khan. Guidelines were prepared to ensure that the visitors would not be disturbed.

"You can film them as they arrive and when they shake hands at the end of the meeting. Other than that, you can only catch them incidentally during the demo," Alderman said crisply.

"I was planning for a few words from Yonezawa and MITI," the producer protested.

"Mr. Arai and Mr. Matsuda speak only Japanese."

This aspect of the international scene had never occurred to the producer.

By the time Bennet Alderman was ready to call it a day, it was almost eight-thirty and the summer sun was sinking toward the horizon. But the film crew was packing up, and a press release was in final draft.

"You'll have to stay on and get this typed," he told the only remaining secretary. "It should be ready for distribution first thing in the morning."

She looked at the much emended script for which the producer was waiting and said resignedly: "Yes, Mr. Alderman."

"You toddle along," the producer said. "I'll be going myself as soon as she has my copy ready."

"Fine," agreed Alderman, who had no intention of wasting his time on empty ceremony. "See you tomorrow morning."

Once outside, he took a deep breath of the balmy evening air, hooked his suit jacket over his shoulder, and began trudging back to his car. When he entered the long alley formed by the concrete loading docks on one side and the blank facade of the high-temperature testing laboratory on the other, he was walking due westward. Behind him, his shadow cast an elongated streak across the yard, ahead of him, the sun shone directly into his eyes.

The sound of an approaching motorcycle had accompanied his progress, but like everyone else in Birmingham, Bennet Alderman had learned to discount a noise that was engulfing the entire area. Even the roar of acceleration did not attract his attention until the charging cyclist loomed into sight at the end of the alley. Already halfway along its length, his eyes dazzled by the golden aureole outlining the intruder, Alderman reacted instinctively. Leaping sideways, he stumbled against a loading dock and fell to the ground.

The end came quickly. For only an instant he was conscious of the foreshortened monstrosity bearing down on him. Then its menacing blackness swelled to gigantic proportions, blotting out the sun, the sky, and life itself.

Chapter 30

The second motorcyclist arrived at the brow of the hill just in time to witness Bennet Alderman's death. Although he did not know it, Gene Fleming was occupying the spot from which the murderer had conned the MR compound, impatiently waiting for his victim to emerge. Now it was Fleming who had a bird's-eye view. He saw the killer race through a rear gate and swerve onto a lower road, he saw figures rushing from a building toward the crumpled body. Appalled by what he had observed, unconsciously impelled by the motor throbbing between his knees, Fleming plunged down the hillside to give chase.

As soon as he rounded the first curve, his quarry was alerted to the pursuit. The distant helmet turned once, the hunched figure crouched even lower, the banshee wail of the engine strained into a higher note.

Twenty years in the world of motorcycles had made Gene Fleming an expert. He knew that he was trying to overtake a machine that was heavier and more powerful than his own. Balancing his handicap, however, was the fact that he was, by far, the more skillful cyclist. On a twisting secondary road, he could close the gap.

"So he'll head for the nearest highway," Fleming muttered to himself.

But after ten minutes he began to appreciate the strategy that was unfolding. They were closing in on the one area of Birmingham with which he was familiar — the speedway that he had left only half an hour earlier.

It was not difficult to understand the choice. As a final burst of speed brought the whole duty area into view, Fleming could see hundreds of motorcyclists milling around. His adversary, already well camouflaged, no doubt intended to work his way through the crowd and slip out by some other road.

Fleming, however, knew every inch of this terrain. Instead of wasting time on a futile search, he swept around the perimeter. The fleeing rider might be just another indistinguishable speck in a sea of uniformity, but that motorcycle was as individual to Gene Fleming as any face could have been. And the very same aficionados who were providing cover for a killer formed a knowledgeable body of witnesses.

"Have you seen my mate?" he called out. "He's on a vintage Harley with crash bars and a fiber fairlee."

At his first stops, the inquiry evoked only blank stares. At the third, there was instant heated response.

"That sod practically crashed into my bike," a grimy youth complained. "Why the bloody hell doesn't he learn to ride!"

Fleming sped off, satisfied that he had gained precious seconds by his tactics. He realized that he was going to need that edge when he caught sight of the familiar black machine on a level, unimpeded road.

Twilight was deepening with every passing moment as they raced east. Calling on his rudimentary knowledge of the environs, Fleming had a sinking feeling that he knew their objective. The Harley was now perceptibly lengthening its lead. If it could break contact long enough to arrive at Birmingham's major interchange, the chase would be over.

In broad outline this fear was justified; in detail it was erroneous. Unknown to Gene, there was a minor version of the larger junction a good deal closer.

"Christ!" he snarled as he skidded to a halt at a five-way rotary.

In the spirit of staking all on one throw, he swerved onto the broadest road. Within seconds he knew this was a mistake. Night had now fallen. To make matters worse, the clear skies of the afternoon had given way to thickening clouds, with no single gleam of moonlight. Ahead he could see the twinkling of many headlights. It no longer made any difference whether or not this was the right road. Without the familiar silhouette of the Harley to guide him, Fleming was defeated by the traffic. He sped back to the rotary and, this time, shot down the narrowest road.

In less than a mile it degenerated into a twisting, hilly lane. The lone headlight that became visible from atop the first rise could have been anything.

"All I need now is some teenager out for a joyride."

But in his bones Fleming knew that solitary adolescents gun their machines on good roads. It requires the spark of competition to take suicidal risks at night. And Fleming, his experienced eye glued on that wavering beam, could read its message clearly. The rider was pressing his motorcycle beyond his ability to control it, and every turn was now being taken by guess and by God.

As the chase continued, however, Gene's conviction lessened. If he had been the one in flight, he would have ducked into one of the many side tracks and doused his headlamp. With a lurching stomach he began to wonder if he himself had unwittingly become the spark igniting some mindless seventeen-year-old.

But when he climbed to the next crest of the lane, his doubts evaporated. That will-o'-the-wisp beam of light had vanished. Ahead there was nothing but stygian blackness.

Moderating his speed, Fleming for the first time realized that he was not in a deserted wilderness. He had been so intent on the chase that he had failed to register the background roar of heavy traffic. Somewhere, not too far distant, there were all the sound effects of urban movement — the acceleration of diesel trucks, the squealing of brakes, the hooting of emergency vehicles.

Maybe this was the explanation for their lunatic pace. The helmeted rider had been determined to reach a particular cut-off. He would remain immobile until Fleming was gone, then scoot off to merge into that unseen stream.

His ears cocked for any betraying noise, his eyes straining to penetrate the night, Fleming pressed on, examining a multitude of exits. In one sense his task was easy. All the tracks led uphill from the near side of the road, while to his right the ground fell away steeply. In another sense, it was hopeless. He was simply looking at a series of black holes. After several miles Gene was ready to admit failure and turn around.

"I just hope there's a sign for the speedway

somewhere," he muttered as he pondered the problem of finding his way.

But he forgot all about directions when he caught sight of a smashed guardrail. Sitting in the middle of a tight turn, it told its own story. Someone, driving too quickly, had lost control.

Coasting to a halt, Fleming took the precaution of angling the beam of his headlight downward. But even with this assistance, he could barely discern, through a tangle of scraggly bushes and stunted trees, the blurred shape some fifteen or twenty yards below. He slid down the scree into the shadowy murk, grasping at branches to brake his progress. The light was barely sufficient to reveal that there was no rider on the smashed motorcycle.

"Anybody here?"

When no answer came, Gene was inspired by a sudden doubt. This accident could have happened hours ago. Precariously balancing himself with one hand on the saddle of the machine, he ran his other over its outline. Yes, there were the crash bars, the heavy fiber screen, the unmistakable bulk of an older Harley.

"Anybody here?" he called again before recognizing the futility of his action.

If the rider had not been seriously injured, he was making his getaway from the scene.

Otherwise he was probably unconscious, somewhere in the dark.

A very sober Gene Fleming scrambled up the hillside, remounted, and sped back several miles before finding a public phone. Tensely he dialed the emergency number, reported his discovery, and promised to wait for the police. With a sigh of relief at the prospect of re-inforcements, he began to cradle the receiver.

When it slipped in his grasp, he looked down and saw that his left hand was covered with fresh blood.

Shortly after ten o'clock John Thatcher and his companion returned to the Albany. They had barely cleared the threshold before the desk clerk produced an artificial smile and greeted them across the width of the lobby.

"Good evening, Mr. Thatcher and Inspector Hayakawa!" he said in clarion tones.

A police constable instantly materialized and shepherded them to a rear office, where a plainclothesman pelted them with questions.

Where had they been? Where was every-body else? Could they vouch for cach othcr from eight o'clock to nine o'clock?

Delaying their own curiosity, they produced an account of their evening.

"The staff of the restaurant will be able to confirm our presence," Thatcher concluded.

"What is this all about?"

The detective had lost interest in them the moment they ceased to be suspects and was already instructing a subordinate to monitor the switchboard. Over his shoulder, he said shortly:

"Mr. Bennet Alderman was run down by a motorcyclist at Midland Research almost two hours ago. It was deliberate murder."

Thatcher and Hayakawa exchanged startled glances.

"We were too slow," Thatcher said regretfully.

The inspector, however, was considering broader issues. Subjecting the scene to a cool professional scrutiny, he said: "In one respect, at least, our killer is a clever man."

Thatcher was not certain he knew what had prompted this remark. "He's had a long run for his money. Is that what you mean?"

"No, I was referring to the fact that each attack has occurred in a different jurisdiction. Superintendent McLeod was so ignorant about the Tokyo background he was also forced to consult me. And now the Birmingham police are in the same position about what happened in London."

But steps had been taken to remedy this situation. Within fifteen minutes, the superintendent was standing in the doorway, his raincoat spangled with moisture from the drizzle now falling. After consulting with his local colleague, he came over to Thatcher and Hayakawa.

"You realize what this means? Matsuda must have been shot by mistake," he said without preliminaries.

"We had come to the same conclusion," Hayakawa agreed. McLeod was still digesting the news that had hauled him to Birmingham.

"Smashing people with motorcycles, for God's sake! If you ask me, our man has gone berserk."

"Possibly, but he retains enough sense to choose his timing," Thatcher demurred. "Everybody in our group seems to be missing."

"Matsuda is the only one in the hotel. He went to his room immediately after dinner, and according to your watchdogs," McLeod said, turning to Hayakawa, "they haven't so much as blinked since then."

Hayakawa nodded. "Under the circumstances, I would accept their assurance."

Both policemen knew that there was nothing like a slipup the first time to keep a surveillance team on its toes.

"As for the others, the desk says that Kruger and Hodiak went out separately. And Arai canceled the reservations for his entire party yesterday morning. He may not even be in Birmingham yet. Then there's Mr. Iwamoto, always circling around the fringe of things. The Shima people have a big crew at the speedway. The first time we called, they said he was somewhere around the track. Now they admit he took a motorcycle out a couple of hours ago."

The last item, delivered in tones of ominous suspicion, convinced Thatcher that this was not the time to volunteer information about the Sloan's own motorcycle enthusiast. With luck it would turn out that Fleming had spent the critical period with some old acquaintances. Fortunately the superintendent had passed on to his own arrangements.

"I'll make my headquarters here, where I can catch the others as they come in," he told the plainclothesman. "So fetch me that witness you've got at the station."

The television producer was understandably sulky when he arrived. After recovering from the initial shock, he had reverted to type. Here was a major news story, Birmingham's biggest crime in years, and he had been stuck in a wretched police station.

"I've already told them everything I know," he protested.

"Now you can tell me," McLeod growled.

"Well, we'd worked for a couple of hours,

setting things up for tomorrow's taping, and —"

This attempt to rattle off his account was stopped in its tracks.

"Wait! Let's go back. Had this session been arranged beforehand?"

"I'd told Mr. Khan we needed to do preliminary work."

McLeod shook his head impatiently.

"Not you! When was it decided that Alderman would join you? After all, he was still in London this morning."

"Oh, I see what you mean. Mr. Kruger sent him over as soon as he found out about the coverage. At least that's what Bennet said. There was a press release to write too."

"Very well. They tell me that Alderman had to walk the length of the yard to reach his car. Why?"

The producer became defensive. "Look, they told us to go to the administration building, so we parked there. I noticed that we took all the spaces, but I didn't expect anybody else to be coming."

"A very natural thing to do." Now that McLeod had his witness rolling, he became benign. "So you worked for several hours. Were there any phone calls for Alderman? Did he tell anyone when he was planning to leave?"

But the television crew had taken over more

than executive parking.

"We were on the phone all the time, calling back and forth to the studio. I don't remember Bennet using it at all. You could ask the girl."

The superintendent knew that the secretary had been heavily sedated.

"I suppose that Alderman didn't say anything about his plans?" he asked. "Whether he was meeting someone, or anything like that?"

"Not a word." By now the producer was actually thinking. "And I doubt if he would have made a firm date. He couldn't tell how long the work would take. We could have hit a snag and been there much later."

McLeod nodded encouragingly. "A good point. But Alderman didn't stay till the end, did he? You were still there."

"Well, I was just waiting for the girl to finish typing the script. My people had all gone."

The picture that was emerging had possibilities for McLeod.

"Why didn't Alderman wait with you?" he prodded.

"Actually I told him not to bother. But I don't think he had any intention of staying."

"Are you saying he was in a hurry to get somewhere?"

The producer frowned. "It's difficult to tell.

You see, he'd been busy establishing himself as the man in charge, the one who had the final say about everything. I assumed he was just emphasizing our relative positions."

"That makes sense." McLeod was remembering his own experience with Bennet Alderman. "All right, so now we come to the moment when he left."

"He walked out, and we went on working. But right away we heard that motorcycle. It kept getting louder and louder. I remember the girl stopped typing and we both looked out the window, even though you couldn't see that part of the yard. I know I wasn't thinking about Bennet. I was just waiting for something to happen, and then there was this god-awful noise. It wasn't what I'd been expecting, it wasn't a crash into a building. It was" — the producer gulped, hesitated, then forged on — "it was more like a hideous squash. Anyway we rushed out the door and from there we could see the body."

By now his voice had risen and he had begun to stammer. "That bloody alley was a perfect death trap. Poor Bennet never had a chance."

McLeod moved to steady his witness. "Forget about how Alderman looked. Describe what else you saw."

The producer gritted his teeth and continued. "The light was in our eyes, you understand. I couldn't see clearly then."

"Then?"

"It didn't take much time to realize Bennet was beyond help. So I went along to the end of the alley, and from there I could see this motorcycle on a road outside the gates."

"Did you notice what kind of cycle?"

"It was like all the others around town." The producer shrugged. It took a Rolls-Royce to rouse his interest. "I was trying to look at the rider. But he had on one of those helmets."

McLeod had assumed as much. Only a madman would have dispensed with that effective camouflage.

"So you couldn't tell anything about his head and face. How about his size?"

"He was hunched into a big blob. I tell you there weren't any details you could pick up at that distance. Nothing except . . . ."

The producer's scornful rejection had turned into surprise.

"I forgot all about noticing his clothes," he said, his voice tinged with discovery. "He was wearing a green windbreaker and khaki trousers."

"*What?*"

John Thatcher sat bolt upright as every head swiveled in his direction. There could no longer be any delay in making his disclosure to the authorities. But even as he was framing the distasteful sentences, he was forestalled.

First there was the heavy tread of approaching footsteps. Then the door swung open. Finally a trio of newcomers entered in military formation. Two rigid uniformed constables were escorting a white-faced Gene Fleming.

Chapter 31

". . . The police who answered my call already knew what happened at Midland Research. They were the ones who told me Alderman was the victim," Fleming concluded his story some time later. "So as soon as I showed them where the crash was, they hustled me back here."

Like a good organizer, McLeod first turned his attention to the ongoing work. "What's being done at the scene of the crash?" he demanded.

The escort replied that a detail was examining the site, with instructions to report directly to the hotel.

Nodding, the superintendent turned an expressionless face to Fleming. "You're probably lucky you didn't catch up with him. What did you think would happen?"

Fleming considered this question for the first time. "Why, I would have identified him."

"If you were still alive. My God, this killer's not fussy about the methods he uses; he simply lashes out with anything. He could have shot you, hit you with a rock, or run you down."

Before Fleming could defend his actions, Inspector Hayakawa seized the moment. "About that shooting," he said. "Mr. Thatcher and I were comparing notes and came to the same conclusion. If Alderman was the intended victim all along, that would provide an explanation of Mr. Matsuda's remarkable attitude."

The superintendent was obviously so dubious that Thatcher came to his companion's aid.

"That would mean they were both telling the truth about the note. Remember, the entire hotel was buzzing about Alderman's behavior at the trade show. Everybody knew that he had threatened to choke the truth out of Matsuda and, therefore, would be very receptive to an invitation from that quarter. At the same time Mr. Matsuda would have been shocked and very curious if he realized someone else was using his name."

With growing interest, McLeod said: "And it would explain the swimming pool. If Matsuda wasn't supposed to take part in the meeting, a location like that wouldn't make any difference."

Thatcher continued his persuasion.

"Having set that trap, the murderer naturally expected only one person to appear," he said. "When the door opened, he fired instantly."

Hayakawa was sensible enough to allow time for the digestion of this material before adding: "I was so convinced by this theory that I intended to consult you about protection for Alderman. Of course it was already too late." He paused, before going on deliberately. "I thought bodyguards might have made Alderman more inclined to cooperate with a request from Mr. Thatcher."

McLeod bent shaggy eyebrows accusingly toward Thatcher. "And what would that have been?"

But Hayakawa, now zeroing in on target, rushed on. "Mr. Thatcher hoped to persuade Alderman to show us the material he received from Lackawanna. Now," he continued cunningly, "it is simply a matter of inspecting his belongings."

McLeod hesitated only long enough to deal with a messenger who had just arrived.

"Yes?"

"That Harley-Davidson was reported stolen from the university at nine-thirty."

"What are the time limits?"

"The owner left it at seven o'clock."

"Very well." McLeod nodded dismissal. "Now let's see what's in Alderman's room."

There was no need for an elaborate search.

The three-page letter was lying on top of Alderman's other papers. It came from a firm of private investigators and, at the beginning, held no surprises. Apparently Alderman had already requested inquiries into Pamela Webb's personal life. Tony Cella listed the steps being taken in Lackawanna and offered, if so instructed, to extend his activities further. But a rigorous probe of Carl Kruger's life, Cella continued, was going to require far more time and money. He concluded that if nasty surprises were to be avoided, there was no alternative to a massive, thorough-going effort.

Hayakawa was shocked. "Alderman was ready to threaten his superior."

"I see that," McLeod growled. "It's the last sentence I don't understand."

Thatcher, however, did.

"Alderman didn't need any justification for investigating most employees at Lackawanna. But when it came to Kruger himself, there had to be some decent coloration. This firm thought Alderman was interested in Kruger's viability as a political candidate. It's really quite clever. Alderman could appear to be working in Kruger's interests while demanding that no stone remain unturned. But it was all a smoke screen, because he started this right after his fight with Kruger."

"It's really not surprising the man is dead," McLeod commented. "Didn't he realize what he was stirring up?"

Both Hayakawa and McLeod expected Thatcher to know about American hard-nosers.

"Alderman was in the habit of thinking he was more unscrupulous than everybody else. He forgot there was a murderer loose!"

"It's happened to blackmailers before," McLeod agreed, as a sergeant from the traffic detail arrived.

"First of all, what about *his* story?" the superintendent asked, jerking his chin toward Fleming. "Is it corroborated?"

"Yes, sir. He was riding one of those light-weight models. Trying to run somebody down with it would be suicidal."

Gene Fleming was outraged. Half choking, he sputtered: "You suspected me?"

"Everything has to be investigated," McLeod said stolidly before turning back to the sergeant. "I see it's raining heavily now."

This was an understatement. The drippings from the sergeant's gleaming black cape were already forming wide pools of water.

"It's been coming down hard for the last hour, sir. But we have established that the rider of the Harley isn't in the immediate vicinity. The nearby roads are being patrolled, and we've put tarps over the cycle itself. I don't know how much good that will do."

"How much damage was there?"

"The machine isn't operational."

"Never mind about that. What about the rider?"

The sergeant collected his thoughts. "That's impossible to say, sir. The rain was already washing away some of the blood by the time we got there. But the main problem is that there are two lots. It's obvious that the mess in the front section comes from the collision at Midland Research. But the rest — on the saddle and the midsection — could come from MR or the road crash. The driver was certainly injured, but we can't tell how seriously."

McLeod's frown had become more forbidding with every word. "If he's badly hurt, he could be lying out there in the dark and we won't find him until daylight. I don't like that, but I like the alternative even less. He must have planned to abandon that Harley somewhere, which means that he had other transport available. He could be already behind the wheel of a car. What good does it do to have patrols looking for a man limping out of the bushes?"

Hayakawa had listened with mounting concern. Now he flashed an unspoken message toward Thatcher, who was still reluctant to voice an accusation that could never be retracted.

"But surely there's no long-term problem, Superintendent," he temporized. "The thing that's holding you up is the absence of so many people. Sooner or later they will return, and presumably only one of them will bear signs of having been in an accident."

McLeod snorted. "What makes you think they'll all return? If I were this killer and I could manage it, I'd already be on my way to the first plane out of the country."

Thatcher was relieved to have a newcomer interrupt their proceedings.

"Mr. Thatcher," the hotel manager announced. "There's an urgent call from your London office. They asked me to interrupt you."

With a last cautionary glance at Inspector Hayakawa, Thatcher rose and left. As he plodded down the corridor, he realized that he was not immune to McLeod's reasoning. Let the killer escape, and the damage that remained might be irreparable. If the police could act tonight, there would still be a terrible price, but at least it would be confined to the guilty.

Shaking his head, he accepted the phone.

"Is that you, John? I've been trying to get

you all evening. And now they tell me you're with the police."

Toby Lemieux, bright as a penny, sounded like a voice from another planet. Fortunately he did not wait for an answer but rattled on.

"My man reported back at five. You were absolutely right, John!"

Until that moment Thatcher had not realized he was holding his breath. He was only conscious of a great weariness. The pathos of the whole situation was growing almost unendurable.

"Just tell me what he found," he said somberly. Any weapon that could shorten this ordeal was welcome; nonetheless Lemieux's cheeriness still jarred.

Simmering down, Toby read from his notes. Then, when this elicited only silence, he said cautiously: "Someday you must tell me what put this extraordinary notion in your head."

"Tomorrow, Toby," promised Thatcher, hanging up without further explanation. After all, the first news bulletin that Lemieux heard would make it clear why voices emanating from Birmingham were brusque and unforthcoming.

For a moment Thatcher braced himself. Further delay was out of the question. Slowly he retraced his steps, to offer McLeod his single, damning fact. He arrived to find the superintendent still outlining a grim future.

"And what if they do all turn up? If the injuries aren't immediately apparent, I can't have them all stripped."

Thatcher's moment, like it or not, had come.

"That won't be necessary, Superintendent," he said, making heads swivel. "I think I can tell you where the murderer is right now."

Thatcher could not provide the exact address, but McLeod already knew it. Within twenty minutes, the three of them were in a large, unmarked police car, piloted with reckless speed. Behind them was a backup crew. As they raced out of Birmingham, Thatcher occupied himself by wondering about their destination.

"Two miles beyond Lower Nettleby," the driver announced, slewing the sedan off the main road onto a narrow, twisting lane. Progress slowed, and they were almost at a crawl when they sighted a beacon to steer by.

Only when they came to a halt did it resolve itself into an ordinary country cottage, several hundred yards beyond its nearest neighbor. It blazed with light — from the windows, from the lantern beside the front door, and from the door itself, which stood open to the driving rain.

Swiftly and silently McLeod moved up the path, with the others keeping pace. On the threshold, they were stopped short. Beyond the hall they saw a warm and beckoning living room, where bowls of yellow roses glowed. It was as unreal as a mirage.

Because in the damp, chill hallway, a woman with crazed eyes was slumped against the foot of the stairs. Blood stained the front of her simple dress as she rocked back and forth, cradling a man's body.

"Ali's dead," said Pamela Webb without looking up. "He crawled inside, then he died. He died in my arms. I tried . . . but . . ."

She did not know what she was saying. When one of McLeod's men tried to remove her, she began to scream. She was still screaming when they led her off.

"What's the connection between Ali Khan and this Webb woman?" someone asked brutally.

"According to public records," said Thatcher, "she was his wife."

McLeod had a long list of things to do. "Pity," he said perfunctorily.

"Yes," said Thatcher slowly. "A very great pity."

Chapter 32

"It's hard to believe," said Don Hodiak at the end of a crowded week. "That Pamela and Ali milked MR to the tune of five million!"

Inspector Hayakawa nodded. "That very simplicity misled us all."

"It also constituted the major threat to Khan and Pamela Webb," Thatcher remarked. "Once you stripped away all the Recruit atmospherics, what was left? Two relatively insignificant men had been murdered. Mr. Ushiba had expressed public doubts about the accounting statements from Midland Research and was killed within hours. Bennet Alderman proposed to investigate Pamela Webb and was attacked the next day. If you recalled that she had financial oversight of MR, the situation deserved investigation — to say the least."

"That's easy enough to see now," Gene Fleming said ruefully. "But with everybody worried to death about Recruit, it was hard just to forget about it."

At his side, Rick Iwamoto agreed. "It looked like a question of identifying which company had tried to buy MITI. Anything else didn't make sense."

"Why not?" Thatcher challenged. "Why should it be harder to imagine employees of Lackawanna embezzling than to imagine Mr. Matsuda accepting a bribe?"

Everyone turned to look at Mr. Matsuda, who was in the chair of honor, flanked by Mr. and Mrs. Kruger. Theoretically they had gathered to celebrate the successful conclusion of the MR hearings and the future flow of Lackawanna goods to Japan. But Matsuda had other reasons for joy. Apologies in many forms were arriving on his doorstep, and some of them were taking very meaningful forms. In Western parlance, today he would not call the king his cousin.

Inclining his head graciously, he said: "I confess I was totally bewildered. Nobody had even approached me with a bribe. And only a foreigner, abysmally ignorant of MITI, would have been foolish enough to deal with Mr. Ushiba."

"We all dismissed Mr. Ushiba too quickly, but then we had all been preconditioned," Thatcher pointed out. "It was not only the Japanese government that was absorbed by the problems of Recruit. Everyone planning to do business in Japan was subjected to crash courses on the topic. Stan Zaretski was emphasizing its importance to Lackawanna, while Gene instructed us at the Sloan. Even you, Haru, helped lead everybody down the garden path by explaining how the workplace has become a primary source of affiliation."

"I said that about Japanese men," Haru replied indignantly. "I never pretended to understand what motivates somebody like Pamela Webb."

"Nonetheless," Thatcher continued, "if the rest of us had never heard of Recruit or *uchi*, we might have set off in the right direction."

"Even the police were puzzled," Hayakawa remarked. "In spite of the length of this scandal, there has never been any violence. Not until foreigners appeared."

"Then," Thatcher rejoined, "it would have been logical to search for non-Japanese motives. In other words, to remember that great pools of money lying around are an inducement to theft, as well as to bribery. But we had an expert at smoke screens taking full advantage of our preconditioning."

Mr. Matsuda adjusted his glasses and assumed the air of a scholar. "If, during your great Watergate scandal, a body had been discovered in the offices of the Committee to Re-Elect the President, it would have been difficult to ignore the political implications.

Nonetheless I blame myself for not paying attention to Mr. Ushiba. I was simply annoyed at his failure to understand what was germane to MITI. When he questioned MR's lack of profitability, I should have realized he was disturbed by the magnitude of their expenditures."

Matsuda received assistance from an unlikely quarter.

"Hell, Ushiba said he was working on Pamela's numbers in front of me, and I never gave it a second thought," Don Hodiak said handsomely.

He had accepted the fact that Lackawanna had carried its own problems to Tokyo. The lesson was coming harder to Carl Kruger.

"But who could think of Pamela as behind all this?" he burst out.

In the midst of his triumph, Kruger was not sharing the general euphoria. As soon as the hearings had concluded, the voice of duty had compelled him to make a prison visit. He had been despondent ever since.

"I'm afraid she stuck out like a sore thumb as soon as one began thinking along the right lines," Thatcher said gently. "Quite apart from her financial association with MR, she was noted for her skill at diversions. That made her a prime candidate once you accepted the fact that someone had deliberately cast the

411

mantle of Recruit over the murder of Mr. Ushiba."

Curiously enough, Rick Iwamoto was enjoying the party more than his host, even though he had lost his battle to keep Kruger's generators out of Japan. Shima had been publicly absolved of any wrongdoing at MITI, and Iwamoto knew he would live to fight another day.

"Given the times we live in, the fear about bribery was a natural mistake, wasn't it?" he suggested.

"But it wasn't left to chance," Thatcher pointed out. "Because if there was no bribe, that Swiss letter had to be a plant."

"Even though its authenticity was proven beyond a doubt," Hayakawa hastened to remark.

"The letter could be genuine and still have nothing to do with MITI. Only the MR notation suggested a bribe."

"All right, all right," agreed Hodiak. "But even if you spotted Pamela, why drag in Ali?"

To Thatcher, the question seemed to answer itself.

"For one thing, in Birmingham, he was very much the man in charge. But the main reason is that they were a natural team."

"A team?" Hodiak gulped. "They didn't have a thing in common."

Audrey Kruger removed her concerned gaze from her husband long enough to snort. "Oh, come on, Don!"

"I mean it. They lived on two different continents. She was American, he was Pakistani; she was a vice-president, he was . . ." Hodiak's voice died away uncertainly.

"Exactly what was he?" Thatcher asked. "I think you may have underestimated him because he was climbing a different ladder. But in fact, they had both come a great distance in a short time, soaring past their contemporaries. She was an officer of Lackawanna. His advance in robotics was the focus of international bidding. And that was simply the outward measure. On a personal level they were two of a kind. They were overwhelmingly self-confident, and above all, they were convinced that the world was theirs for the taking."

Kruger might have been reviewing his own past as he said reflectively: "A lot of people think like that until they get straightened out."

"The process seems to have been delayed with them," Thatcher retorted. "Calling them high achievers is bowing to current jargon. What they really shared was the quality of being the brightest sixth grader in school. They were convinced they were cleverer than everybody else. Of course they presented themselves differently. Pamela openly paraded her ability and even her sense of mischief. Ali, on the other hand, preferred to play the provincial."

"Are you trying to say they enjoyed their little scheme?" Hodiak asked incredulously.

"Until they had a murder on their hands, I'm sure they did. Ali relished the knowledge that he was outsmarting you all. To make matters worse, he was a man with a grievance. In his book, the corporate world had tried to steal his work."

"I didn't steal anything from him," Kruger protested.

"According to our London manager, the damage was done before you got him."

Mollified, Kruger admitted there was some merit in this reading of Ali Khan.

"In a way you're just saying what Pamela told me this afternoon," he said dejectedly. "When Ali was down-and-out, everybody told him that money simply had to be poured into MR to save it. He figured that if people were so damn free with their cash, they'd never miss what he took."

Audrey reached for her husband's hand.

"I know it wasn't easy to see Pamela, honey, but you'd be feeling even worse if you hadn't."

"I suppose so," he said. "But I hardly recognized her. She's so broken up by Ali's death, she talks about everything else as if it happened twenty years ago. Do you realize this all started the first time she came over to MR? She discovered Ali's hand in the till, and the only thing that bothered her was the chicken feed he was taking! They were already in love, and she figured that together they could skim enough to seed a new company. She made it sound like the most normal decision in the world."

"To her it probably was," Thatcher observed. "The reason the Japanese investigation was so ineffective was that they were dealing with two rampant egotists who acknowledged no outside loyalties."

Mr. Matsuda was shocked. "That would be impossible in Japan. Passion may overtake unfortunate individuals. But if there is no appropriate solution, they simply commit suicide."

His stately assurance was too much for a firm believer in a changing Japan.

"Maybe in the past," said Haru Fleming, wrinkling her brow doubtfully, "but I wouldn't rely on it these days."

Thatcher would not have been surprised to hear her explain that being raised with one's own bedroom made suicide unacceptable, but she was forestalled.

"To hear Pamela tell it, everybody else should have gotten out of her way." Kruger was still troubled by the unknown woman he had met that afternoon. "Mostly she sounded half dead. The only time she showed any emotion was when she was blaming other people. There wouldn't have been any problem if Ushiba had known his job. And poor Benny had no right to dig into her personal life. But the one who really got to her was Mr. Matsuda. If he hadn't come nosing around, Alderman would have been killed in London and Ali would still be alive. Nobody had any rights except her. How the hell did I fail to notice this before?"

"Maybe because she adopted company coloration when you first knew her?" Thatcher suggested. "She was planning to do her climbing at Lackawanna then."

Rick Iwamoto was more interested in facts than in personality profiles. "Just a minute," he directed. "I still don't know any of the details. What exactly did happen?"

Shima's president had been far too busy with the future to spare time for the past. After the media explosion, one of the first voices to break through from the outside world had come from Anchorage, Alaska. Len Ridgeway was eager to sign on the dotted line. And in the burst of jubilation from Tokyo, the Japanese penalty against Shima had gone virtually unnoticed.

"I expect it all started when Mr. Ushiba queried the amounts flowing through Midland Research," Thatcher hazarded.

Mr. Matsuda could not contain the old exasperation with his incompetent subordinate. "Ushiba was too limited to understand Miss Webb's irreproachable analysis, so he just looked at the end result."

"Yes, but after you snubbed him, he was probably afraid he had overlooked something obvious," said Thatcher. "So when Khan came back from lunch early, Ushiba would have drawn him aside to ask for an explanation. It was a fatal mistake. Over the years, Khan had accepted Pamela's assurance that her paperwork could defy examination by Lackawanna. Suddenly everything had changed. MR was about to be sold, Khan was summoned overnight to Japan, and then, out of the blue, a clerk with imperfect English was announcing suspicions. Knowing just how valid those suspicions were, Khan lost his head and attacked."

Rick Iwamoto was frowning. "If Khan was in such a panic, how come he set up that red herring about the bribe?"

"He didn't," Kruger half groaned. "That was my clever Pamela."

"Khan would have raced to the women's coatroom to warn her," Thatcher reasoned. "And she certainly demonstrated her ability to think on her feet. She must have had the notification from their Zurich agent with her. So she scrawled the initials MR and slipped it into Ushiba's drawer. Then she sauntered into the meeting, casually referring to the distance she had to cover. It was a brilliant stroke. After that letter surfaced, the Japanese government was so consumed with its own jeopardy it could think of nothing else."

Matsuda could scarcely believe his ears. "She might have toppled not only the Prime Minister but the LDP!"

"All she cared about was entangling Ushiba's murder with Recruit. When I sat next to Khan on the plane to Anchorage," Thatcher recalled, "I accepted his explanation for taking a very roundabout route home. Of course he simply wanted to reach foreign soil as rapidly as possible."

Matsuda was tepid in his appreciation. "I admit that her feint succeeded. Why, then, did she start sending messages that purported to come from me?"

"Because she had taken immense pains to create a scheme that would elude the auditors, but she never contemplated being investigated by detectives," Thatcher replied. "I'm sure she and Khan exercised normal discretion about their association, but they were vulnerable to a real probe."

"You can say that again," said Kruger, who seemed to be grunting his way back to equanimity. "When I first heard about all this, it seemed so incredible I did a little checking. And sure enough. When Pamela went to the Bahamas for a week, so did Ali. And they were both in the south of France last summer."

Audrey nodded in a knowing fashion. "And I'll bet they relaxed when they were in England. After all, Ali lived outside of town. So Pamela probably felt free to come and go. That's the kind of thing that people do, and it works until somebody starts really digging."

"I can see that their relationship was open to discovery," Inspector Hayakawa said restively, "but who cared that she was a loose woman?"

"Nobody did." Thatcher searched for a telling example. "If you go into partnership with the man who will actually run the business, you don't hire his wife to protect your interests. The minute that Alderman released his results, Carl would have known he was in exactly that position."

"I sure would have," announced the new Kruger. "I would have torn the place apart."

Looking at that outthrust jaw, Thatcher realized that Pamela Webb's next move had been inevitable.

"She decided that Alderman had to go before he did irretrievable damage, but she was still determined to use Recruit as cover. The Matsuda note was more than a lure. If Alderman had been found dead with that note in his pocket, we would have been sucked into another diplomatic brouhaha."

Matsuda gasped as he realized he had been the beneficiary of more than one near miss. "If I had not been the victim, everyone would have assumed I was the murderer. That she-devil! That unprincipled harpy!" His feelings threatened to overcome him. "And she wasn't even a competent planner. Both attempts on Alderman were fiascos."

"But not by much," Thatcher said before Matsuda could boil over. "After all, if Khan had made it safely back to the cottage, they would have alibied each other. And don't forget, we had two other people in the MR group associated with motorcycles."

Fleming and Rick Iwamoto exchanged glances that were more congratulatory than alarmed.

"By the way, John," Gene asked, "what was your reaction when they told you that someone in a green windbreaker and fatigues had sped from the scene of the crime?"

"I realized that, alert as usual, you were in hot pursuit," Thatcher said blandly.

Fleming projected skepticism. "I'll bet."

Hastily Thatcher reverted to Pamela Webb. "The final irony is that Bennet Alderman would never have understood the financial implications of her involvement with Khan."

"That really is incredible," Gene marveled.

"No more so than insane chases by middle-aged men who ought to have more sense," Haru said dispassionately.

Her husband eyed her warily. "They make it sound more dramatic than it was," he muttered.

The men were all too craven to venture into an area of marital discord, but Audrey Kruger proved that some things transcend the minor variations of East and West.

"It was two motorcycles roaring around in the dark, wasn't it?" she challenged. "And you did say your oldest daughter has graduated from college?"

Gene grinned at her. "You're trying to tell me I should be acting like a grandfather."

"Why not? She tells *me* that all the time," Kruger said affectionately.

Audrey soared above these trifles. "How could Bennet have seriously believed there was anything between Carl and Pamela? I always thought he was simply jealous of her importance."

At this display of conjugal trust, Kruger preened himself too soon. "Benny didn't know me like you do, honey."

"It's not that you've never strayed," she said severely. "But not with crisp efficiency and a mind like a steel trap. They've never been your weakness."

Before she could tell them what his weakness was, Thatcher came to the rescue. "There had been a good deal of gossip when Pamela first joined Lackawanna. The reason it never died down was the absence of another man in her life. I suspect that made her uneasy with Alderman, even if she felt safe with Carl and Don."

"What's that supposed to mean?" Hodiak demanded.

Thatcher grinned maliciously at his contemporaries. "Those of us in the grandfather generation grew up in a simple corporate world. The executives were men, and most of them were married. The others were quiet about their arrangements. But Pamela and Alderman belonged to a different society. She should have been living openly with someone. As she didn't want Alderman wondering about that, she fostered his belief in the gossip. I noticed she was different in Audrey's presence, but that was all too explainable."

Audrey sniffed. "She could never have fooled me."

"She had enough sense not to try," Thatcher said gravely.

In the face of this generosity, Audrey admitted her own error. "Pamela was always so quiet about her personal life, I just assumed there was a married man somewhere. I guess I belong to my generation too."

Neither Kruger nor Hodiak was particularly grateful for this analysis.

"All right, all right, so we're decrepit," Hodiak growled. "But Pamela wasn't so smart, either, tying herself up to a guy who committed murder at the first sign of pressure. She must have been out of her mind when she realized what she was dealing with."

Thatcher shook his head. "I meant it when I said they were two of a kind. Khan may have lashed out in a panic at MITI, but when Pamela scented danger from Alderman, she responded with a cold-blooded trap. Just look at the development. The morning after the trade show, she learned from you of Alderman's threats against her. At eleven this is confirmed at the fax station. By five the note intended to incriminate Mr. Matsuda is waiting in Alderman's mail."

"And Khan didn't have to be in a panic

to be vicious," Gene Fleming added. "I'll never forget the way he lined up Alderman in that parking lot."

"They must have been living on their nerves for days by then," Kruger commented. "I'd sent Pamela up to Birmingham, where she couldn't take another crack at Benny."

Inspector Hayakawa had a confession of his own. Turning to Kruger, he said apologetically: "When we read Alderman's correspondence that night, I had last-minute doubts. It seemed possible that if Miss Webb had told you what was in that letter, you might have tried to kill him."

"It's not surprising you were confused," Kruger conceded. "By that time I was scared stiff. If Benny had engineered the disclosure of that Shima export violation, he was a lot cozier with Yonezawa's boys than I'd realized. But when I blew up at him, damned if he didn't turn the tables on me. He said I'd practically admitted I blew the whistle on Shima. Of course I thought it was just Benny trying to weasel his way clear."

Rick Iwamoto was tolerantly superior. "How come you overlooked the obvious? Back at Shima we were never in any doubt that Yonezawa was responsible for our troubles."

"It was just like Mr. Arai to take out some

insurance," Gene Fleming agreed. "He probably got the goods on you the minute you became his big opposition. Then he kept it at the ready in case of need."

"Well, that dummy of ours in San Francisco handed him a gift package," Iwamoto concurred.

They could speak freely, as Yonezawa was not represented at the table. Mr. Arai had barely waited to append his signature to the agreement before flying off.

"Never mind about the Shima scandal," Audrey Kruger said to Hayakawa. "You mean you seriously suspected Carl because Bennet was up to his dirty tricks?"

For some strange reason, Audrey never put a foot wrong with Mr. Matsuda. She was in some danger of becoming his ideal of Western womanhood.

"I am sure it was a momentary lapse on the inspector's part," he now said soothingly.

"After all, we had just learned of Alderman's murder, and the letter was mostly about Carl," Thatcher said, continuing the good work. "But the inspector soon remembered that Pamela had seen only the first page."

Hayakawa was far too sensible not to accept shelter from wifely indignation. "Besides, as soon as I paused to think, I realized the murder method made Mr. Khan the major suspect."

"Exactly," said Thatcher. "Khan made the arrangements with the TV crew, knowing that any mention of their presence would bring Alderman to the scene, and he made sure that they would fill the executive parking strip. He was also the only one familiar enough with Birmingham to know where he could steal a motorcycle, where he could abandon it, and where the rally was."

Don Hodiak still had more trouble with the relationship between Pamela and Ali than with their criminal conspiracy. "Even if they were in it together, what the hell made you think they'd gotten married?"

"If Pamela Webb was the kind of woman I thought she was, she would have looked around for protection before she agreed to take risks. In their situation, marriage made a good deal of sense. It not only shielded them from testifying against each other; it enabled her to weld their financial arrangements so tightly that neither of them could simply walk away."

"They couldn't keep it a secret forever," Hodiak objected.

"They didn't have to," Thatcher told him. "By complaining about the Japanese, Khan was laying the groundwork to leave MR. Probably Pamela intended to join him at a new company. Her friends could say she preferred entrepreneurial risk to the corporate hierarchy. Others, like Alderman, could say that having failed to hook a man at the top, she was settling for one on his way."

Frowning, Audrey said doubtfully: "And then they'd live happily ever after?"

"Just so," Thatcher said briefly.

He preferred not to consider the prospect of two murderers locked together forever.

Fortunately Gene Fleming, still gnawing at his own personal bone, prevented any exploration of this topic. "All that business about being familiar with the speedway, knowing about the rally, and being able to steal a bike didn't point just to Khan. I was right on the spot, and you could say it applied to me."

"I couldn't," Inspector Hayakawa said instantly. "Not when they told us what you were riding. After all, I spent my first two years with the police on a motorcycle."

No sooner were the words out of his mouth than Rick Iwamoto was subjecting him to narrow-eyed appraisal. "Let's see, that must have been about twenty years ago," he calculated. "So if you were with the Tokyo prefecture, you were using our model FJ-4."

Hayakawa nodded enthusiastically.

"That was it. It was a wonderful bike," he recalled on a wave of nostalgia, "except for one thing. When it came to cornering at high speed —"

"I always said that was its weakness," Gene Fleming interrupted. "When we were designing our TX-1 to compete with it, we tried . . ."

Within seconds all three of them were positioning salt shakers and cutlery in a complex discussion that unconsciously slipped into Japanese. Even Haru Fleming was sucked in when she responded to a query from her husband. At the same time, Don Hodiak and the Krugers were retreating into a low-voiced conversation about their forthcoming return to Lackawanna.

It remained for Thatcher to shoulder the burden of entertaining the guest of honor. This was not difficult in view of the generalized benignity with which Matsuda was gazing on the world.

"An extraordinary tale," he was saying. "And while mistakes were made, the original conviction that foreigners were responsible has been more than justified."

"Moreover, MITI emerges untarnished," Thatcher murmured, acknowledging the unspoken priorities.

"On the whole, it has been a pleasure doing business with the Sloan Guaranty Trust," Matsuda said, matching cordiality with cordiality. "Perhaps the occasion will arise again."

For a moment Thatcher did not reply. Unbidden, his mind had unreeled the past and frozen the frame of Pamela Webb and Ali Khan jogging into the Tokyo Hilton. There they were, preserved for all time as the incarnation of glowing youth. Beneath that bright, shining surface, however, lurked the common impulse that had carried them beyond the claims of honesty or decency or compassion. Haru Fleming would say that they had been insufficiently socialized. Whatever its name, their fatal flaw had drawn them remorselessly into a spiral of tragedy.

But murder and embezzlement, like the promise of youth, are ephemeral. The gross national product of Japan is not.

Rallying, Thatcher answered in a voice of unmistakable sincerity.

"I certainly hope so!"